# AFTER THE PARTY

A.K. RITCHIE

Copyright © 2021 by A.K. Ritchie

Cover Photos by Jc Siller and Lucas Pezeta

ISBN 978-1-7779061-1-5

ISBN 978-1-7779061-0-8 (ebook)

*For my family and friends who knew I could do it, even if I didn't.*

1

My first black eye of the year came only seconds after midnight when the band began playing everyone's favourite song. I stopped my search for Will long enough to take in the scene, to smell the stale beer and body odour. I appreciated those kids—the ones pressed against me, the ones I saw every weekend, the ones who accepted me when I showed up uninvited. Caught up in it all, I forgot about Will and absorbed the music. The voices singing together, the vibrations of the bass. Everyone surged toward the stage, screaming the band's lyrics back to them.

When the crowd shifted again, the blonde guy in front of me tumbled backwards, his body knocking the plastic beer cup from my hand before his elbow collided with my cheek. He crashed to the ground and disappeared as the crowd filled in around him.

Ignoring the sharp pain, I pushed two boys out of the way and reached down to grab the guy's sweater. The DeKay House etiquette said if someone fell, we picked them up. His honey-coloured waves were easy to spot in the sea of black clothes. A blue-haired boy and I linked our arms beneath the guy's and hoisted him to his feet. The moment he stood the crowd rushed in, their feet stomping down in the exact place his fingers had been.

The pain in my face yanked my attention away from the situation. Since the guy seemed stable, I let go of his arm and moved through the mass of people, hand clutching my cheek, to find Will and get out of here.

"Hey," the guy shouted, over the band. "Your face."

I turned to tell him not to worry about it, but stopped when I saw him properly. He wasn't just some random blonde guy.

I'd seen Chase Reid many times, but never without his guitar. Only the week before I'd watched him jumping around and sweating on a stage downtown. In the year since I found Forever July's music, I'd never missed one of their shows. I'd seen him in clubs and venues all around town, but he didn't belong at The DeKay House. He was from a different scene, a different world.

I waved him off, before turning toward the stairs. I needed to be outside in the cold air. I needed to find Will so I could go home.

All my expectations for New Year's Eve crumbled. The best I could hope for would be to come out of the night without my eye swelling shut. A few hands patted my shoulder and back as I passed them, but they kept their focus on the band. I used the shaky railing to climb the stairs of the old punk house. The pain in my face and the humidity of the basement made my head feel light, as if I was drunk, not mostly sober.

I made it into the graffiti-covered hallway at the top of the stairs. I pulled the phone from my pocket and sucked in a deep breath of cooler, drier air as I unlocked the screen. The only message was Kay, saying she'd made it home already—and she had put water and Tylenol next to my bed.

Then Chase Reid's voice came again. "Hey!"

I glanced up—he was standing on the top stair, sweat

plastering wavy strands of hair to his forehead. He looked like the Chase that appeared on stage. I didn't know what to say to a guy like that, a guy like Chase Reid. I didn't know why he was slumming it in a punk house. Chase belonged in proper bars and clubs, not houses that should be condemned. The DeKay House had become a place for those with nowhere else to go. But he wouldn't have been the first to come to a show at the House to say they'd done it once, to see how the other half partied. I didn't want anything to do with his slum tourism.

I ran my thumb over the spot where his elbow collided with my cheek. The skin beneath my left eye was smooth and hot to the touch.

"You're Peyton, right?" He asked. "Peyton Young?"

"Yeah. How'd you..." I trailed off. I tried to focus on the ache instead of thinking about the fact Chase Reid knew my name.

"I've read your blog," he said.

I tugged at my hair, trying to hide my flushed face without being too obvious. I tried to gauge his reaction. I'd made a suggestion about the band I couldn't imagine he would like. I pointed out that Chase Reid couldn't handle lead guitar as well as vocals.

"Can I get you some ice or something?" he asked, nodding his chin toward my face.

"It doesn't hurt." I didn't want to talk about my face anymore. To figure out why Chase Reid was speaking to me, I asked, "Sorry, what were you saying? About my blog."

"You made a solid point about my band in your post." He stepped up and shifted against the door frame to let someone into the basement, but he never took his eyes off me.

I tried not to look away, wanting him to know I was listening, despite my pathological fear of confrontation.

That post went up weeks ago, right after the band played at the Horseshoe Tavern. I had stayed awake until four in the morning, trying to detail my thoughts on the entire thing: about how Forever July had become one of the most popular local pop-punk bands, how they'd landed themselves a decent record deal with a great label, and how their lead guitarist, who also held the position of vocalist, couldn't do the band justice. I wrote about how he, Chase Reid, couldn't do the band justice if he refused to give up lead guitar.

It never occurred to me that any member of the band would read my blog. I was sure none of them knew I existed. We didn't have any of the same friends. Outside of shows, we didn't hang out in the same place. But there stood Chase Reid, in a crumbling punk house letting me know he read my blog.

"If I'd known you were going to read it—" I stopped myself and shook my head.

"You would have still written the same thing?" Chase asked. He hadn't raised his voice. It didn't waver. There was no sign if he was on the angry side or the annoyed side of the unimpressed scale.

"I would have still written the same thing," I admitted, pressing myself against the wall, shoulders braced for whatever he might say next.

An excited holler came from the kitchen, and a bunch of people cheered. It would have been the perfect reason to escape, but I didn't want to move. Kay had gone home early and Will had disappeared. I didn't know who to run to.

"You weren't wrong." He shoved his hands into the pockets of his jeans and went on, "You said we needed someone stronger on guitar. It's a slap to the ego, honestly. But we decided to switch things up to see what would happen. As you probably already know, it worked. So, we made our rhythm guitarist our lead."

"Mitchell, right?" I asked. From the videos on their website, I knew Mitchell's guitar skills outweighed Chase's. Chase's polished vocals worked and he had great range, but

Mitchell needed to take the burden from him, to carry the music. Chase needed to focus on the lyrics and his vocals. Actually, in the first draft of the blog post, I made the direct suggestion that Mitchell take over the more intricate guitar pieces, but Kay said it felt like pushing the critique too far, and to let the band make their own decisions. At the time, the suggestion annoyed me, but standing in the hallway with Chase Reid I was grateful to Kay, saving me from awkwardness yet again.

"Yeah. Would you be willing to listen to a track we recorded? Let me know if you think it works?" Chase took the phone from his pocket and waited.

The question threw me. The blog was where I expressed all the thoughts I couldn't say out loud. No one at the DeKay House knew of it. It became a place I expressed things without having to face the audience. I assumed no one cared to hear my opinions, so I could go off without consequence.

The party kept moving on around us, but Chase still held the phone in front of him, an eyebrow raised. "I know you just saved my fingers from being totally obliterated down there, but could you do me one more favour? In the spirit of the holidays and all that?"

People don't always enjoy hearing the truth, and when they heard it, their responses didn't always come out rationally.

"It's a new song. You'd be the first to hear it," he said.

I pressed my lips together, hoping the word 'yes' wouldn't slip out. It would be an honour to be the first to hear a new Forever July track. Their self-titled album, released before they were signed to the label, occupied a spot in my top ten albums of all time. It embodied a sense of melancholy I craved in my music. With their track record, I knew the new song would be excellent and I would love it, but if I'd been wrong about Mitchell's abilities, the truth would come out. And the night was already a disaster.

"I really need to find my friends," I told Chase. "Another time?"

The corners of his mouth tugged downward. He shoved his phone into the pocket of his jeans.

"How about this?" he asked. "I'll put you on the list for our next show in a couple weeks and you can give me your honest feedback then."

I tried to keep my voice light. "You want me to write a review for one song?"

He let out a deep chuckle and said, "No. Let us know, in person, if we still suck. If you're cool with that."

"I highly doubt it'll suck." I attempted to smile, but the aching in my cheek doubled.

Chase laughed again. "So, is that a yes?"

My phone rang and we both glanced down at the screen. A picture of Will and me stared back at us, faces pressed together, glistening from post-mosh pit sweat, eyes bloodshot from too many beers. I muted the call.

"I didn't expect that," Chase said. His words came out high, like a question.

"Expect what?" I asked, turning the screen of the phone toward the ground.

"You and Will, I guess," Chase said. His smooth forehead creased.

"You know Will?" I asked.

Chase shrugged. "I used to come here all the time with my brother. I know Will well."

Everyone who went to the House knew Will, his quirks, his moods. No one minded his attitude. They chalked it up to Will being Will. It never bothered me that people knew all those details about him, but for some reason, I didn't want Chase to know. My stomach tightened. "I should go. I should call him back," I said, staring at the phone in my hand. "Thanks for helping me down there."

"Someone goes down, you pick them up. Those are the

House rules." I gave a small wave, then turned and headed toward the front door.

I yanked my coat from the pile on the uneven stairs with one hand as I called Will back with the other. The phone rang against my ear as I pulled the door open.

Icy air wrapped itself around me as I stepped out onto the porch. My teeth chattered, making the pain in my cheek double, maybe triple. The weather had been mild last week, but it turned bitter during our night at the DeKay House.

"Peyton," Will's voice yelled at me through the phone. "Hunter's having a party."

"What? Where are you?" I listened for familiar voices on the other end, but I couldn't make out any distinguishing details.

"I'm at Hunter's."

A lump formed in my throat. I swallowed it away and listened to Will shouting at someone for another round of shots, something stronger. His words slurred. I didn't want to go to Hunter's. Will got out of hand when he was around that group of friends and I didn't like how he acted when he drank too much.

"Alright. I'll see you in a bit," I said, even though I had no intention of showing up at Hunter's party. It was better not to argue, not to ask why he didn't take me with him. By morning, he'd forget he'd called me at all.

On top of it, I didn't have enough money to get an Uber all the way to the east side of town, especially on New Year's Eve. The rates would be inflated until at least three in the morning, when the majority of people had already turned in for the night. I didn't even know how I would get home from the DeKay House.

Unsure of what to do, I started walking, and called Kay. It rang and rang, but kept going to voicemail. Despite the snow, I sat down on the curb and pulled the coat tighter around me. Every time my fingers reached for the cellphone in my pocket, I had to remind myself I had no one left to call. To top it off, my charge was down to 2% and I could feel the tears start to well in my eyes.

New Year's Eve held so many expectations for me. I'd expected the night to make up for my lack of Christmas celebrations. I'd never had a real Christmas, and my first two years being out of my childhood house, I just wanted my own version of holiday celebration. But Will and Kay went to be with their families and I stayed alone in the apartment for three days, waiting for someone to return.

The sound of steps on the sidewalk caused me to duck my head so whoever it was wouldn't see the tears and the swelling beneath my eye. With the toe of my shoe, I pushed down the fluffy piles of snow until they were flat and marked with my tread. The person stepped off the sidewalk and stopped right in front of me.

"Hey," Chase said when my eyes met his. Despite the cold, he wore only a sweater, with the hood over his head.

"Hey. Waiting for a cab."

"You'll be waiting for a while. I'll give you a ride." Chase extended a hand. "I basically broke your face. It's the least that I can do."

A lopsided smile crossed his face as he wiggled his fingers. I took his warm hand and he pulled me up from the curb. When I was on my feet, Chase said, "And I hope you know, I'm going to force you to listen to that new song I was telling you about."

I wiped my cheeks dry with the sleeve of my jacket. "I think I can handle that."

2

WHEN I FIRST MOVED TO THE CITY, I REMEMBER WALKING HOME from the bus station to the room I found from an ad online. I saw a hand-drawn sign stuck to a lamppost. It read, PUNK SHOW. THURSDAY. DEKAY HOUSE. The address was crammed into the tiny space along the bottom of the flyer. I had to squint to read it. The most enticing part of the poster were the words NO COVER CHARGE. The first night I showed up at the DeKay House, I had expected little more than a place to hang out for the night.

Five minutes after I walked into the DeKay House, Kay approached me with an energy drink and asked me my name. She said she noticed I was alone and asked if I wanted a tour, asked me what my story was. I gave her some version of the truth and she accepted it. Before the night came to an end, she offered me her couch for the night so I didn't have to walk home alone. Within a week, after she met the intense woman I'd rented the room from, I'd officially moved into Kay's spare bedroom.

Kay strolled into our living room with a mug in one hand and a bag of frozen peas in the other. Day-old eyeliner smudged straight across to her hairline.

Despite being sober by the time I got home that morning, the day dragged like any other would have after a DeKay House party. My stomach roiled. My head ached. I flinched when Kay tossed the frozen peas in my direction. The movement made me notice the plastic wrap covering her bicep.

"What did you get done? And when?" I asked, nodding at the new tattoo on her arm.

Kay grinned and curled up into her Lazy-Boy, twisting her body so I could see the colour added to her tarot tattoo. The black cloak of Death stood out against her pale flesh. The various shades of red in the roses added splashes of colour to her mostly black work tattoos.

Kay's chuckle rumbled out of her, like stones in a tumbler. "Turns out Alain is a tattoo artist. That's where we went when we left the House." She wrapped both hands around her mug of coffee and stared back at me. Her smile faded as she scanned my face. "What happened last night?"

I'd been waiting for the question. My body tensed and readied itself for the interrogation. To compose myself, I picked up the bag of frozen peas and pressed it against the warm spot on my cheek. A jolt of pain radiated out across my forehead and down to my jaw. The skin beneath my eye had turned deep red with flecks of purple and black. It would only get more hideous in the days to come. I knew the process well.

"I took a hit in the mosh pit and then I came home."

Kay ran a hand through her raven bangs and asked, "That happened in the mosh pit?" The pitch of her voice felt accusatory, like she assumed I had been caught in a lie.

I sighed and pulled the peas away from my face. "I was looking for Will."

"Where was he?"

"Hunter's, apparently." Without wanting them to, or meaning to, the words came out sharp. Somehow the questions always came back to Will. What he was doing? Where he was going? Kay never pretended to like him, but I wanted her to. I wanted her to say hello when he showed up instead of rolling her eyes and finding excuses to leave the room. I wanted to have a conversation where I talked about something Will and I did, without her judgmental eyes watching me for signs of something that didn't exist.

"Hmmm." Kay sipped her coffee again.

"It wasn't like that, Kay. I'm not some pushover…" Like my mom, I wanted to finish, but held it to myself. I folded my arms across my chest. "And he's not a bad guy."

Kay blinked. Nothing I could have said would make her change her mind. The conversations hadn't been original since I started hanging out with Will. Kay didn't like him and she'd never kept it a secret.

I watched her sip her coffee and wondered if she had always been so cynical or if it came after.

In the nearly twice years I'd lived in Kay's apartment, she only spoke in vague statements about what happened before I knew her. What I picked up came from people at the DeKay House. There weren't any pictures in the apartment or on her social media. The only details I discovered could be counted on one hand: his name was Daniel; he liked getting high; he wasn't picky about substances; he died. Not surprisingly, Kay had yet to recover.

I glanced at the painting above the bricked-over fireplace. For months after I moved in, I saw nothing but smudges of greys, blacks, reds across the canvas. That changed when someone let it slip at a party the previous August that it happened to be the second anniversary of Danny's death. I started to see the shapes in the brush strokes; The hands reaching out for each other, the distance they could never close.

"Who drove you home?" Kay asked. She shoved some

books away from the edge of the coffee table to set her mug down.

I picked up the thawing peas and pressed them against my cheek. "Some guy from the DeKay House," I said. My cheeks began to feel warm. I moved the bag of peas to hide my embarrassment.

"Really? Who?" Kay curled up with her legs tucked in and head against the back like she might fall back to sleep.

"The guy who gave me this," I said, lifting the peas off my face. "He says he used to go there all the time with his brother or something, but he was really clean cut."

The car ride turned out to be far less awkward than I suspected. We talked about music and about how he had to drive out of the city to pick up his girlfriend from a house party in Milton. I told him about my job on Queen Street and how I both appreciated and loathed tourists. It had been easy conversation, especially when we both got caught up singing along to the music. The ride made the night feel less horrible.

"Oh, someone I know?" Kay asked. She adjusted herself in the seat until she sat upright.

"Doubt it. Chase Reid. He's in this band, Forever July. I think I told you about them." Just mentioning his name caused heat to flood my cheeks. How ridiculous Chase and I must have looked getting into his car together. A mix-matched pair.

"Forever July..." Kay drifted a minute, then found it. "You wrote that blog post about them a bit ago."

"Yeah. He's the lead singer."

"That was nice of him. Are you going to see him again?" Kay asked.

I wondered if she had mistaken my earlier blush for something more than it was. A golden boy like Chase Reid didn't date girls like me.

Before I had to answer, an aggressive buzz came from the intercom. We both jumped, startled. I pushed myself from the couch, taking the peas along with me. Without asking who wanted in, I pressed the white button to let them enter. Another buzz filled the apartment, letting us know the main door was unlocked. I made my way back to the couch and settled in.

Kay gathered her books from the table, never setting down her coffee. "I'll be in my room if you need me."

"Why?" I asked, but she didn't answer.

I watched her walk toward the hallway and disappear around the wall. Even if it was Will coming up to the apartment, she never left so abruptly.

Maybe she didn't believe me about the black eye. It wouldn't be the first time she assumed Will did something that he didn't do.

The front door opened and Will walked in with two paper cups from the cafe below our apartment. The ever-present circles under his eyes were deeper than normal. He strolled over and kissed me. He tasted like beer and cigarettes.

"What happened to your face?" he asked, handing me one cup of coffee. He tossed himself onto the couch next to me, tucking his feet under my thighs. The physical touch made me smile. I enjoyed closing my eyes and feeling his heat next to me.

"The mosh pit last night," I asked.

"Sounds like we both had a crazy night. I don't even remember how I got to Hunter's place."

A small piece of me wanted to remind him of how he had left me alone at the party. Another part of me, the large part, knew it wouldn't be worth the fight. If Will got defensive, it would be days before his anger subsided.

I took a sip of the coffee. The bitterness caught me off guard.

"I think I got your coffee," I said, handing the cup over to Will.

He sipped from the cup in his own hand before shaking his head. "Nah, they're both black. What did you want in it?"

"No, this is good," I lied, squeezing his knee.

I pushed myself up from the couch, grabbed the thawing bag of peas, and headed into the kitchen to get myself some cream and sugar.

3

"I CAN'T BELIEVE I LET YOU TALK ME INTO THIS," WILL SAID, AS he slipped between a group of guys with three tall boy cans of beer. It had only taken two bands before he started complaining, so I considered it a win. I accepted the beer with one hand and tapped the last comments into my phone with the other. I wanted to remember that the drummer of the previous band was inconsistent, but the vocals were solid. I also wanted to note how hectic their movements were on stage, how their antics fit the chaos of their sound.

My phone stored details to keep me inspired for the blog post I'd type up later that night. Since I'd reviewed Forever July's live show several times, I finished the last of my thoughts and slipped the phone into the back pocket of my jeans. With the work complete, I could just enjoy the rest of the show.

"You act like I'm torturing you," I said as he worked his way against the wall next to me.

A couple on one side of us were too busy making out to notice we had taken over the space one of them had occupied earlier. On the other side, a group of friends in their late twenties were talking about what it was like when they were young enough to slam around in the mosh pit. It felt safe there, hidden behind the crowd.

I knew how much Will hated going to anything but shows of the most intense political punk bands. I'd only asked him to accompany me a handful of times, because going alone was easier than trying to make sure he had a good time. Going to shows alone didn't bother me, but that night I needed the backup. If Chase Reid didn't remember inviting me to the show, I didn't want to look like a fool standing alone, like I was waiting for him.

It had been almost three weeks since Chase and I had talked, since he'd said he would put me on the guest list for the show. When we got to the door, I handed over tickets I bought the week before. I couldn't bring myself to ask if he'd given them my name for the list. I didn't know if I'd be able to go in if they said they had no one with my name on record.

"This is torture. I can't believe you like this music. It's watered-down punk. It shouldn't even have punk in the name. It makes a mockery of real punk. I didn't know you were into this shit." Will shook his head in disappointment. He chugged his beer, dropped the can on the floor and crushed it with his boot. Meanwhile, I hoped everyone around us was too busy to hear his rant.

"I'm sorry I'm ruining your night," I mumbled before taking a large mouthful from my own can. I wanted to have a good time and I wanted to see how things had changed since Mitchell took over lead guitar.

Having Will there made it different. Going to shows outside of the DeKay House had never been a social activity for me; it was more like meditation. Surrounded by people, yet I didn't need to talk and didn't need to worry if someone else was having a good time. I could focus on the lyrics, the vibrations of bass in my chest, the melodic guitars. I wanted to get back to that, but I couldn't.

"If you stay at my place tonight, we can call it even," he said, leaning over and planting a kiss on my collar bone.

I glanced around to see who might have seen. I turned my face away from everyone, toward him. "Your mom hates me."

"They're out west until next week."

I shrugged. "All right, deal."

The crowd stretched out in front of us, becoming denser as it neared the stage. The opening bands had drawn the audience in, but when Forever July would come out, things would erupt.

The double doors that led backstage opened and a photographer I knew from other shows walked out. The door swung shut behind her and I turned away.

"Are you in a mood?" he asked, staring at me with a raised eyebrow. He wrapped an arm around my waist and whispered loud enough to be heard over the music, "Did something happen at work today? Were the tourists pissing you off again?"

The question made me realize I'd made a mistake. Asking Will to come with me didn't make sense. If I ran into Chase and he mentioned inviting me there, I'd spend the night trying to mitigate Will's anger.

"Yeah, the tourists." The lie made its way up my spine, straightening my back under Will's touch.

If I'd told him why I had wanted him to come, the whole truth, he wouldn't be pressing his cheek against mine. It would hurt him if he knew I invited him because of Chase Reid. It would devastate him if he knew that I begged him to watch bands he hates, because I was worried about what another man would think about me.

"We should go." I slipped my hand into his. "Let's just go back to your parents' place."

"That sounds like a way better plan than this," Will grunted.

I turned away from him and straight into the

photographer from earlier, Camila Gutierrez. She had one hand gripping the lens of her camera, the other perched on her hip.

"You're Peyton, right?" Camila asked.

I nodded. I had seen her work online. Not only did she have an eye for live shows, capturing the perfect moments when they jumped, screamed, spit water into the air, she always took great portraits of bands, and great candid shots of them backstage.

"I'm Camila. You free after this?" she asked. She shifted her weight from one foot to the other and watched me, waiting for me to say something.

"Um, I'm not sure. What's up?" I asked, hoping my voice came off more confident than I felt.

She might have been a few inches shorter than me, but her shoulders were squared, her head was tipped high. Her confidence intimidated me. I knew how many followers her social media accounts had and I saw first-hand the way people gravitated toward her.

"I actually gotta get back up there," Camila said. Then the lights dimmed. "Stick around after the show for a few minutes? I have to talk to you."

She didn't wait for an answer, but gave a short wave and jogged toward the stage. I couldn't tell if she didn't have time to care about the answer or if she was just confident that I'd wait.

The crowd's collective voice rose and hands shot up in the air. Over everyone's heads, I caught sight of Chase Reid strolling out in front of the crowd with such ease, like he entered a room of friends. He waved to a few people up front before pressing his lips to the microphone. His eyes turned in my direction or at least, I felt like they did.

"If we're staying, you're buying the beer for the rest of the night," Will shouted over the sound of Forever July crashing into their first track.

FOREVER JULY NEVER PUT ON A DISAPPOINTING SET, BUT THAT night felt surreal. Their timing was flawless. Their energy was high. Mitchell's guitar riffs were on point. Chase's voice had elevated since the last time I watched them. Between songs, their fans kept moving, so not to miss the beat when the next one started. It was a show that fans of Forever July would talk about for months.

Many nights, I left inspired after their performances. Heading home, I'd still feel the vibration of the bass notes through my body, still hear the lyrics looping in my head. Nights like that I had to get it all down before the feeling faded or became ground down by the monotony of everyday life. That was how my blog began.

But only a few moments in my life felt like that night, like a shift in the world as I knew it.

I felt it the morning I found the envelope of money hidden in my mother's box of tampons. It was there the night I stole the money and shoved it into the bottom of my backpack. I also felt it the first time I went to The DeKay House, the night Kay offered me a place to stay.

A shift in the atmosphere. The pressure filled the space around me I stood there.

The house lights came on and the night ended. The crowd shoved their way out the exits while some people stood around to chat with each other.

Will sighed and said he was going to have a cigarette while he waited for me.

I reached for his hand, but by the time I thought of the right way to ask him to stay, he'd already put more distance between us than I could reach across.

Alone, waiting for Camila was excruciating. I kept my eyes on the stage, watching the crew tearing down the equipment. Every time someone stepped out of the wings, I sucked in a breath, hoping it wouldn't be Chase. I didn't want him to see me pressed against the wall and think I'd stuck around to see him.

The double doors next to the stage opened and Camila walked out with the camera around her neck. Before the door swung shut, Chase Reid followed her out, talking as he and Camila strode toward me.

I uncrossed my arms, crossed them again, unsure of what to do with my hands. I wished I had a drink to make me look busy.

Chase grinned at me.

"I heard you two know each other," Camila said, gesturing to Chase.

"We started the new year as new friends," Chase said.

I pressed my lips together to keep from smiling too wide.

"I was going on and on about this idea I had and Chase mentioned your blog," Camila said. She dug into the sleek, brown camera bag across her chest, pulled out a card and handed it to me: her social media details, phone number and email. The embossed black letters on the stark white card looked so professional.

"Good thing you came tonight," Chase said as he tugged on his sweat-soaked t-shirt.

I raised an eyebrow.

"I have a proposition," Camila said.

My stomach tightened.

Chase chuckled. "It's a good one."

Camila swatted at him to hush. "I like your blog a lot. I read all your posts in a day. I think we could team up and make it something next level."

When she'd asked me to wait after the show, I hadn't thought about what she wanted. If I'd known, I might have left with the rest of the crowd. My blog wasn't meant to be next level—I never dreamed that big.

"I'm a shit writer. I can't form a grammatical sentence to

save my life, but I had this dream of one day creating a publication." Camila pulled out her cellphone and turned the screen toward me. "I'm only decent at web design, but I'm a good photographer, so I can bring something to the table."

The screen showed some logos for my blog name, *Eternal Spin*. My favourite had to be the small 'A' being replaced with a record and tonearm.

She swiped, and the next image made my breathing hitch: a mock-up of my blog, expanded. Headers read *Music, Shopping, Venues, Resources, Eats,* among others. The colours were simple. The page was mostly white with the banner in black and soft yellow, typeface black with the same yellow dividers. Sleek and professional.

"Wow." I was staggered. It was a mock-up of what the blog could be.

"When we get some traction, we'll sell ad space. Get a calendar together for shows and events. You already have the foundation, but together we could turn it into something not just profitable, but bigger than both of us."

The idea was too big. I had no chance of pulling off something like that—and the thought of working with Camila Gutierrez was overwhelming.

"This isn't something I can do on my own," Camila said.

I'd never been the person people relied on. I didn't know how to take the request.

"And I would like to create it with someone who has a similar vibe," she went on. "I get that from your work. I get that from you now."

"You do?" I said with a laugh.

"Yeah, I'm looking to avoid ego. I've dealt with egos. It's not my thing. I want someone honest, someone I could see being my friend, not just a business partner, you know?" Camila gave a small shrug, like those demands weren't a big ask.

But I was drawn to her concept. I didn't know if I could

keep up with Camila and her vision, but I liked the idea of spending time with her. We liked the same music and I liked the idea of sharing that with someone. I knew how massive her photography following was and the attention she'd bring to my blog. What I couldn't decide was if that's what I wanted.

Sensing my withdrawal, she said, "How about this? We collab on a post about tonight. You do your thing, write your review of the show. I'll post one picture on my Instagram and mention that the others will be on your blog. We can see how it goes? If you don't want to do it, it brings a little attention to your blog and we go our own way."

"As a fan of both of you, please do it." Chase chuckled. His enthusiasm made its way to me, running up my fingers, tingling through my chest.

"I don't really have followers to promote it to," I confessed.

"How many visits do you get on your blog?" Camila asked.

"Only about four hundred—I don't promote it," I admitted. "But I could try, try to promote it."

I'd been working on the blog for a year and a half, averaging the same steady numbers every week, the same people clicking on my page, looking for updates, and links to new music. My followers weren't growing daily, like Camila's.

I pushed the hair behind my ears and glanced at the group of kids who were still hanging around, waiting to get Chase's attention.

"Okay, that's lower than I thought," Camila said with a shrug. "But we can work with four hundred views a month—and with…"

I cut her off. "Oh—a week, sorry."

"You get four hundred views a week on your blog?"

Chase's eyebrow arched upward. "Without promotion? Without tags? Without SEO?"

"SEO? I don't…" I shrugged.

"Search Engine Optimization."

"Chase," someone called from the stage. We all turned to look: it was a woman wearing a Forever July t-shirt, hands on her hips.

This must be Chase's girlfriend, I assumed. I could tell by the polished look. Her hair had immaculate waves. I didn't know anyone who looked as classy as she did in jeans and a t-shirt.

She ran her fingers through her long, blonde waves and said, "We're heading out."

He raised his pointer finger. She tipped her head with a smile and headed backstage.

"Think about it and text me, alright?" Camila said. "I think together we can do something really awesome."

Will's fingers on my waist made me freeze..

He nodded at Camila, ignored Chase, and asked me, "Ready to go?"

"Hey—" Chase said. "You two should come to a party I'm having next week before we head out on tour. It's on a Thursday, so I know it might be—"

Will raised a hand to stop Chase short. "Your party?" His laugh came out in a snort.

I flinched.

"Yeah, my party," Chase responded. His voice was steady.

I couldn't bring myself to look at him, to see his reaction to Will's tone.

Will said, "You sold out, and now you want us to come to your party? You need us to give your party an edge?"

I squeezed Will's hand urgently. I didn't want him to start a fight, to see him and Chase come to blows.

And I could see Camila's face change. I panicked. If the conversation didn't end soon, Camila would send me some excuse as to why our partnership wouldn't work, before it even began.

"We'll have drinks and food, just show up," Chase said, ignoring Will's outburst.

I expected Will to argue with him, to protest, but he only grumbled and motioned for us to leave.

"When you text Cam, she'll send party details, cool?" Chase said to me.

I searched his face for a reaction. His eyes were light. His nod was easy. He'd taken Will's comments in stride.

A smile tugged at the corners of my mouth. "Yeah, cool."

Chase gave me a wave, then turned around and headed for the stage, thanking a few lingering kids for coming as he went.

I tried not to stare.

"Definitely, message me," Camila said, pointing to the card in my hand.

"Sure, yeah."

Will grabbed my hand and made for the exit. When I glanced back, Camila was on her phone already.

We were outside in the cold, damp air fast.

Will pulled the hood of his sweater over his head. "You know there's no way in hell we're going to that party, right?"

I knew better than to respond. His reaction to Chase had been minor on the scale of Will's moods, but once his emotional temperature starting rising, it didn't take much to hit the boiling point. I wanted to go to Chase's party, but I didn't plan on telling Will that night.

As we walked through spitting rain to the car, I thought about Camila's proposition. It would bring in traffic to my blog, like she said, but I didn't know if it mattered to me. I didn't know if I wanted something more than I already had.

But then I thought about the easy confidence she showed. It didn't give her pause to walk up to a stranger and propose an idea. She didn't seem to mind expressing her weakness in writing and she held no embarrassment saying what she excelled at. Maybe spending time in her presence, some of that strength would rub off on me.

It would only be one post, I reminded myself.

I pulled the phone from my back pocket. When Will became distracted with his own phone, I took out Camila's card, tapped her number into my contacts, and sent a message.

*I'm willing to try one blog post.*

4

FORTY-EIGHT HOURS AFTER THE POST WENT PUBLIC, KAY AND I walked into the DeKay House—the night was in full swing when we arrived. Since I'd spent my entire shift at Ever Black Vintage Clothing thinking about the blog post Camila and I had created, I'd fallen behind on inventory that needed pricing. All the bathroom breaks I took to check the view count climbing had put me two tasks behind when the store closed at nine-thirty. Because of it, it was almost midnight by the time we crossed the House's threshold.

A few people waved and we waved back.

Kay kept her faux leather jacket on, but I tossed my jean jacket onto the pile that accumulated on the stairs. We made our way down the graffiti hallway.

"What do you think?" I asked.

"Well, I always thought this was for fun, so what are your actual goals for the blog?" Kay asked as we walked into the kitchen. She nodded at the guy standing behind the two kegs. He took ten dollars from each of us and handed over blue plastic cups.

"I thought no one would care about it, honestly," I admitted.

Kay filled one cup, handed it to me and took the other from my hand. I took a sip of the beer, feeling the foam against the tip of my nose.

"And now?" Kay dropped the keg nozzle into the bucket of ice.

A band started in the basement, making the floor vibrate. A group of people next to us turned to head toward the sound.

I watched them go, wondering why I couldn't have a night of unthinking fun. "I like that people are reading. People have commented on my old posts, saying they're checking out bands I mentioned. One band emailed me, asking if I'd do a review of their newest album for my blog, and that they would give me a free copy on vinyl for it." That email had stuck with me through my whole shift—wondering how to respond that would sound more professional than *hell yes*.

We made our way back into the living room. I glanced around for Will. He'd texted close to eleven, saying he had arrived, but I didn't see him.

"And what has Camila said?" Kay asked.

"That she likes seeing her work next to mine and she's in, if I am."

Kay's perfect eyebrow arched. She tapped the plastic cups with one of her rings.

I listened to the band in the basement, a staple for The DeKay House: a group of teens paying tribute to LA punk bands like X and the Germs. They were sloppy with their sound and their lyrics were half-baked, but they brought the energy, so people enjoyed the performance.

"You should do it," Kay finally said. "It's a good project for you. You don't have to quit working retail, you can keep doing basically what you're doing now, but it gives you something to look forward to, to see it grow."

For my entire life, the goal to get out of my parents' house occupied my plans for the future. Since leaving, my focus changed to all the things I could do without being under their rules, away from the fear of making a mistake.

That first weekend in Kay's apartment, I stayed up until four in the morning watching television until my eyes watered. I ate sugary cereal. I put on make-up. I wore clothes that showed my shoulders, even if I couldn't bring myself to expose my thighs. Setting goals hadn't been high on the priority list. I never assumed I'd make it long enough to worry about the future.

"What are your goals?" I asked Kay. "I mean, your just got your accounting degree, but now what?"

Kay swirled the liquid around in her cup and watched it steady before saying, "I had a lot of goals before."

The *before* spoke volumes. I didn't say anything, but nodded to let her know I was listening.

"I wanted to start a gallery and…Well, we wanted a family."

While she rarely said his name, I knew 'we' meant her and Daniel. I wondered what it was like to think about someone so much that using their name didn't feel necessary.

"We had it all figured out. My sister was going to be our surrogate. Daniel wanted to open his own guitar shop." Kay glanced up from her cup and shrugged.

I gave her time, hoping she would expand on things with Daniel, but I should have known better. She tipped the cup into her mouth and swallowed its contents.

"You can still have that," I said. Having kids never crossed my mind. The thought of taking care of someone other than myself seemed exhausting, impossible. I knew how easily parents messed up their kids.

"I think that dream is dead," Kay said. As the words passed over her lips, her forehead and eyes crinkled. She held up her empty cup. "I'm going to grab another and then say *hey* to some people. You want to come?"

I shook my head, leaving out the part about finding Will, and let Kay walk from the kitchen before taking my phone from my back pocket.

The night before, I'd moved the website app to the main screen on my phone. I tapped it open and looked at the view count.

We were reaching a thousand views for the day again, two thousand in forty-eight hours. I'd more than doubled my monthly views in two days. I hadn't even implemented all the ideas that Camila shared with me to help promote my blog. I grinned at the screen.

I didn't know where I wanted the blog to go, didn't know what I expected to accomplish, but the idea of being able to work on my website without having to work another job felt like a good goal to have. Camila suggested selling ads, making revenue from the views, and merchandise if people liked us; she talked about her goals for what she called *the publication*. Office space, interns—other writers on staff. In our text messages since the post went live, I'd felt a spark of excitement with each idea she suggested.

Kay's goals were bigger. She got her degree and wanted to work in a gallery and start a family. Those were life-altering goals, things that would carry her into the next phases of her life.

As I searched for Will, I stopped to say hello to a few people I knew, before heading outside onto the back deck, which had begun slanting toward the overgrown yard. Despite the risk of its collapse, there were always people out there and usually Will.

That night was no exception.

Will stood against the far side of the deck, leaning on the banister, all of his attention focused on a girl with a shaved head.

I didn't recognize her. She laughed with her head thrown

back, her long neck exposed. Will's entire body leaned toward her.

It reminded me of the night I'd gotten to know Will, when I was still the new girl at the DeKay House. I'd been standing in the kitchen, picking at the skin around my nails. People said hello, as they did to everyone. No one was rude, but only Will came over to ask where I came from, what my name was, if I liked the band playing. I'd been standoffish and uncomfortable, but the next weekend he did the same, and the weekend after that. Within a month he had me laughing at his jokes the way the girl with the shaved head was laughing at them now.

He asked me once if I wanted a relationship. The question had come when we'd just started spending time together. The only relationship I knew was my parents. Committing made me nervous. I didn't know if it meant we'd have to spend all our time together. I didn't know if it meant that I'd have to ask his permission before Kay and I went out. I didn't know if it meant I could no longer go out at all. So, I said no. He smiled, nodded, and said we were on the same page. He said that I got it and no other girls got it. It made me feel good that he thought I was special. The question never came up again.

Because I said no, I knew I needed to push the rising heat from my stomach back down. We didn't own each other, as he'd reminded me before. I couldn't tell him to keep his hands off her arm. I had no right to complain about how he leaned in to talk to her. He could flirt with whomever he wanted.

"Will," his friend Hunter called out.

Will turned to look at him and then to me. "Hey, Peyton," Will said, waving me over. "I want you to meet Molly. Molly, this is Peyton."

Molly stopped laughing. She stopped smiling all together. "I should go find my friends," she said. Her eyes never landed on me as she excused herself and darted back into the house.

"You're in trouble now," Hunter snorted, nodding his head at me.

Will flung an arm over my shoulder. "Nah, Peyton isn't like your uptight bitch of a girlfriend."

My entire body stiffened. I'd only met Hunter's girlfriend on a few occasions, but she was sweet. From what I remembered, she didn't like when Hunter got blacked-out drunk or when he did cocaine with his sketchy neighbours. To me, those were reasonable things to be upset about.

But unlike her, I never said those things to Will. I didn't want to nag him. I remembered how much my father hated to be nagged. I released my fists.

"You're lucky," Hunter said, slapping Will on the back. He turned to. "Hey Peyton, why don't you leave this clown? I'll treat you better than he ever could."

I tried to laugh, but the sound wouldn't rise in my throat. I mustered up a weak smile.

Will kissed my neck and asked, "Were you looking for me?"

"Yeah." I leaned into him and said, "Can I ask you a weird question?"

"What up?" He reached out and wiggled his fingers at Hunter. Hunter passed the joint he was holding.

Will's willingness to answer the question surprised me. I figured he must be high already. While he was in a good mood, I had to take advantage.

"What are your goals?" I asked as he put the joint between his lips.

Will let out a loud chuckle and exhaled smoke into the air in front of us. "My goals?"

Hunter and their two other friends snorted with laughter.

I stared into the cup of beer warming in my hand and

asked, "Like, for the future or whatever. Do you have any goals?"

"Yeah, sure. Goals. My goals are to get fucking wasted tonight." Will and the guys high-fived at the answer.

"But what about long term? What do you want out of life?"

"Life? Who knows. Live for the right now, Peyton," Will said, handing me the joint.

I took a small puff before handing it over to Hunter. I should have known better than to ask for a genuine answer, especially in front of his friends.

"Wanna go watch the bands?" I asked.

"We'll meet you in there," Will said, turning his attention back to Hunter.

My phone vibrated as I headed back into the house. It might be Camila, telling me we passed two thousand views, or Kay asking where I was.

Instead of a name, my phone displayed a local number. I tapped the message and sucked in a breath as I read, *Hey! It's Chase. Got your number from Cam. Hope that's cool?*

I had the urge to write back something with at least one exclamation mark, but I didn't want to be too needy, too excited.

After a deep breath, I tapped out a response.

*What are your life goals?*

I slipped into the hallway where Chase and I had talked on New Year's and waited for an answer. The longer I waited, the more I regretted sending the text. In my head it had seemed like a smooth response, but it might be too much. We didn't know each other. It would be a stretch to say we were friends.

After chugging the rest of my beer, I rested my head against the wall.

"Peyton, you coming?" Kay called as she headed into the basement.

I pushed myself off the wall and said, "Yeah, coming."

My phone vibrated again.

*Good question! Tour with Jimmy Eat World. Buy a house. Maybe open a recording studio? And eventually have a family. What about you?*

I smiled at my phone and tapped out a response before heading into the basement.

*Not sure yet. Working on it though.*

5

KAY'S BEDROOM WAS ONE OF MY FAVOURITE PLACES IN THE apartment. It smelled of vanilla and incense that followed her home from her work. Salt lamps on her dresser and the windowsill cast the space in a warm glow despite the white light of the overhead bulb.

Canvases were stacked with their painted fronts toward the grey walls. The secrecy of her work made me want to peek at them, but I knew better. On one occasion I did sneak a glance at a single stack of canvases: all portraits of people who looked tormented, creased foreheads, screaming mouths, teary eyes. I didn't recognize any of the faces. Actual people, or images she created on her own? I'd never asked, afraid I'd broken an unspoken rule by looking at them.

"Why don't you come tonight?" I asked as she sat on the bed in front of me.

Kay rolled her makeup cart closer with her foot to pick up a second eyeshadow. "Alain and I are going to get ice cream and go for a walk," she said, tapping a soft brush into the eyeshadow pot.

I closed my eyes. "You two are spending a lot of time together."

The feeling of the brush sweeping across my lid was calming. All day I'd felt nervous about going to a party at Chase's parents' house. I was on edge about Will possibly finding out, nervous I wouldn't have anything to say to Camila outside of the blog, concerned that people would see I didn't belong at a party like that.

"It's not romantic," Kay said.

"It would be okay if it was," I told her.

"I know, but it's not. I'm not ready for that."

She tapped the brush onto the edge of the eyeshadow lid. I opened my eyes and she studied me, one hand on my chin to turn my face from side to side.

"If I'd known you were ready to learn more about makeup, we could have started *before* you actually planned on wearing it," Kay said. She picked up a natural eyeshadow palette.

"I was just going to wear mascara, but thought maybe..."

I tried to be subtle, asking for her help, saying I didn't want to look washed out in photos, if Camila took any.

"There's nothing wrong with wanting to do your makeup," Kay reminded me. She held up the brush with a cream-coloured eyeshadow, a signal for me to shut my eyes again. I did. The brush moved across my lid toward my temple in long, gentle strokes.

Makeup had been forbidden growing up. The only things in my mother's drawer were tubes of concealer, one of which I'd kept to hide my teenage acne. When she realized I'd taken it from her, she suggested I leave it in the shoe box in her closet so I didn't get caught with it. She promised I could use it any time I wanted. That single tube of too-dark concealer was my only makeup experience until I moved in with Kay.

"Relax your face." Kay's breath warmed my cheek as she spoke.

I exhaled, trying to push the tension out of my forehead and jaw.

"Do you like this guy?" Kay asked.

"What guy?" I asked. I knew she meant Chase, but I didn't want to admit he was the first person that crossed my mind when she asked.

"The guy whose party you're going to."

"He seems nice. We've been texting."

Kay stopped moving.

I opened my eyes and she blinked before turning back to the palette. She gave me a tight-lipped smile. "Oh, you didn't tell me."

I didn't know how to explain how texting Chase made me feel. Emotions layered like sedimentary rock. Periods of calm or happiness squished between layers of guilt, panic, and self-doubt. Other than our first message, we texted about superficial things like movies or albums we were listening to, but something about it still felt private. Even saying I texted him a dog picture might raise questions I didn't want to answer. I didn't want her to see how he made me smile when he sent a video of his parents' little dog chasing a bee, or how I typed out lyrics to a song I'd been listening to on repeat. I didn't want her to spot the signs of guilt when my phone vibrated. Especially when Will and I were together.

"It's just nice to have another friend." I shut my eyes as she raised her hand with a new brush. "So I don't have to be so dependent on you."

Kay let out a deep chuckle. "You're fine without me."

"Barely. Remember all the red flags you pointed out about the lady I was renting a room from? I would have never realized she was sneaking into my room when I was out," I said, arching a single eyebrow.

I tried to think of how to say thank you in a way that sounded genuine, but nothing I could think up felt big enough.

"There you go," Kay said. Her weight shifted on the bed as she picked up a mirror and handed it to me.

The airbrushed looked of my skin, the brightness of my eyes, took me by surprise. Kay had gone light like she promised, but I was used to seeing my face with just mascara and lip gloss. I still looked like myself, but with the edges smoothed over.

"Just one more thing," Kay said, reaching to the dresser without standing up. She handed me lipstick. "Take this one with you. I did a natural look on the rest, so red lip will give it that party vibe."

I glanced down at the tube in my palm. Camila and Kay looked elegant in a red lip. They looked badass. I didn't know if I could pull it off.

My father's voice rang in my ears, his vocabulary for a woman in red lipstick, short skirts, and bare arms. He held very little back, even in public.

"Give it a try," Kay said, taking the mirror and holding it up.

I popped off the top and twisted until the colour appeared. Blood red. I focused only on my lips in the mirror. But when I capped the lipstick again, I felt shocked to see it against my skin. I didn't feel bold or elegant. I looked like a clown.

I turned my attention away from the mirror and handed the lipstick over to Kay.

"No, you'll need to reapply. Keep it," Kay explained as she got up. "It suits you."

I stood up. She might notice if I left the tube on the dresser.

My phone vibrated on the bed. A text from Camila.
*Outside!*

"Your ride here?" Kay asked.

I nodded, tucking the lipstick into my pocket along with my phone.

"I'm not working in the morning, so if you wanna come

home before Camila's ready, let me know. If Alain and I are out and about, we can get you," Kay said.

"Thanks, Kay."

She smiled at me as I grabbed my jacket from the back of the chair and snatched up a tissue from the box on the table. Kay held the door open for me while I slipped into my shoes.

"Have fun and be good." Kay chuckled as I stepped out into the stairwell.

I gave Kay a wave as I jogged down the stairs. At the bottom step, after listening for the sound of the door shutting, I used the tissue to rub the red from my lips.

---

6

EVEN THOUGH CHASE HAD TOLD ME THE PARTY WAS AT HIS parents' house, I wasn't prepared for the reality of it. I hadn't been inside a friend's childhood home since middle school. I couldn't remember now whether they stopped inviting me or I stopped going because the contrast to my own family made visiting too heartbreaking.

The Reid household made me wonder if this thing sitting heavy on my chest was culture shock. Family pictures on the wall: all wearing similar colours, little Chase next to his brother—cheesy, adorable outfits and poses filled every frame. I watched Chase grow from one frame to the next. His perfect blonde-haired, light-eyed family smiled down at us as we headed down the hall.

I'd never been to a party where candles sat in the centre of the coffee table, where people used actual glasses and not plastic cups, where guests moved around the house like they owned it. Everything looked too clean to be hosting a party of at least fifty people.

Camila stopped to speak to a group of women who beamed at her and laughed at everything she said. Even though their eyes never left Camila's, I could tell they were paying attention to me. I picked at the skin on my lip.

"I'm going to find Chase," I whispered to Camila before weaving through the pockets of people. A few people turned to watch me go. I pulled my hands into the sleeves of my shirt.

Chase stood in the kitchen, leaning against the counter, a group of people close around him, trying to soak up every word. I hung back. He stopped to let someone else speak, nodding as he listened.

Between the heads of his friends, our eyes met. The corner of his mouth pulled up and he excused himself from the group. I sucked in a breath and held it as he approached.

"For some reason I didn't think you'd come," Chase said.

We stepped to the side to keep from blocking the kitchen door. He pushed the hood of the burnt orange sweater off his head, his teen heartthrob waves falling back into place.

"I said I would," I told him, trying not to stare.

"People say a lot of things. But I shouldn't have doubted you," Chase said. I looked up at him and smiled. He took a sip of the beer in his hand and went on, "I'm glad you guys came all the way out here. I've been looking for apartments in the city, since we're making enough money now, which is..."

"Kind of unreal?"

He let out a quiet chuckle. "Super unreal. I thought I'd always be working for my dad to support the band, you know?"

"You too good for club shows now? Are you going to start doing amphitheatre events and making people pay hundreds of dollars to see you?" I asked with a raised eyebrow.

"Never," he said with a deep chuckle. The skin around his eyes crinkled with amusement. It made me smile.

A woman cut in next to me. "I don't know why he's so afraid of success."

Both Chase and I turned to look at Chase's girlfriend. She

shoved her hands into the pockets of her dress and leaned into Chase. His response seemed automatic: he moved the beer from one hand to the other and the empty hand took hold of her waist. When she rested her head on his shoulder his head tipped toward her.

"Peyton, this is my girlfriend, Melissa. Melissa..."

"Peyton of the *blog*," Melissa said. Her wide smile held so much confidence. Up close she was stunning.

"Yes, I'm Peyton of the blog. It's nice to meet you."

"I heard you and Camila are going into business together?" She raised a single eyebrow like she actually wanted to hear the answer.

"Oh, I'm not sure."

"You should do it," Chase said. "The two of you have amazing talent. I can't imagine what you could do if you worked together."

"Do an interview with Forever July," Melissa suggested. "It would be good publicity for you and Chase won't get so nervous about what questions are going to be asked."

Chase being nervous had never crossed my mind. I glanced up. I wondered where he tucked the nervous version of himself away when he stood on stage, when he did interviews, when he posed for photoshoots. I envied his ability to hide it.

"I don't know if I'm ready to start interviewing anyone," I said with a short laugh. "I'm not exactly a people person."

Melissa pulled a hand from her pocket and took my wrist. I bumped into the wall behind me as she stepped into my personal space. Her eyes locked onto mine. The harder I tried not to blink, the more I did.

"Helen Keller said that life is either a daring adventure or nothing at all," Melissa said. Her eyebrows moved up and down, as if telling me something without words.

I kept blinking.

When someone called out to her, I sighed with relief. Her

hand left my wrist and attached itself to Chase's, tugging him.

"We'll be right back," Chase said.

Melissa turned her attention to a couple in the living room who had just arrived. Chase mouthed 'sorry' as he followed behind her.

I had an urge to follow them—I didn't want to be left standing in the kitchen alone and Camila was nowhere to be found. At the DeKay House, people just assumed they knew everyone else; people approached strangers, making them feel welcome. There was comfort in it. I didn't know how to talk to the people around me, didn't know their interests for an ice breaker. I didn't know how to approach someone when we had nothing in common.

The atmosphere at the party gave off more of a high school vibe with cliques and groups of girls heading off to the bathrooms together. I glanced around at all the small huddles of people wondering who I could approach. Posing in the middle several women I saw Mitchell Rizzo, Forever July's lead guitarist. Someone must have asked to see his tattoo because he'd pulled up the side of his shirt, showing off the dips and slopes of his toned torso. I recognized the image tattooed on his ribs. Two robots leaning on each other, headphones over their robot ears. I crossed the dining room to where Mitchell stood.

"The Get Up Kids, right?" I said, nodding where his shirt fell over his body.

He looked up and stared at me for a minute and grinned.

"The girl from the blog," Mitchell said. "The only person who saw my true talent."

I laughed and shrugged. "It's Peyton."

"Wanna do a shot, Peyton?" he asked, then held up a finger. "Wait, are you old enough to drink?"

"Twenty-one."

"Still a baby," he chuckled, waving at me to follow.

"Compared to who?" I laughed. "You guys are what? Twenty-five?"

"Twenty-six, dear child," Mitchell said over his shoulder. A space had opened at the kitchen island, and he slipped between a few people and took over the spot, asking me "How do you know Chase?"

Bottles and cups cluttered the countertop. Mitchell opened the right cupboard and grabbed a couple of shot glasses. They clinked as he set them on the marble countertop.

"I met him on New Year's. At the DeKay House," I explained.

He filled the two glasses with tequila and slid one toward me. "Do you know his brother?"

We picked up the glasses, clinked, and tipped them into our mouths. The tequila still burned, like all tequila, but smoother. I didn't even think about salt or lemon. Mitchell grabbed two cans of beer from the fridge and set one on the counter in front of me.

"No, I don't know his brother," I said. "Does he hang out at the DeKay House?"

Mitchell glanced around before running a hand over his coiffed hair. "Nah, I just thought maybe you were from around here. So, you're not from Toronto then?"

"Nope. You?" I asked.

"Nope. Came for school, but dropped out for the band. You here for school?"

"Just to get away from my parents," I admitted.

He looked up from pouring a second shot of tequila and nodded.

Only a few people knew I'd left home to get away from my father's rage, away from my mother's compliance. The only times I said it out loud I found sad eyes staring back at me. Mitchell didn't have pity; the nod he gave me said he understood. The same nod Will had given when I told him I had nowhere to go for Christmas.

"To escaping shitty lives," Mitchell said, lifting his shot glass for a second time.

"Escaping shitty lives," I said in return. I coughed a little as the tequila slid down my throat.

"Are you celebrating our partnership?" Camila asked, appearing next to me with a beer in her hand. After a wink, she introduced me to Dylan and Mohammad, known as Mo to his friends. I knew them as the other two members of Forever July. "These boys are my two favourite people." She draped an arm around each of their shoulders. A little beer spilled from her can onto Dylan.

Dylan swatted her away and said, "I was taking this shirt on tour with me—now I'm going to have to wash it before we leave."

"You should wash it anyway," Mo said with a single raised eyebrow.

"Agreed," Camila laughed.

Dylan glared at both of them.

I stood back with my beer and watched them together, bickering like siblings, teasing without concern someone might get offended. They knew and trusted each other. In high school, I'd watched groups of friends who knew each other well. Over time, they learned all of their friends' quirks, their likes and dislikes. They had a bond I'd never experienced.

As I grew up, I wondered if it was my family, the lack of closeness with my parents, that made it impossible to build those types of relationships with other people. The only friendships I had in high school were lunch company, people I nodded at in the hallway. I couldn't remember if any of them even gave me their phone number.

From what Camila told me, her friendship with Mo started as kids. Chase and Dylan came later in high school. It had been the music that brought them together.

"Put on *My Friends Over You*," Dylan told Camila.

Within seconds, she had hijacked the Bluetooth speaker and the song played out through the kitchen.

"Peyton. Dance with us," Camila said while she bounced around to the music.

Mo waved at me to come join. Other than slamming around in the mosh pit, I didn't dance, but I forgot that detail as Dylan grabbed my hand and pulled me into their circle.

"I'm glad you came tonight," Camila said. Her words were slurred from too many drinks, but I knew she meant it by the way she gave me a side hug, our heads resting against each other.

"I wanna partner up," I told her, keeping my voice low so only she could hear. "The Eternal Spin thing. I want to do that."

She let out a loud squeal and wrapped her arms around my neck. Emotional display felt out of character for Camila, at least what I knew of her, but I took it.

---

AFTER MESSAGING KAY THREE TIMES TO TELL HER I WISHED SHE'D come with me to the party, a rush of relief came over me to see her name on my screen. I slipped away from the group to find somewhere quiet. I headed upstairs and down the quiet hallway. More family photographs lined the hall like the ones downstairs, but more casual: family vacations, backyard BBQs, a picture of Chase with Forever July.

I sat cross-legged on the hallway's plush carpet and rested with my back against the wall. I tapped Kay's contact to call her back.

"You didn't tell Will that you were going to Chase's?" Kay asked.

I sucked in a breath.

"Peyton?" She asked.

"I'm here."

"I told him Camila just stopped by and begged you to come last minute, so that's the story." Kay chuckled into the phone. "I figured if you didn't tell him, you probably had a reason."

I exhaled. "You know how he can be when he's drinking."

"Sure do."

"Are you at home now?" I asked.

I glanced up at a frame on the wall. It surprised me to see a picture of Chase and Melissa standing together, holding each other, smiling at each other. Younger, softer faces, leaner bodies. Melissa deserved to be on that wall among his family. They looked perfect together. I tore my eyes away from Chase's younger, rounder face and glanced down at my sock feet.

"Yeah, just sketching. How's the party?" Kay asked.

"You grew up in a house like this?" I asked her.

She chuckled. "Yeah, I grew up in the suburbs."

"It's really nice. I mean, the houses are close together and that's weird, but there's so much house, and it's pretty. And they have family pictures everywhere," I told her. I could feel myself rambling, but tequila kept the words flowing.

"Yes, I'm sure you had embarrassing baby pictures on the walls too," Kay said.

I realized that my half-baked stories about my family had worked. Kay assumed my life had been some version of normal. I must have come off as just another kid whose parents didn't understand them, disgruntled because their dad didn't buy them a car. I wanted that, when I first moved in with Kay. I didn't want to push her away with my stories like I'd done to my friends in school. I didn't want to burden anyone else with my sob story.

"Peyton?" Kay asked.

"Yeah?"

"You good?"

"Yeah, for sure. I should go back the party," I told her.

"If you need to talk when you get home, wake me, okay?" She offered.

"Thanks, Kay."

"Little word of advice, they may have pretty lawns and more square feet, but they still have the same problems."

I didn't know if Chase would ever be able to understand the problems I faced, the problems that Kay faced.

After telling her I missed her at the party again, we hung up. Instead of going back to the party, I opened a document on my phone and typed.

*Where family photographs might have been, cheap hotel art hung. Where a child's art or report cards might have been stuck to the fridge, there was only grocery lists and coupons. No toys on the lawn. No Barbies on the floor. No sign at all that a child lived in the room at the end of the hallway. Just the way her father wanted it. One day she'd leave and no one would remember she'd been there.*

"Hey." Chase's voice startled me. I dropped my phone into my lap and turned my attention up to him. His cheeks were flushed. His lips looked poutier. His fingers ran over a damp spot on the chest of his sweater.

"Sorry. I just needed a quiet spot to call my roommate, tell her I'm okay," I told him.

"No problem. I wanted to show you something anyway," he said. He offered his hand and I took it with my own. His palm was hot to the touch. I tried not to wonder if my own palm felt too clammy or too dry. Before I could get too into my head about it, I was on my feet and he'd let go.

I followed him through an open bedroom door.

Even the navy-blue walls couldn't diminish the size of the space. There were shelves of books, a desk that appeared untouched, and two dressers. I didn't own enough clothes to fill a single dresser, let alone two. Three guitars sat on stands beneath a window. Two acoustic and the electric guitar I'd watched him play many times. The band posters on the walls surrounded a record in a glass frame above the bed. I moved closer to the frame. Inside, Forever July's most recent, self-titled album.

"You don't have your first album up here?" I asked.

Chase crouched at the shelf that held albums and record player. "I've been meaning to get it pressed. The label also offered to re-release it. Maybe when they do? I'm not sure I'm ready yet, ready to put those songs back out there."

He stood up with a record in one hand and turned to me. His forehead creased. I waited, hoping he would give me some insight into what he was thinking.

My thoughts were foggy from all the alcohol. I tried to remember what the songs were about, what he might be unsure of approaching by re-recording. I wanted to think about the deeper meaning to the tracks, but I could only think of one line.

*"I started thinking about you, so I turned the music up,"* I spoke the lyrics to him.

*"I raise my glass and whisper your name for luck."* Chase smiled, but with his heavy eyes and the slump of his shoulders, it became the saddest smile I'd ever laid eyes on.

"It might not be as polished as your self-titled album, but the emotion of *Summer's End* feels more real, more honest than the more fun songs of your self-titled."

I wanted to tell him how the songs helped me through my difficult time. I wanted to ask what happened, for him to write lyrics so filled with sorrow. I didn't know how someone who lived in a house like that, with a family who clearly adored him, could write lyrics full of such heartbreak. I wanted to believe what Kay said, about his family having their own issues, but looking around, it was hard to see where such secrets would be hidden.

Before I could ask what he'd written about, he raised his arm to show me the album in his hand. I knew the cover well. I had a copy in my own collection which was only a quarter the size of Chase's, but I didn't recognize the markings on the cover. I took a step closer, my leg bumping into the edge of his bed.

"Are those signatures?" I asked. "Please tell me that's real. Like, is that Blake Schwarzenbach's actual autograph?"

"I'm not proud of how much I paid for this," Chase said with a short laugh.

He handed it to me. I took it with light fingers, not wanting to damage the unflawed sleeve, or get oils from my hands on the cover.

"This Jawbreaker album was the first material thing I ever bought myself," I told him. My very first bank account, my first job, my first pay cheque all came after I moved in with Kay. The morning the money hit my account, I walked down to Ossington to the record store I'd been browsing in since I arrived in the city. With the album in a paper bag, I walked back to the apartment, singing their lyrics to myself.

It felt surreal to be handling an autographed copy. I handed the album back in fear of damaging it. The responsibility felt like too much.

"I thought you'd appreciate that." He turned to put the album back into his collection.

"How did you know?" I asked, turning to look at a picture frame on his dresser. Chase and his brother standing together holding skateboards in some skate park. Chase looked about fifteen in the image.

"When I drove you home on New Year's. You nodded your head to everything, but you actually sang that one line out loud. *Survival never goes out of style.*"

I groaned. "Oh god. I didn't even realize I sang out loud."

He laughed. "It was cute. You were just so into it. I told myself if we ever hung out after that I would show you this album. Figured you'd appreciate it."

I sucked in a breath. I didn't want to get caught up in the word 'cute'. The way Chase hugged his friends, the easy way he smiled at people. I knew words like 'cute' didn't seem out of character for him to use with his friends, but I couldn't remember if anyone used it when speaking about me before.

"Well thank you for showing me, even if you had to embarrass me at the same time," I said.

Chase cleared his throat. "Thanks for coming, even if I haven't been able to hang out much tonight."

Being invited to his house party was an honour. Camila, Mo, Dylan, they grew up there, they knew those people. I stood out among his friends, but Chase had invited me anyway.

"Thanks for having me," I said, glancing away. "I had a good time."

A picture stood on the dresser next to the one of Chase and his brother. It was a group photograph in a club or bar. I took a step closer to make sure—I could pick out a few familiar faces in the picture, but I knew her better than anyone else. Her hair was shorter, the lines of her jaw sharper, and her clothes were baggier, but I recognized her right away: Kay.

I picked up the frame. "Where was this taken?"

"My nineteenth birthday," Chase said over my shoulder. "The bar shut down a couple years ago now."

"You guys look young."

"Look at Mitchell," Chase said, tapping the glass. "I just met him that summer. He was just an awkward kid, not the handsome devil he is now."

I forced a laugh to match Chase's.

"That's my brother," Chase said, moving his finger to the face next to hers. "And that was his girlfriend, Kayla."

Kay had known Chase when I brought him up. She'd known about him the entire time and pretended she hadn't. What could Chase's brother have done to make Kay pretend not to know him? What kind of heartbreak had Kay faced, that she would lie about it? I wondered if Kay avoided the party assuming Chase's brother would be there.

Footsteps down the hallway pulled our attention away from the picture. Chase took a step back while I set the frame back where it came from.

"There you are." Camila leaned against the doorway. She raised her camera and snapped a photo of Chase and me. Before I could protest, she said, "Mo's ready to drive us home, and this boy has to get some sleep before they leave on tour tomorrow."

I stood still. I had questions about Kay. I wanted to know what Chase knew about her, what happened between her and his brother. I had questions and despite it being two-thirty in the morning, I no longer felt tired.

Chase put a hand on my elbow and said, "I'll walk you guys out."

7

A SENSE OF DREAD WOKE ME THE MORNING AFTER CHASE'S party. The memory of the phone call with Kay came back to me. While drinking, I'd felt so confident that going to the party without Will would be fine. I'd brushed the whole situation off by believing that lie Kay told him would protect me.

I rolled over and glanced at my phone. Five text messages. One from Chase, four from Will. I flinched as I opened Will's conversation.

*so you bailed on me for chase fucking reid*

*do you consider omission lying*

*I'm coming over after class*

*on my way*

The last message had come almost an hour before. It surprised me he hadn't already arrived. I thought about getting out of bed, trying to pretend a hangover wasn't pulsing through my body. I didn't want him to think I'd had fun without him, even though I had.

The air in the room was suffocating. I rolled onto my back and pulled the blankets off. Just like I assumed, Kay had left a glass of water and Tylenol. I sat up and popped the lid off the bottle, shaking two into my palm. The door to my room opened as I swallowed room temperature water. I choked a little and covered my mouth to keep it down.

Will said nothing as he walked into the room, tossing his sweater onto my desk chair. As he threw himself onto the bed, I could smell the sweet smoky scent on his clothes. He'd smoked weed before showing up. I felt a pang of relief—a high Will was a calm Will.

He pulled the comforter over us and said, "How was the big party you went to without me?"

"It was okay," I mumbled. I tried to push the duvet cover off, but Will pulled it up around his neck covering me again.

"Only okay?" Will asked. He gave an exaggerated roll of his eyes. "I saw the pictures on Camila's Instagram story. You were really loving your time with all those basic girls."

"I just hung out with Camila," I told him.

Guilt spread through my entire body. I didn't want him to bring up Chase. I didn't want him asking. I tried to pinpoint what part of the night I felt ashamed of, but couldn't. Chase and I were friends and only friends. I didn't know what bothered me so much about it.

"You could have told me you were going," Will said, tucking a hand behind his head.

"It was last minute." I hoped that was what Kay had told him the night before. I picked at the skin around my nails.

Will let out a long sigh as he shifted to pull the cellphone from his pocket. "I know I said I didn't want to go, but I can't believe you didn't at least invite Kay."

I didn't like the accusation that I'd left Kay behind. More than anything, I had wanted her to be there. It must have been the post-drinking emotions making my eyes well up. I didn't want Will to see me cry. He'd told me many times how his crazy last girlfriend cried over everything.

"She didn't want to go," I said. My words quivered at the end.

Will rolled onto his side to look at me. "Can you blame her? After everything that happened with the Reid family?"

"What..." I couldn't finish the sentence. My voice shook too much.

"That's cold, Peyton." Will shook his head.

I wanted to ask what happened, what he meant. Chase showed me the picture of Kay and his brother, so I knew they'd been together. Kay had mentioned losing a lot of people from her old life. She said people hurt her. If one of those people happened to be Chase's brother, it must have hurt her to know I was hanging out with Chase and that I'd been in his family home. She'd never asked me to stay away, but Kay never would. She'd always put me first.

"A couple people are going to a metal show on Wednesday and to Sneaky Dee's after. You wanna come?" Will asked.

"I'm supposed to be meeting with Camila after work, maybe I can change it to another day," I said.

I didn't want to change my plans. I didn't want to go to a metal show. On the drive home, Camila had made me promise we'd sit down and determine what we wanted out of the blog-turned-website. I'd been looking forward to it—the thought of cancelling on her, or even postponing, made my stomach ache.

"I see how it is. Fine. Hang out with your *new* friends." Will gave a chuckle heavy with sarcasm. "It'll just be me and the guys anyways. Have a girls' night, paint your nails or whatever."

"I can cha—" I stopped.

"Whatever," he said as he pushed himself up from the bed. "I'm going to see what's in the fridge."

I picked up my phone to text Camila and ask her to reschedule. I wanted to hang out with her, but if it meant Will would be moody for days on end, it wasn't worth it.

I opened my messages, ready to tell Camila I had to

reschedule, but instead I found the unread one from Chase. I opened it.

A picture of him yawning with the hood of his sweater pulled up took over the screen. Mitchell's face in the left-hand corner, sticking out his tongue, made me laugh. The text had come in at seven-thirty in the morning. They'd hit the road already.

I sent a quick text to let him know I saw his message.

*You should have kicked us out so you could get some sleep before hitting the road.*

Before I could set my phone down it vibrated with a response.

*no way. totally worth it!*

"What are you smiling at?" Will strolled back into the room eating one of Kay's yogurts.

I made a note in my phone to pick up more yogurt for Kay after my next shift.

"What?" I asked, setting my phone face down onto my nightstand next to me.

Will climbed into bed. "Who you were talking to?"

"Just Instagram."

"Hmmm." Will slid off his socks. Between mouthfuls of yogurt he asked, "So, you coming to the show on Wednesday or are you still ditching me for your rich friends?"

I picked up my phone and texted Camila.

8

WATCHING CAMILA WORK WAS AN HONOUR. TAKING A photograph, she noticed things in the background most would never see, like a piece of glass in the grass or where the grass grew slightly longer. She didn't seem to stop and think about lighting, but instinctively knew where the band needed to stand for the best shot. She didn't pause to decide what pose to suggest next or where to stand to get the right angle on her subjects. I watched in awe.

The band, Sheetrock, stood in front of an abandoned farm house. Parts of the roof had caved in over years of neglect; curtains left in the windows were bleached of all colour and the fabric had fallen apart. Camila knelt in the long grass, framing the shot from the ground. The band kept straight faces and stiff stances as she clicked again and again.

I glanced around at the trees. The woods appeared to stretch on for ever. I grew up in a town surrounded by forests and fields, but I'd never been allowed to venture far from my house. Standing in the middle of nature, I realized how much I'd missed. After moving to Toronto, I came to terms with how many things I never experienced—I'd become so comfortable in that part of my life, I hadn't realized what else people took for granted. It appeared there was still more to uncover.

"As I mentioned, Peyton is my partner at Eternal Spin," Camila explained to the band as she crouched even lower. "So, if you guys are cool with it, we could post a shot or two from today and do an interview about the new album coming out."

"Like, an article or something?" one of the guys asked.

Camila stood up. Her knees were wet from the ground, but she didn't seem to care. She took a few steps back and squatted. "We could link to your single, maybe do a small piece or question-and-answer type thing, something to let people know about you."

What she offered felt like my domain. The last time we talked about the direction of the publication, she mentioned I'd be in charge of interviews and all written content. I would be handling when it came time to start creating content outside of reviews. That time had arrived.

"Is that something we could do right now?" the lead singer asked. "Is that's cool?"

The world tilted and I closed my eyes to make it stop. Reviewing bands didn't require back and forth, didn't require actual interaction. Reviewing gave me time to sort out the finer details before anyone saw them. If someone ended up hurt or angry, I didn't have to deal with it face to face.

"Like, right now?"

"Yeah. Let's do it!"

The grin across Camila's face encouraged me, but the rate of my heart reminded me how unprepared I was.

"Okay," I mumbled.

"Let me finish up a few more shots and then we'll take a break." Camila turned her attention back to the band and the scenery around them.

While they were distracted, I slipped back to the car to find the pen and paper in my bag. After pulling up a list of interview questions on Google, I started to write down things I could ask a band I didn't know anything about. I couldn't find a website or Twitter account with any details I could research, but they had a half-empty Facebook page and a few pictures on Instagram. Going into the interview blind terrified me, but I didn't know how to say no.

Camila tapped on the hood of the car, bringing me out of the panicked brainstorming session.

I pushed the car door open. "Now? Like, I have to do this now?"

"Do you not want to do it?" she asked, ducking her head inside.

I sat back into the seat. "I've never interviewed anyone before."

"You told me."

"I'm unprepared." Some of the anxiety loosened its grip when I said it out loud.

"We all know that."

For some reason, the fact Camila knew I didn't have a clue made the whole situation easier. I picked up the notepad I'd been scratching ideas on. "This could be a disaster."

"At least you have the excuse of being unprepared," Camila said, arching one eyebrow.

I handed Camila the notebook. "Anything you'd add?"

"Nope. You got this." Camila tipped her head toward the band, standing around the cars they'd arrived in. I gathered my stuff and followed Camila to them.

"We're honoured to be your first interview," the bassist said.

I forced a smile and set my notepad on the hood of the car, unlocked my phone and tried to find the audio recording app. It didn't seem to be where I remembered it. I flipped through pages of apps over and over until Camila reached out and tapped on the right one. If I couldn't do that on my own, I couldn't imagine pulling off the interview.

After asking them their names and positions in the band, I asked, "So, how long have you been a band?"

It wasn't one of the most unique questions, but none of the other questions made good openers either. I glanced down at the list I'd come up with and realize none were unique. They were questions I'd heard and read in every interview with every band.

While the band laughed and joked about how they began, about how they met working construction one summer, I tried to come up with something interesting. I became so caught up I didn't realize they'd stopped talking.

"That's cool," I said with a smile. The question list trembled in my hand. "Where did you come up with the name Sheetrock?"

"As we said, during that summer working construction, we teased Brandon about calling it sheetrock and not drywall, so it just became our thing," the drummer said.

I glanced at Camila, trying to silently plead with her to end the whole thing. I'd already made a fool of myself and I feared the longer it went on, the worse it would get. Camila either didn't understand my wide-eye scream or she didn't want to acknowledge it. She gave me a smile before saying she would be right back.

"I'm sorry," I said, turning back to the boys. "This is... This is a disaster."

"Don't even sweat it." The drummer laughed. "The first show we had was so bad I said I wouldn't play another."

"But he did."

"What happened?" I asked.

Brandon, the lead singer, said, "Alex was so hungover he had to keep running off stage between songs to puke. Tim kept speeding up our tempo and messing us up. I forgot the words to one of our songs and ended up just humming the whole thing."

They all laughed, but with each other. They didn't pass the blame around. They'd already moved on—I admired that.

I let a laugh escape. "That's rough."

"Too bad you missed it."

"What kind of music do you play?" I asked. Then a thought occurred to me. "I mean, without saying anything genre-specific."

The boys took time discussing it with each other. They made jokes and debated the band's key elements. In the end, the bassist leaned in toward my recording phone and said, "Songs for sad twenty-somethings who still want to slam around in the mosh pit."

"Sounds like a band I'd like," I told them as I picked up my list of questions again. "So, when is your album coming out?"

9

Being alone in the apartment still made me uneasy. Every time a voice shouted from the street below, every time the door across the hall opened or shut, I glanced up from my work. Since moving to the city, being alone was something I learned was freeing, but from time-to-time old, concerns resurfaced. I couldn't keep focus knowing I was alone and the article I needed to complete about Sheetrock suffered because of it.

My mother taught me never to assume we were alone. She told me never to leave my clothes on the floor for even a minute, never get carefree with things like singing or dancing —definitely no sharing secrets. One of the last nights I spent in my parents' house I'd let my guard down.

Instead of cleaning up the Sheetrock article, I opened another document. My fingers trembled as I typed out the first few words on the stark white of the screen.

*She sat by the bedroom window with all the lights turned off. The music coming from the neighbour's house made her smile to herself. Every time they had a party, she strained her ears to hear the words of bands she would later learn were punk rock legends. The Ramones. The Misfits. Black Flag.*

*For a moment she lost herself. She knew the lyrics. She knew that song by heart. As the words flowed from her lips, euphoria overcame her. She wanted to sing forever, wanted to feel that moment for the rest of her life.*

*But she wasn't alone. She was never alone.*

*It had been almost a month since her father's last episode. Her mother reminded her it had been going well, but she messed it up. Her mother told her she should have just gone to bed. If she had been asleep, she wouldn't have woken her father who worked so hard to keep a roof over their heads. If she had been asleep her father never would have slammed the window shut on her fingers.*

My phone vibrated on the table. I jerked at the sound, sending the laptop to the floor. After checking for damage, I scooped up the phone. A text from Chase popped up on the screen. A double tap brought up a picture of him in bed with the blankets pulled up around his neck. I glanced at the clock in the top corner of the screen. Two-thirty in the morning had crept up on me.

*It's a little early for you to be turning in?*

Chase's name appeared on the screen with the words 'incoming call'.

I swiped to accept the call. "Hey."

"He-e-ey." The way he dragged out the single word made him sound exhausted. The yawn that followed only solidified that.

I chuckled into the phone. "Why aren't you out partying, living that rockstar lifestyle?"

"I came back to call Melissa. It's our nightly thing," he explained.

I wondered what Will's reaction would be if I asked him to call me every night before bed. Embarrassment rippled through me at the thought of asking him. Often days would pass without a word from him. I'd learned pretty quickly not to follow up with him anymore—I waited.

"But what are you doing up? Are you working tomorrow?" Chase asked. His words were heavy.

I smiled. He remembered I always worked Mondays.

I hid the grin from my voice before answering. "I work tomorrow, but I wanted to finish the Sheetrock article tonight. I'm struggling to stay focused."

"Something on your mind, or just not in the mood to write it right now?"

"I don't always like being in the apartment alone," I admitted before I realized what I said. I laughed. "I'm not freaking out or anything."

I expected Chase to laugh. I expected him to make a joke about me being a grown adult who jumped at the sound of a car door, but he fell quiet for a few seconds. I held my breath, waiting for him to say something.

"I'm sure Will would come over if you called him."

I squeezed my eyes shut. I didn't want to talk about Will with Chase. It felt wrong, like I needed to take a side. They'd made their feelings about each other clear.

"He has early class." I couldn't admit I didn't know what Will was up to that night, or why I didn't hear from him. Chase didn't need more reasons to dislike him. Anyway, conversations with Chase were limited. I didn't want to spend our time talking about Will.

"If I were in town I'd come hang out until your roommate got back," Chase said. The weight of sleep in his voice and the words themselves made my stomach feel light, fluttery.

I swallowed. "That would be nice."

Neither of us said anything for almost a full minute. I listened to the sound of him breathing from somewhere in Florida. It occurred to me he'd fallen asleep, that I should hang up.

Then he spoke. "Would it help if I told you that you might be in the apartment alone, but you're not *alone* alone?"

"It helps."

"Good."

"You should sleep. You have a long drive before the show tomorrow, right?" I asked him.

"Yeah. I know I should sleep. Just wanted to say hey."

"I'm glad you did." I squeezed my eyes shut and tried not to think about Chase thinking about me when a country separated us. My whole body felt fluttery at the idea, but then reality hit and I nearly sighed into the phone. He'd gone back to his room to call his girlfriend for one of their adorable, nightly conversations. The type of things couples like them did, while I sat around waiting for my kind-of-boyfriend to tell me when he wanted to hang out next.

"You should have at least one crazy night before the end of tour," I told him, trying to change the subject away from me. I didn't want to think about Melissa or Will.

"We'll see." He chuckled. "I'll be home in a week."

"I'm looking forward to it."

"Goodnight, Peyton."

"Goodnight."

The sound of keys in the doorway caught my attention. I set my laptop and phone on the coffee table as Kay let herself into the apartment. She said hello as she tossed her jacket onto the coat rack.

"I thought maybe Will was here," Kay said as she slipped out of her shoes.

"No, why?"

"I heard you talking to someone as I came up the stairs." She headed into the kitchen, toward the refrigerator.

I thought about the picture in Chase's bedroom, about Chase saying Kay and his brother had dated. Since moving in with her, I'd gathered that dating hadn't been easy for Kay, that men didn't always treat her with the kind of respect that Daniel did. I feared that Chase's brother might have been one of those people before Daniel, one of the ones that hurt her.

I needed to know if my hanging out with Chase made her uncomfortable. I wanted to know if I hurt her by starting a friendship with him, by looking forward to talking to him. The conversation needed to happen and it was as good a time as any.

"Chase just called to say hey," I explained.

Kay pulled the water jug out of the fridge. I watched for a reaction and for the first time, I saw it. For a brief second, she paused. I tried to remember if she stiffened the same way other times I mentioned his name, but I couldn't recall.

"So, do you know Chase? Like, from before?"

Kay made an effort not to glance in my direction as she pulled a glass from the cupboard, filled it and gulped it down.

I wasn't ready to give up my friendship with Chase, but I would if Kay asked me to, if he'd hurt her in some way. I owed her everything and it was the right thing to do.

"Did he say something to you?"

"No. I'm not sure he knows you're my roommate. I just saw a picture."

"What picture?" She still didn't look at me.

"A picture of you with Forever July. When you were younger. Before they were Forever July"

Kay stared at her glass of water before taking another sip. She set it on the counter and said, "Yeah. We knew each other."

"Did his brother—Did he hurt you or something? I know—"

Kay raised her hand and turned to look at me. Her eyes were heavy, with annoyance or hurt, I couldn't tell. She set the glass of water down on the counter a little harder than necessary, before saying, "If I wanted to talk about it, I would talk about it. Alright?"

"If it makes you uncomfortable, I don't have to hang out with him," I told her. I didn't want her to say it would make her feel better. I didn't want her to tell me that it made her uncomfortable when I spent time with him.

"You can hang out with him, Peyton," Kay said with a sigh.

She put the water jug back into the fridge and turned off the kitchen light. I wasn't sure she meant it, but I couldn't bring myself to push her anymore.

Mumbling a goodnight, she went through the living room toward her bedroom.

I made a point of never upsetting Kay and now I had. I wished I hadn't said anything to her about it.

Something was wrong and she wouldn't tell me. I thought about texting Chase, to find out what happened between them, but it would be a breach of Kay's trust. I didn't know Chase well, but the thought of giving him up made my entire body feel heavy.

I picked up my things and headed into my room. Only when the door was closed, when the lights were off, did I hear it. The sound of Kay slamming things around in her room.

SOMETHING ABOUT THE SMELL OF COFFEE AND THE SOUNDS OF chatter made it easier to focus on my work. Being in Camila's presence, seeing her excitement for everything I suggested, made me want to produce more, encouraged me to get things done. Not only had I come to our meeting at a family-run café with a rough but completed draft of the Sheetrock article, I also put together a brief review of the café we were sitting in.

When Camila handed me back the article with notes in the margins, I turned my laptop around so she could read what I've written while she went over it.

"You did this right now?"

I shrugged.

"I'm going to share this doc to my account so we can edit and upload it soon, cool?" She tapped around on my computer and said, "This part is brilliant. '*You come for the coffee, but you find yourself staying to people-watch, to enjoy the soundtrack of friendly voices and the tapping of fingers on someone's keyboard next to you.*' Love that."

Overhearing the excerpt, the man typing on his laptop next to us glanced up. In one fluid movement, Camila pulled a card from her laptop case and slid it across the bar top we sat at. She nodded at him and said, "It'll be published on our website, Eternal Spin, by Friday."

He took the card and tucked it into his pants' pocket before going back to his laptop.

Camila oozed professionalism. We had gone to a show the night before, bands that we knew from the local scene. She said it wouldn't be a night for work, but a night for fun. But the whole time she told people about our project, about our plans for it. She introduced me to every single person she knew and even some she just met. She suggested everyone check out the website despite its lack of content. It worked. The numbers were going up every day.

"I went back through your reviews," Camila said as she made a note in her 'content' notebook. "I have pictures from almost eighty percent of the shows you went to. If you're down, I can get my brother to take your older reviews and put them together with my photographs and then at least there's more content on the review page."

"Do it," I said.

Camila tapped out a text and said, "Cool. He'll have it done by the weekend."

"Are you paying him?" I asked.

"Girl, no. *We're* not even getting paid yet. However, that should be changing soon," Camila said. "We'll be making money from ads in no time. And I had this idea for a fundraiser eventually. I mentioned it to Forever July and they said they'd play. Mitchell said only if I take some pictures of him shirtless for his Insta. Worth it, I guess."

"You have high expectations for this whole thing." I laughed.

"Don't you?" The way she squinted I wondered if she questioned my commitment to Eternal Spin.

"Of course," I said, glancing down at my hands.

I enjoyed spending time with Camila. It kept me committed. If she wasn't sending me emails about business, she texted me about a new band she found or a movie she watched, but we never hit topics below the surface. Her goal was to get the website into a place it could be considered a career. I wanted to know why. Not only did I want to understand her better, but I wanted to know how people made those types of plans for the future.

"What made you think of creating something like this?" I asked her as I picked up my iced coffee.

Camila sat back in her chair and ran both of her hands through her curls. She thought about it for a minute. "When I was a kid, my mom always read magazines. She and her friends would share copies and talk about the articles together. I tried, you know, to read them with her when I got a bit older. But they never really fit me, you know? I mean, I did learn tips on how to flirt and put on make-up, or how to put together outfits."

"And your outfits are great," I said nodding at her attire. She wore all black, but somehow made it stand out with gold on her ears, neck, and fingers.

"Thanks," Camila said with a wink. "So, like… I didn't hate those magazines, but they weren't meant for me or maybe for our generation. Like, they didn't talk about social issues, they didn't have clothes I wanted to wear, they didn't talk about music that I liked. Everything felt so binary and it didn't make sense to how I saw the world. If that makes sense. I don't know."

I nodded.

"I was kind of sick of seeing 'fifteen ways to please your man' and as if only straight people want to read make-up tips. I wanted to make something for people like me, but also for people who care about their city and their scene."

"I like that." I smiled. I liked the glimpse into Camila. The topic might have still been stuck on work, but it made sense for her. The one thing I'd learned about Camila: work made her happy.

"What about you? Why did you say yes to doing this?" Camila asked.

"I guess it felt like a natural progression from what I was already doing, plus, I kinda needed a goal. I heard that's a normal thing to have." I hoped that sounded playful and not self-deprecating.

"I wouldn't know any other way to be." Camila laughed, but I could feel the honesty in the comment.

I wanted to believe Eternal Spin could be that for me. I wanted to believe it would be the thing I could get behind, see myself doing for a long time, but I could tell the difference between Camila's motivation and my own.

Even slogging through the boring bits, Camila seemed thrilled. I could see the same exhilaration when it came to Chase and Forever July. They didn't see their jobs as work, but art. I'd come to realize they almost needed it.

I understood it, to a degree. I knew the need to write, to get it all down. But I never thought about the possibility of making a career out of it, doing something I was passionate about for money.

Growing up I knew one thing for sure about my father. He hated his job. He mentioned it often. He said that he worked to keep my mother and I fed, to keep a roof over our heads. He worked for money. It would never be more than that for him and I'd always assumed it would be the same way for me.

"Hey," Camila said, sliding her phone across the table. "Found a band you should interview on Saturday."

I looked at the band's social media. Once I got used to the idea of doing interviews, maybe I would find that excitement too.

BETWEEN MY RETAIL JOB AND WRITING FOR ETERNAL SPIN, I didn't do much else. Keeping busy made me feel accomplished, but the need for rest weighed me down. Kay had made me promise I would take a night to myself, actually watch The Menzingers' show without working. Even though Camila would be busy the entire show, I decided Kay was right. A break was on the agenda. I wouldn't say it out loud to anyone, mostly because of Will, but I wanted to be rested for when Chase returned the next day.

A few people turned to look at me where I stood against the wall. Once I could just melt into the crowd. Now, eyes landed on me instead of glazing right past. The wait between bands never stretched when I made notes or got another drink, but the attention from the few people made me uncomfortable. It took me back to my years in high school.

The first time I showed up to school with a black eye, it was grade nine. Soon the rumours started. Hiding in the bathroom at lunch, I overheard two girls whispering that I'd gotten into a car accident while drinking and driving. No one questioned how I'd do that at fourteen. In my sophomore year when I showed up with two stitches in my chin, the rumour changed again. One of the girls I spoke to during lunch period asked me if my boyfriend hit me, because that was the rumour going around school. When I said I didn't have a boyfriend, she responded with, "That's what I thought." No one asked me where I really got the black eyes or the split lip. No teacher questioned it. I never wanted to go back to feeling like that again.

A hand touched my wrist. I jumped away, wrapping my arms around myself instinctively. But seeing who stood there, I let out an awkward laugh, trying to hide my reaction.

Chase tilted his head while staring at me. "Peyton?" The lines on his forehead deepened as he watched my attempt to relax my face.

I tried to school my expression, but the sharpness of the panic didn't dull fast enough. I forced out another laugh. "Sorry. Just surprised—that you're here. I thought you weren't coming back until tomorrow."

He refused to match my smile and I figured he saw right through my attempt to change the subject. I couldn't think of anything else to say to distract him and braced myself for whatever he might ask. The weight of his question turned down the corners of his lips.

Before the words made it off his tongue, Mitchell collided into us, throwing his arms around our shoulders to pull us close. As Mitchell alternated between kissing both of our foreheads, I was very aware of Chase's shoulder bumping against mine.

Chase wrapped an arm around me and I had to push through my thoughts to tell my body to do the same.

"Peyton," Mitchell slurred. "We missed you."

Chase gave me an affectionate smile. "It's good to be home."

The entire time they'd been on tour, I'd missed being around Chase. Seeing him made me realize how much so. Even though our friendship only consisted of a few days spent hanging out, him being gone was comparable to a habit that had been broken, like I was forgetting to do something each day. While life continued on as it always did, I noticed his absence. That was all.

"I don't have to share a bed with this asshole anymore." Mitchell laughed as he fell out of the group hug.

Chase's arm lingered around me for a second or two longer.

Mitchell took the beer from my hand and sipped it before handing it back to me. "I'll buy the next round."

"Keep it." I handed the beer back to him. "It's warm anyway."

"Cold beers, coming right up!" Mitchell spun in the direction of the bar.

Chase shook his head. "We might have had a couple drinks with my parents and Melissa at dinner."

"When did you get in?" I asked.

"Around three this morning. We decided to just take turns driving all night so we could get home. I needed a shower and clean clothes."

"Well, you look, and smell, clean. I'm still surprised to see you here." I wanted to hug him, but I didn't know if it would be appropriate.

"I'm moving in a couple days, so I didn't know when I would have time to see people. I knew you and Camila would be here. I missed you guys so much." He reached out like he was about to touch me, but stopped.

My cheeks burned at his hesitation. I wanted him to touch me, even if to just pat me on the shoulder. I wondered if his girlfriend ever became so panicked people were afraid to touch her. I doubted it. She had so much poise, so much confidence. She attracted people, never repelled them.

It made sense that Chase and Melissa worked. They were a perfect pair.

"Well, I'm glad you drove all night," I said. I hoped he

knew how much I meant it.

Before either of us could say anything further, the house music cut off and the light dimmed. The band rushed on stage to screaming fans. Chase and I moved away from the wall, following the intensity toward the mosh pit.

The sound rumbled all around us. With songs I loved, combined with the excitement dripping off the people around me, I forgot about my awkwardness with Chase. I forgot about the reminders of my past popping up. All my insecurities disappeared as I bounced on the balls of my feet, shouting my favourite lines toward the stage. Chase did the same, his fist pumping the air between us. He bumped into me with excitement and I wished it was intentional.

Being with Chase wasn't like being with Will. In the beginning with Will there was this excitement that someone noticed me, that they wanted to be around me. I was starting to wonder if I would have experienced that feeling with anyone. With Chase, it was different. All the cliché things, like butterfly stomachs and jelly legs applied. There was a deep want I'd never really experienced before and it surprised me.

Mitchell returned and his presence reminded me that it was just a friendly hangout. He pushed tall cans of beer into our palms while he shouted lyrics into the air. He wrapped his arms around our shoulders as the music played on and saying, "This is so fucking great" every few minutes. The band broke into my favourite song of theirs just as Camila appeared with Mo.

"You got me for this song," she shouted over the music. "I know it's your favourite."

Without waiting for her to make the first move, I wrapped my arms around her neck, showing my appreciation with a squeeze. We pulled back, but not entirely. She grabbed my hands and we sang as loud as we could.

I got that feeling again. Like the first night at the DeKay House, when I met Chase for the first time. If I were doing the same thing with anyone else, it might have been good, maybe even great, but it couldn't touch what happened right there with those people. I never knew a happy moment could bring me close to tears.

I didn't want the song to end, but when it did, Camila pointed at every one of us and said, "Sneaky Dee's for drinks after, alright?"

"Drinks!" Mitchell pumped his fist in the air.

"And food," Chase said, tilting his head in Mitchell's direction. I watched as Chase offered to hold Mitchell beer for him when he went into the mosh pit. He switched out my nearly empty can for Mitchell's, and said, "Gotta keep an eye on him sometimes. He can be his own worst enemy."

"I know a little something about that," I said before I could stop myself. Trying to play it off, I chuckled. "But that's nice of you to look out for him."

"It's nothing. It's just what you do for people you consider family."

The next song started and I thought about that statement. Maybe standing up for and taking care of your family was second nature to him, but I'd been learning it a little bit at a time. Kay's kindness, the ease with which she accepted me, had shocked me when we first met. It never became easier to confront that open expression of caring.

"I love this song," Chase shouted to me over the music.

It pulled me out of my thoughts and back to the present. "Me too."

Obviously caught up in the moment, he grabbed my shoulders and sang the lyrics straight to me. I couldn't hear the music over the pounding of my pulse in my ears. All I could hear was his voice. All I could see was the grin on his face.

I closed my eyes, trying to clear my mind, but when I opened them again, I couldn't help smiling back. I was in trouble, and I knew it.

"Makes sense Eternal Spin is doing so well. You two were already established names in your own mediums," Mo said as he grabbed a nacho from the massive plate between us. He pointed at me with a guacamole-filled chip. "Eat, before Chase gets them all."

I picked up a chip, but I only nibbled on the edge before putting it on my plate. With Chase's thigh only inches from my own I struggled to think about much else. I did however, think about how terrible it was to be thinking about Chase's thigh when I knew he had a girlfriend—a beautiful, sweet one.

Despite how busy the bar was, the four of us had snagged one of the graffiti covered booths. When Camila slid in next to Mo, the only choice was to take the seat next to Chase. Mitchell had disappeared with some girl he met at the show. Dylan tried to convince Camila to go with him to an after-hours club in the Village, but disappeared when she told him no for the third time.

While I liked the intimacy of the four of us at the table, it meant I needed to have a clear head to contribute to conversation, the one that everyone had been holding without me. Camila watched me from across the table. So she wouldn't catch the guilt on my face, I pulled out my phone and typed a message to Kay, letting her know I would be home kind of early, just getting some food.

"Nothing sets us apart from any other publication," Camila said. "We've got the photography, the reviews, the interviews, whatever. It's just like everyone else's."

"And the business owner section is limited to people in the city," I explained, repeating the line Camila had texted me several nights before. "It doesn't have appeal for the majority of people. Maybe some tourists."

"Exactly. We need something bigger, something that

appeals to a wider audience, but is still unique." Camila tossed her hands up like she was defeated.

"I thought of something—but it might be a hard one to get people on board with," I said. "Or to actually commit to doing it, I should say."

"The tour diary thing?" Camila asked.

I nodded. "I think it has lots of potential."

"What if you could get someone to do it for free? Just to see what the feedback is?" Mo asked.

"Do you want to do it?" I asked Mo, hoping he would say yes. If it caused clicks, if it provided ad revenue, then we would know it was worth it before taking the only money we made and spending it on a long shot.

Mo glanced across the table. "Chase, why don't you let them use your postcards?"

Chase looked up from his phone too quick to play it cool. He stared at Mo.

Mo laughed and said, "Why are you looking at me like that?"

"They're personal," Chase said. He set his phone onto the table and turned to me. "Sorry. They're like—a journal. Mo's never read them. No one has, honestly."

"I just thought that you'd want to support your favourite publication." Mo chuckled as he reached for another chip.

"It's okay. If they're personal, I understand." I smiled at Chase, hoping it was reassuring.

Chase nodded at me.

Camila's phone rang. She sighed as she answered it. "¿Qué quieres?"

"You going to eat that?" Chase asked, pointing to my plate.

"Nah, have it." I pushed it toward him. "I'm still full from the beers at the show."

"Guys," Camila said, pulling out a twenty-dollar bill from

her camera bag. "My brother locked his keys in his car, so he's sitting outside my parents' house."

"Want me to drive you back?" Mo asked. "I gotta visit all the family tomorrow anyway, so an early night wouldn't be the worst thing."

I tried to hide my disappointment that the night was coming to such an abrupt end, after only a few hours with Chase.

Camila pulled on the sweater she'd discarded when we first got inside. "Chase, you coming back with us?"

"I'm good. I'm crashing at Mitchell's tonight." He turned to me. "You going to stick around until we finish the nachos?"

"I don't have any other plans," I said.

Camila pointed at me and said, "Don't forget, we're interviewing two bands tomorrow. Do your research."

"I have, but I'll do more tomorrow," I promised her.

Before they could leave, a couple of guys stopped next to the booth to tell Mo and Chase how much they liked the band, that they couldn't wait for new material. The boys took it in stride, thanking them, but telling them to have a good night before the conversation could escalate. I realized it must happen to them a lot, not just in town. Sometimes I forgot Forever July were not just some local kids playing to a couple hundred people. While they might not have been mainstream, they weren't a small band. They'd definitely outgrown the city's fanbase.

When we said goodbye, Chase moved to the other side of the table. As he slid into the booth, he grinned. "Now I can see you better."

I glanced at my hands before looking back up at him. "How was the tour?" I asked. "Did you allow yourself to get a little reckless?"

Chase ran a hand through his hair. "We partied one night and I blacked out."

I laughed. "Did you do anything wild?"

"No. Well, Mo said I sat with Dylan while he vomited into some bushes at our host's house. Forgot to call Melissa that night though. That's probably the most reckless I got."

While my knowledge of Chase might be limited, his blacked-out caregiving didn't surprise me. His friends only said kind things about him. So, why did Kay act so elusive about what happened between them?

"Can I ask you something kind of awkward?" I asked, sitting up straight.

Chase raised a single eyebrow. "Off the record?"

I laughed. "Everything between us is off the record."

"You just have this very business-like vibe about you all of a sudden." When he smiled the muscles in his jaw flexed. "But ask away."

I wrapped both hands around my empty glass and sucked in a deep breath. It might have been easier if he stayed on my side of the booth. It would have been easier if I didn't have to look right into his eyes as I asked.

"So, you know Kay? Kayla Black?" I blurted the words out before I lost my nerve.

Chase waited two long seconds before saying, "Yes. I assume you do too?"

I nodded.

"She was my brother's girlfriend for like three years. How do you know her?"

"She's my roommate, and my best friend."

Chase nodded. "Does she still hate me?"

"I don't know," I admitted. "Should she?"

Chase rubbed the back of his neck before picking up his beer and taking a sip. He set it down, but still didn't look at me.

My mind went to dark places trying to figure out what might have gone wrong. Over time, Kay made it clear she'd been bullied most of her life. Back when she hid her true self, before she came out as transgender and moved to the city. She explained she dated men that forced her to keep their relationship secret and how some fetishized her. Kay told me how cruel people were to her and I didn't want to think that Chase might have been one of those people. I needed to know.

"It's interesting that I ran into you on New Year's Eve," Chase said. "I went there looking for Kayla. I've been wanting to talk to her for a long time but I didn't know how to get in touch with her anymore."

I didn't know what to ask, so I said nothing at all. I rolled the empty glass back and forth in my hands, giving him time to find the words.

"I said some things that hurt her," Chase said, "Things that—"

"Peyton?"

I heard Will over the music and voices of all the other patrons.

My head whipped up to find him stumbling through the door with a group of his friends. I didn't recognize the girls they were with. All drunk. Even from far away I could see the heaviness in his eyelids that set in when he drank too much.

"Is that..." Chase turned in his seat to confirm his suspicion.

"Chase fucking Reid," Will said, pointing across the room. I winced as he made his way toward us, weaving in and out of people doing their best to avoid him. I regretted not getting up as soon as I heard his voice.

I slid out of the booth, telling Chase, "I'll be right back."

I caught Will a few feet from the table and took hold of his wrists to keep him from moving toward Chase. Distraction was necessary to keep things from escalating. I feared what would happen if he made it to the table, and didn't want to deal with whatever might trigger drunk Will.

"I asked you to come out tonight," Will said. "I asked you

to come to Antonio's party. You ditched me for Chase fucking *Reid*?"

"I didn't ditch you. I went to the show I invited you to. We just stopped to get drinks after with a couple of people."

"A couple of people? Looks like a fucking date to me," Will hissed.

I turned my face away from the whiskey on his breath, trying to keep my composure despite the tremble through my body.

"Hey," Will said, moving me out of the way.

I stumbled as he pushed me to the side. Even intoxicated, he was stronger than me.

He pointed at Chase and said, "Just remember, she's my girlfriend, got it?"

My heart slammed around inside my chest. I opened my mouth, but closed it again. In all the time Will and I spent together we'd never used those words. Never once did he say I was his girlfriend, not to his friends, not to his family, and definitely not to me. A small part of me sighed with relief, but a larger part of me curled into itself.

Chase stood so he and Will were inches apart, face to face. They had nothing in common. Not their attire, stature, taste in music, and definitely not their personality.

"You're reading too much into this," Chase said to Will. "We're just friends getting something to eat after a show."

My stomach ached. Staying with Chase, while a strong contender, meant making Will upset. Upsetting Will only ended up one way; it was already teetering on the brink. Will's mother left him when he was seven. Despite her return, he had serious abandonment issues. Me leaving him to spend time with Chase would only make the situation a lot worse. I knew how it was and I didn't want to be someone to inflict that on someone else.

Also, Chase had to get home to call Melissa.

I stepped between the two of them, putting a hand on

Will's arm. I tensed as he ripped it from my grasp.

"Come on," I whispered. "Why don't we just go back to my place? Just the two of us."

The muscles in his jaw tightened. When I glanced back, Chase stood tall, but his hands were in his back pockets. Nothing threatening about his stance. I wished Will could be like that. Calm, attentive, and sweet. But guys like that had girlfriends like Melissa and I didn't blame them for that one bit. They were a perfect fit.

"Will, come on. I wanna go home," I said, touching his face. "Just let me pay and I'll meet you outside."

"You think I'm just going to let this go?" Will yelled. He reached around me, shoving Chase and knocking me back at the same time.

I grabbed onto the back of someone's chair to brace myself and heard the clinking of glasses on the table. Chase had stumbled from the impact. I became aware of people around us watching, filming, taking pictures. One of the bartenders left his post and headed toward us.

I tried to hide my face, but the damage was already done. "Will, let's *go*," I said, putting my body weight against him. "You're gonna get kicked out."

"They'll have to drag me the hell out of here," Will shouted.

"You guys stay," Chase said. "I'll go."

While my shoulder remained pressed against Will, I turned to look at Chase. His eyes didn't meet mine. He grabbed his coat and tossed more money than necessary on the table.

"Hey man." One of the bar's bouncers appeared and out a thick hand on Will's shoulder. "Let's grab a smoke outside, all right?"

Will shrugged off the bouncer's hand. I could see the shift in his body language. The muscles in his arms tensed. He took a step back with one foot.

I backed away from him, bumping into Chase before the first swing.

Will's fist grazed the bouncer's chin. Before Will could straighten up, the bartender and a second bouncer were on him, dragging him from the bar while the patrons all turned to watch him go.

I needed to get out of there, away from all the eyes. "I'm so sorry. This got out of hand. I should go to him." I kept my eyes cast down while I grabbed my bag and sweater from the booth.

"You're gonna have to go," the bouncer said, taking my arm. The other bouncer was apologizing to Chase for not getting to the situation sooner.

I fumbled with my things, dropping my bag to the floor. My notebook and pen spilled out and Chase and I both crouched to pick it up.

"I'm sorry," I said as I reached for my bag.

Chase put his hand on mine and the urge to cry overwhelmed me. Will's behaviour was bad enough, but the bouncer asking me to leave made it much worse. They never asked who I was with—because I didn't look like I belonged with Chase. One look at me and they knew I should be out on the curb with the drunk.

"Peyton, you don't have to apologize for anything."

I shook my head, hoping enough hair would fall into my face to hide the shame burning my cheeks and neck. "I don't know why he's acting like this."

"I guess he feels threatened."

I let out a sarcastic laugh. "Of what? You said it yourself, we're just friends."

Chase gave my hand a squeeze. His eyes met mine and he looked as if he were about to speak, but the bouncer grabbed my arm and pulled me to my feet. Chase stood too, handing me my bag and reassuring me with a lopsided smile.

The bouncer directed me toward the exit with a hand on

my back. He didn't let me say goodbye. He didn't let me put my sweater on. I tried to step away, but he kept my arm in a strong grip.

I couldn't breathe. The tightness of the bouncer's hand on me caused my whole body to stiffen. My thoughts came at me fast and I couldn't think straight.

After everything I'd been through with my family, I told myself I would never allow anyone to push me around, to tell me who I could spend time with and what I could and couldn't do. I made that promise to myself when I left the house I grew up in, but something about what happened was comparable to so much I'd been through before coming to the city. The bouncer's grip on me was a stark reminder.

I tried to focus on getting outside, tried to tell myself not to pull away again, but the movements were involuntary. I struggled as he shoved me out of the front door into the damp night. The movement sent an ache through my body. Phantom pains, I'd told Kay one night. Muscle memory, she told me.

"Peyton, let's go," Will shouted as he climbed into the back of a cab.

I wanted to tell him no, wanted him to go to some party and leave me out of it, but I knew I wouldn't. More than enough confrontation for one night. And I didn't want Chase to come out and find me there, or find me walking home alone if he took a taxi past me. I climbed in next to Will and pulled the door shut.

As the car left the curb, I rested my head against the window. Will humiliated me in public. He embarrassed me in front of Chase. I could still feel the bouncer's hands on my arm. I curled my arms around myself.

The same night he told me I was his girlfriend was the night I realized things between us had to come to an end.

12

AT TEN-THIRTY, KAY STILL HADN'T EMERGED FROM HER ROOM. I needed to tell her about Will calling me his girlfriend. I needed to tell her about how those words made me realize I needed to leave him. I needed to share all the things that happened with Chase and Will, how it made me want to cry. But I didn't know if she wanted to hear it. I never found out what happened between Kay and Chase. I couldn't text Chase to apologize again without knowing if he hurt her.

Once I'd paced the hall long enough, I knocked on her door and waited for the mumbled "come in."

I slipped into the darkness of her room. The morning's light remained trapped behind the blackout curtains. The only glow was from the tiny salt lamp on her vanity.

Without word, Kay lifted up the blanket on the other side of the bed. I climbed in, wrapping the comforter around myself. I closed my eyes and listened to the sound of Kay's still sleepy breathing, trying to muster up the courage to tell her that I liked Chase. I wanted to tell her I'd developed feelings for him even though I knew it was useless and that I didn't know how to leave Will without a disaster ensuing.

"While you were out, I realized I was an asshole the other night," Kay said, and then yawned. Her weight shifted on the bed as she turned to face me. She found my hand beneath the blankets and gave my fingers a squeeze. "I should have just told you how I knew Chase."

"You don't have to," I told her. "Especially if you're not ready to talk about it."

My response was selfish. Knowing meant facing what had happened, why Kay hated Chase, why maybe I shouldn't be spending time with him.

I'd been so afraid I'd hurt her by spending time with Chase. But Will took care of that issue the previous night with his outburst.

Kay said, "I know I don't have to. I want to."

I could hear the pick-up in her breathing, and steadied my own. What she said might mean I wouldn't look at Chase the same way again, that I wouldn't feel right spending time with him. I swallowed down bile and focused on Kay.

Kay cleared her throat and pulled herself into a sitting position. "I've been hoping you'd open up about all the things that happened to you before we met. I know your dad sucked and your mom wasn't great either, but I get the sense that it's a lot bigger than that. Then I realized, why would you open up to me about what's going on if I can't be open and honest with you?"

I sat up too, resting against the plush headboard. I stayed quiet, giving her the space to speak when she was ready.

"I met Danny when he got into a car accident. I'd been admitted to the hospital for trying to...Well, I took too many pills on purpose."

I nodded. That part of Kay's life she'd told me about. The stress of the bullying, the confusion about herself and her body became too much.

"We met when he escaped from his room in a wheelchair. He needed a break from his family's attention, I guess. I'd been given privileges to leave the ward during the day and I'd sit at Tim Horton's, drinking coffee, hoping to be inspired to work on my art. He noticed the Black Flag patch on my sweater sleeve and just started a conversation about music."

I smiled at the thought of someone approaching Kay instead of the other way around. Kay approached anyone who looked like a lost soul.

"He was in a lot of pain for a long time. When his leg and ribs healed, he still had back pain and struggled to walk without a limp. I didn't know how much he relied on his painkillers. In the first six months we hung out, I only saw him take them once or twice. Turns out he was already buying them from a guy on campus to supplement what the doctors were giving him, which, honestly, was a lot already."

The story turned quick, from a cute meeting to a tragedy in just a few sentences. I patted Kay's hand, because I didn't know what to say.

"I honestly had no idea what he'd gotten himself into. We had fun together. When he was better, we traveled together. We went on hikes—like, somehow, he got me to hike. He never judged me or tried to change me, which is a lot more than I can say for most people in my life at that time. And he didn't fetishize me for being trans, like others did before him. He just loved me and I loved him. It felt like enough. I thought love was enough." Kay turned her head to look at me. "Until it wasn't, you know?" Kay heaved a big sigh and rested her head against the headboard.

From what I'd heard, I could piece together what happened next. At least the major parts of it.

"We had ups and downs. He got a bit better and then he'd get worse again. He couldn't kick the habit. He no longer reminded me of the Danny I knew. And his family didn't recognize him either. They blamed me; you know. I mean, obviously."

While Kay gathered her thoughts, something Mitchell said

came back to me. The first night we spoke he asked about Chase's brother.

"And Danny is Chase's brother?" I asked.

Kay nodded.

Chase lost his brother. The pain Kay felt, Chase felt too. I thought about his first album, the songs he didn't want to re-record. I thought about the lyrics about a relationship I assumed was a lost friend. It was his brother.

"Why did they blame you?"

Kay grabbed her water bottle from the nightstand and took a few gulps. "He met me at the same time as his drug habit started."

I patted Kay's leg. Words wouldn't have been comforting or reassuring, so I opted to skip them all together. I figured Kay needed the space to say all the things she'd been holding in. I wanted to give her that.

"I hate monologuing," Kay laughed.

"You got this."

Kay pulled her hair back from her face and said, "In May, he went into rehab. While he was gone, I got us an apartment. I planned things to do that didn't involve his friends who used. I made sure to include his family in everything. He got out—and July was honestly one of the best months of my life."

*Forever July.* I closed my eyes, not wanting to get distracted by thoughts of Chase.

"We went out for a walk one night. He was restless and so moody. We'd been fighting on and off for days because living together was hard. We decided it was a good idea to get out of the apartment, to talk about things, but he ran into this one guy, a guy he used to buy from. He wanted to hang out, catch up and I said it was a bad idea. He promised he was fine, but I just had this feeling, you know?"

I nodded, encouraging her to go on.

"We got into a fight. A big one. In public, which is not my thing. I probably should have gone with him, but I was upset. It was just another in the dozen little fights we'd had all week. So, I went home. Like, the minute I reached the apartment, I regretted my decision to leave him. I went back, but I couldn't find him." Tears rolled down Kay's cheeks. She rubbed at her face with the bottom of her t-shirt.

"If it's too much you don't have to tell me."

After a few seconds, she shook her head. "I didn't find him. A man who was sleeping on a park bench did. By the time the paramedics showed up, he was already gone. Gone for a while. And his family blamed me for that too. They said it was my fault because we got into a fight, because I left him when I knew." Her breath hitched. She shoved the heels of her hands against her eyes and sighed. "I mean, they were right. I should have stuck it out, but I let him down."

"I'm sorry," I said. "I can't even imagine what that loss would have been like."

Hands against her face, Kay sobbed. "They told me that if he'd never met me, he wouldn't have gotten into drugs. No one talked to me at his memorial."

"What the hell."

Kay didn't fit into the perfect world that they built. Their son didn't either. The thought made me queasy. I pulled a piece of hair from Kay's damp cheeks. "You deserved better than that."

"I didn't tell you this so you would stop hanging out with Chase," Kay said, between sniffles. "That's not what I want."

"It's okay," I said.

She turned to face me. Her eyes were narrowed in the serious way they got when she believed someone wasn't listening to her. "I'm serious. Don't let my drama with his parents affect your relationship with him."

I didn't want Kay to think she had to shelter me from her

pain. It couldn't be easy knowing Chase and I were spending time together. Chase had admitted he'd been part of what his parents said.

I took Kay's hand from her lap and squeezed it. "Thank you for telling me that story. That must have been hard for you."

"Are you saying nice things just so I don't talk about Chase again?" Kay asked. "I honestly don't want you to think your friendship with him has to change because he and I have old drama. We might have history, but he makes you happy."

After everything she said, I didn't want to turn the conversation back on me. Kay, of all people, deserved some undivided attention. I smiled, instead of arguing.

"Doesn't he? Make you happy?"

"Sometimes," I admitted. "Sometimes I feel miserable, too."

We were quiet for some time. Kay turned the light on and gave me a sympathetic smile.

"I have a feeling some of that misery has nothing to do with Chase," Kay said. She pushed herself off the bed to grab a tissue, and picked up a canvas that faced the wall.

In the painting, Kay stood with her arms around a dark-haired, gaunt version of Chase. The painted Danny even had the same green eyes and expressive forehead as his brother.

I smiled and said, "You two are cute. Even in painting form."

Kay set it up on her dresser so that it looked down over the bed. She stood back and said, "I guess it's time I face this shit, since I assume I'll be seeing Chase around."

I took the cellphone from the kangaroo pouch of my hoodie and checked it. Chase still hadn't responded to my apologies. I put the phone away and tried to forget about Chase and about what Will said to me. Kay needed me and I owed her a day of attention, the kind she'd give me if I were going through something.

"I have to work tonight, Eternal Spin interview stuff. But do you wanna have a day? Black Metal Brunch in Kensington, smoothies, strolls?"

Kay didn't take her eyes off the painting, but she nodded. "That sounds perfect."

13

MOST SHIFTS I SPENT AT THE BACK OF THE STORE, FOLDING clothes, with my phone hidden under the counter to type out thoughts for Eternal Spin. The monotony of the work made it easy to daydream without getting in trouble for slacking. I'd become too distracted for customer service.

But that day was different. I couldn't even fake productivity. Even folding jeans felt impossible—my thoughts kept coming back to Will. My mood fluctuated between sad and angry.

He'd called me his girlfriend and I panicked. I didn't want Will to be my boyfriend. I didn't like the way he spoke to me or the way he disappeared for days on end. Those weren't things boyfriends did when they cared about someone.

I knew I had to do something, but I didn't know how. I didn't want to find out how Will would react when confronted. I didn't want to face his anger.

"I heard you like iced coffee."

My head shot up to find Chase standing in front of me. It had been three days since the incident and I'd given up on ever hearing from him again. My heart sped up.

He handed over the large iced coffee and leaned against

the counter.

I searched his body language for red flags, in case he'd come to tell me it wasn't a good idea to hang out anymore; in case the coffee was a goodbye present, to soften the blow.

The ease of his casual lean and the way one corner of his mouth turned up told me to relax.

I took a sip of the iced coffee. The right amount of milk and sugar. I took a second sip and said, "I needed this. I barely slept and I'm pulling a twelve-hour shift."

"Well, I'm glad I could help, but that's not why I came." Chase pulled out his phone. It looked brand new. He handed it over and said, "I need your number."

"You need my number?" I raised an eyebrow, but I took the phone. I swiped to open the screen and found the contact list.

"I had a little trouble with my phone." He cleared his throat. "This is a new one."

I stopped typing in my number and looked up. "Trouble because of the other night, I assume?"

Chase pressed his lips together.

"Did I wreck your phone?"

"You didn't."

"But Will did?"

Chase shrugged.

I groaned and covered my face with one hand. It all went from bad to worse—yet another layer of horrible added to the whole fiasco.

"I should have known Will would show up there." I groaned. "I feel bad."

"Why is Will's temper your responsibility?" Chase asked.

It wasn't the first time someone had asked me that.

"He's got a thing about you, specifically. I don't know what it is. And I should have known if we ran into him it would end up like that."

Chase had picked up one of the shirts and was folding it

exactly the way the other shirts in the store were. "So, you're not allowed to have friends he doesn't like?"

I finished my number and handed back his phone. "It's not that I'm not *allowed*. I just... should have known it would make him angry." I sucked in a breath, hearing my mother saying the same thing. I remembered the way she scolded me when I dropped a butter knife on the ground while my father slept. It clattered and my father came out shouting, threatening. When he finally went back to bed, my mother told me I shouldn't have been making a sandwich at eleven o'clock at night. I should have known any little noise could wake my father.

"Will and I have history," Chase admitted. He set aside one shirt and picked up another.

"Which is?" I drank some iced coffee and then went back to folding too.

Chase ran a hand through his blonde hair. While he was looking down at the clothes, I took in the splatter of freckles across his nose and how full and pink his lips were. Handsome was an understatement. Beautiful fit better.

I glanced away before he caught me staring.

"Will and my brother Danny knew each other. He didn't like it so much that I'd show up at the DeKay House to drag my brother home from time to time. He thinks my attempts to save my brother meant I looked down on him, on all their friends." Chase grabbed another shirt.

"Until recently, I didn't know Danny was your brother," I admitted.

Chase looked me in the eye and said, "You talked to Kay?"

I nodded.

"Do you think less of me?"

If Kay had told me to stay away, if Kay had said Chase wasn't a good person, I would have taken it at face value. But she wanted me to make my own decision. "Should I?"

"Is there a grey area? I think I'd fit more into a moral grey area."

I chuckled. "I feel like I've been fitting in that myself lately."

Chase moved on to another shirt, smiling. "No way. You're basically a saint."

I shook my head. "I wasn't sure you'd still want to talk to me after what happened. I feel bad about it."

Chase shook his head. "Yeah, don't think I'd give up on you that easily, Peyton."

Heat spread up my neck and across my cheeks. I took a sip of my ice coffee.

"You wanna come by and see the new place tomorrow? I'm moving things in."

I nodded. "Sure. I'm off at four tomorrow."

"Come when you're done—we can order in food or something."

I exhaled and told myself to take it easy, to not look too eager. I nodded. "Sounds like a plan."

"I'll text you details." He grinned, waving his new phone in the air, and left.

I cringed at the thought of how my excuses for Will must have come off to Chase. They were so transparent. For years, I listened to the same excuses from my mother, every time she tried to defend my father.

After running away from that life, I'd allowed myself to get sucked into my own version of it. Even though I promised myself I wouldn't be that person. So many times, I begged my mother to leave, but she always found excuses to stay. I didn't want to make excuses anymore.

Despite the unease in my chest, I wasn't alone in this. I had an apartment. I had friends. I deserved better than the life my mother had and I wanted to get it.

I slipped my phone from beneath the counter and texted Will.

*My apartment for 9, ok?*

14

DESPITE MY REQUEST, KAY REFUSED TO LEAVE THE APARTMENT. She said she'd stay in her room with the music on, but she didn't plan on going anywhere *just in case*. No protest would move her. If we sat on the couch, facing the kitchen, Kay would be less likely to hear my rehearsed speech.

The apartment buzzer went off. I froze. If Will got violent it would impact Kay too. He'd never hit me, but his temper never ceased to shock me. All it took was for the wrong button to be pushed.

The buzzer went again and again.

Slipping around me, Kay pressed the lock release. She gave my shoulder a squeeze and whispered, "You got this."

I braced myself as the sound of heavy steps echoed up the stairs. Suddenly I couldn't imagine sitting on the same couch as Will. I couldn't think about being inches away from him when I told him it was over. I went to the kitchen to get a glass of water, to give him time to sit down first.

"Peyton," Will called as he walked through the door.

The sound of him kicking his shoes off against the wall made me flinch.

"You want water?" I asked.

"Nah, just had a couple beers."

I gripped my cup and walked into the living room.

Will had already taken up the couch, legs spread out across the cushions. I sat in the recliner, clutching my glass.

"I'm surprised you wanted to hang. I thought you were all *mad* at me." Will tossed his head back when he laughed.

I watched his movements, looking for signs he was drunk. He might have been loud, but his body language said he was mostly sober. I thought about apologizing to him, or telling him I wasn't upset. I thought about saying it was no big deal, which I'd said many times before. I knew what to say to keep things from escalating.

But for the first time, I wanted to stand up for myself.

"I was… I was mad."

"What?" His laugh petered out.

I couldn't tell if he was challenging me to say it again or if he didn't hear me over his own amusement. I stared into my water glass.

I could have told him it was over by text. He wouldn't have even given me that.

With him here in my living room, I wished I'd taken the path of least resistance and just ghosted him until he forgot about me, until he moved on to some other girl.

"What is this?" Will asked.

I couldn't speak. I didn't know what to say. This was new territory.

"Are we making a thing out of this?" Will asked. "Are you going to be that girl?"

He made it seem terrible to be like other girls. He acted like standing up for myself against him made me undesirable. He didn't like it if I expressed my thoughts or had my own opinions and he sure didn't like it if I cried.

I didn't care if I were like other girls anymore. I didn't care if he found me annoying.

"Maybe." As confident as I wanted to be, my voice still shook. "Yes."

His feet slammed into the ground as he sat up straight. I couldn't bring myself to look at him. The realization terrified me. I couldn't remember ever looking my father in the eye during a fight. I couldn't remember what colour his eyes were. I'd lived with him for eighteen years of my life and I'd always been too terrified.

I forced my eyes to meet Will's. "You called me your girlfriend."

"Chase needed to remember who you're with."

"You said this was casual. We don't own each other."

"What's your point?" His voice was already getting louder.

"I don't want you to think that…I was just hanging out." They weren't the words I wanted to say.

"Oh, fuck off. Everyone knows you want Chase Reid. I was just trying to protect you. There's no way a guy like him is gonna want you back."

Sometimes I thought Will didn't understand me or my insecurities, but I realized he knew them well. He understood my wants, needs, fears. He used them against me.

I set the glass on the table and shoved my hands beneath my thighs. Not the power pose I planned to convey while practicing in my room after work. "I don't want to be your girlfriend."

"What?" He let out a disgusted laugh. "Because you think you can do better than me?"

I shook my head. I didn't want him to assume it was an attack on him. If he thought he was under attack, he would become more defensive than he already was. If he thought he was under attack, he would see me as the enemy.

"It's not about dating someone else," I told him.

"Because no one is going to put up with your poor, sad girl routine like I did." He got up, hovering over me.

I tried to remember his words were his way of manipulating me, trying to change my mind. My instincts told me to apologize to him, to make him stop yelling. It took all my courage just to look up and meet his eye.

"I don't care," I told him. "It's not about someone else."

"Ha!" He pointed at me. "You're so full of shit. Is this just some game you're playing because you're mad that I don't call you enough or take you out on proper dates or some shit?" When I didn't answer, he leaned toward my face and yelled, "Answer me."

Things were about to go from bad to worse. I wrapped my arms around myself.

"You're too good for me now, huh? Some rich fucks let you hang around with them a couple times and you forget who you are?"

"Don't say that."

"You honestly believe that those people care about you? The poor little runaway? They just feel pity for you."

His laughter gave me goosebumps. He reached out to grab my wrist, but I pulled them way. I pressed myself back into the chair, drawing my legs up onto the seat. I heard my father's voice in my head screaming, *look at what you made me do*.

Will pointed at me, his finger only inches from my face. "You're leaving me for Chase fucking Reid, aren't you?"

I shook my head. "No." It was the only word I could muster up.

"You seem to thinks he's this white knight. He comes in and saves the day so he can say look what I did, I'm a hero, and then he's going to leave you behind, broken, like he did with his own brother."

Kay would be hearing every word that he yelled at me. Everything he said about Chase, about Danny. It would break her heart. I couldn't let him hurt Kay too.

"Shut up," I spat at him. I climbed out of the chair. "I want you to leave. For good."

"You're gonna come crawling back to me when you realize how fucking alone you are. But don't expect me to take you back. You're pathetic."

My eyes stung. I shook my head, trying not to let my insecurities get the better of me. "I don't need you." It was supposed to come out strong, self-assured, but my throat tightened and the words were barely audible.

Then Kay stepped into the living room, arms folded across her chest. Her presence helped me retain a scrap of my composure. I forced my shoulders back and raised my chin.

Will straightened, but his anger didn't lessen. He glanced from Kay and back to me. "I'm done with both of you bitches."

Tears spilled over my cheeks and dripped from my chin. All the things I wanted to say were still inside me. I was going to tell him that we didn't work anymore, to explain that I'd outgrown him. I wanted to give all the reasons why he couldn't treat me the way he did. I should have told him I deserved better, but I couldn't say another thing. All my thoughts were replaced with embarrassment.

He grabbed his shoes from where he'd kicked them off and shouted, "Have a terrible life."

"Fuck you, Will," Kay shouted as he slammed the door.

I collapsed into the chair and covered my eyes with both hands. My lungs couldn't take in enough air—I gasped for it.

Kay put her hands on my shoulders, saying nothing. I focused on the weight of each of her fingers holding on to me. I focused on each beat of my heart, to calm my breathing.

"He was so angry," I whispered after a few minutes, as my breathing steadied.

"You did it."

I uncovered my eyes. "What if he comes back?"

Kay sat on the arm of the chair and said, "Then we call the police."

I stared up at her. "This is the worst."

Will sensed how alone I was, how I was desperate for anyone to see me, understand me. When I came to the city, I'd been alone so long and I feared that loneliness would push me back to my parents, the only constant I'd had. Will took advantage of my weakness.

"It was hard, but you pulled it off."

I nodded.

"What do you need?" Kay asked me.

"I think I need some music and an early night," I told her.

She kissed me on the top of my head and said, "I'm going to stay up and work on some sketches. If you need me, you can bug me, okay?"

Kay and I both stood. She squeezed my shoulder again. "I know that wasn't easy, but I'm proud of you."

I forced a smile. "Thanks, Kay. Took me long enough, right?"

She shook her head. "There's no timeline for things like this."

I thought about my mom. Part of me always blamed her for not leaving my dad, for forcing me to grow up around his anger, letting him take it out on me. Things were different for my mom. Her parents were dead. Her friends had abandoned her somewhere along the way. I'd fallen into the same trap my mother had. Being alone made her stay.

I gave Kay a hug. I wanted her to know how much I appreciated her being there. If it weren't for Kay, I might have stuck with Will. That realization shook me.

I said goodnight and headed into my room. Putting on a playlist full of the saddest songs, I crawled into bed and pulled the blankets up over my face. I tried not to think of the things that Will said to me, the way he knew how to target my insecurities. I knew he said them out of desperation, but it didn't make them hurt any less.

I rolled over and took my phone from the nightstand before tucking myself beneath the covers again. I opened a blank document and typed.

*Her mother woke her in the middle of the night with a hand over her mouth and a sharp shake. They needed to stay quiet. No words were required. Her mother picked up the bag she'd packed and nodded toward the window. They were making their escape. Her nine-year-old brain thought about all the places the two of them could go, all the adventures they were about to experience.*

*Her mother allowed the car to roll down the driveway, away from the house. Once it had coasted into the spot behind the neighbour's car, she started the engine and pulled away.*

*Neither of them spoke for an hour. She had to remind herself to breathe. It wasn't until her mother pulled over for coffee that she asked where they were going.*

*Her mother shook her head and said, "I don't know."*

*Another hour went by. They passed a motel and she wondered why they didn't stop, why they didn't wait until morning to continue. They made sharp turns and followed roads she'd never laid eyes on before. She saw outside of the town for the first time in her life. She told her mother they should drive somewhere that was summer all the time. Her mother turned again and she thought maybe they could go to the east coast, where her mother was raised.*

*But then she recognized the Tim Hortons as they approached. She saw the town sign.*

*"Mom?"*

*Her mother's grip on the steering wheel had tightened. She kept her eyes ahead.*

*"I don't want to go home," she whispered.*

*Tears dripped from her mother's chin. "We have nowhere else to go."*

I put the phone down on my nightstand again and pushed the covers away. I got up and headed out into the living room. Kay sat on the couch with her sketchbook, working on the face of a person I didn't know. I cleared my throat and she glanced up.

"Everything okay?" She asked, setting her sketchbook down.

I nodded.

Kay raised the blanket that covered her lap and said, "Climb in."

I lay on the couch next to her, tucking my feet beneath her legs. Kay covered us both with the blanket and asked, "Do you want to talk about things?"

I shook my head.

It was comfortable, just the two of us. I was lucky to have Kay.

15

IT TOOK LESS THAN FIFTEEN MINUTES TO WALK TO CHASE'S NEW apartment, in the basement of a yellow brick Victorian house. As his text instructed, I headed around back. The walkway between the two houses was so narrow I ran my hands against both walls without stretching. The backyard had been turned into a parking spot, but in an attempt to make the space relaxing, someone had added planters on the fence.

The massive window next to the door looked into the basement apartment. As I approached, I could see into the living space below. Mitchell stood at the bottom of the stairs with a beer in one hand and he waved at me to come in.

I stepped in and removed my shoes at the top of the stairs. Mitchell called out he was getting beer, before disappearing into the depths of the basement.

As I walked downstairs, I realized I'd expected something different from Chase. The walls were dull beige, but the windows at the top of the stairs brought in a lot of natural light. The furniture in the small living room was in shades of grey and black. Masculine, but more modern than I expected. His bookshelves were up, but still empty. Boxes took up all the floor space in the combined kitchen and living room.

Melissa and Chase emerged from the back room, which must have been the bedroom. By the heaviness of his eyelids and his messy hair, I assumed he was exhausted.

"Peyton, hey," Chase said, giving a wave. "Sorry the place is a disaster."

Melissa walked over and wrapped her arms around me. "It's so good to see you."

The gesture took me by surprise, but I hugged her in return. "Hey. It's been a while."

I could smell the sweetness of her perfume. Despite wearing yoga pants and a long t-shirt, she looked put together. She gave me a toothy grin as she pulled back.

Chase took his turn giving me a hug. I wished it wouldn't end so quickly. His cheeks squished into his eyes as he smiled at me. "I'm glad you could come."

Mitchell shoved a beer into my hand. "You come to repair the walls?"

"What?" I asked.

"He's joking. My dad's coming by when he's off sometime this week or next."

Melissa laughed. "These two had too many beers, unloading the truck yesterday, and put a huge hole in the bedroom wall with part of the bed frame."

"My dad has some spackle or whatever," Chase said. "I could do it myself."

"How big is it?" I asked.

"It's not *that* big." Mitchell rolled his eyes.

"It's about the size of a fist!" Melissa laughed loudly.

I took a sip of beer before saying, "Then you'll probably need to patch it first. I can do it, if you want. If you have what you need."

"You can patch a wall?" Mitchell asked.

I nodded.

"My kinda woman," Mitchell chuckled. He set the beer on the coffee table behind him and said, "Gotta piss."

Melissa grinned at me, nudging me with her elbow. "Mitchell's single, you know."

"Yeah, I don't know," I said to Melissa, with an awkward laugh.

"By choice, though," Chase mentioned.

"Seriously. You two have this sexy edginess to you. You'd look so cute together. A power couple or whatever," Melissa whispered.

I pulled at my hair and tried to think how to respond to that. Mitchell was attractive and funny, but I didn't need yet another man who didn't take relationships seriously. Also, it was too soon.

"Mel, come on," Chase said to her, keeping his voice low.

"You two would look like rock stars together, honestly."

"She has a boyfriend."

I swallowed. "I don't, actually."

Melissa clapped. "This is perfect."

Chase looked me in the eye. The way he watched me caused tingles to spread through my entire body. With Melissa in the room, instant regret filled me. I needed to be distracted. "Can I get a tour?"

"Oh my god, Chase, show her that shower. It's to die for," Melissa said reaching out, squeezing his hand.

Mitchell returned and picked up his beer.

Chase waved at me to follow, so I did. He turned to face me with his arms out and said, "Kitchen, living room, office, dining room." He chuckled.

I smiled back. "Fancy."

He nodded and turned to saunter down the tiny hallway into one of two doors. The bedroom was a basic square, full of boxes and a disassembled bed frame. A mattress lay in the middle of the floor, with just a comforter thrown on top. The windows were small and looked out on the house next door. The hole in the wall sat right beneath one of the two small windows.

"Do you honestly think you could patch that?" Chase asked, examining the ruined drywall.

"Yeah. It's simple. I've patched a lot of drywall in my time." I glanced around the room and said, "This is really nice."

He laughed at that. "Not rockstar enough though, right?"

I tried to think about Chase in some loft with bold colours and records and guitars hanging on all the walls. While it seemed possible, it didn't fit with him—the humble basement apartment suited what I knew about him.

"I think it works. It's simple, but bright and kinda timeless."

Chase raised his arms above his head like he was thanking some higher power. "Thank you! Melissa has a lot of ideas on how to make it more Forever July centric, but I think I'd rather it was my escape."

The framed record of Forever July's first album stood against the wall. I walked over and touched it. With the knowledge I gained about Chase's brother and Kay, the lyrics held more weight. I knew I wouldn't be able to listen to the album in front of Kay anymore. I wonder if she knew the whole time who the songs were about.

"Hey," Mitchell said coming into the room. "Drive me to pick up the stuff to fix the wall. I wanna pay for it."

"I've had too many beers," Chase told him.

"I can drive you," Melissa said with a sigh. "I want to get some paint for the accent wall in the dining area."

"Let me just get out of these track pants and we can all go," Chase said.

"You guys stay here. We'll be like ten minutes," Melissa said, peeking into the room. "Plus, I have something to talk to Mitchell about." She winked at me.

I forced a smile. I didn't want to fight it too much, to make her think it was because I liked someone else. Even though I did.

"Maybe you two could start setting up your record player thingy." Melissa kissed Chase on the mouth and grabbed her purse from the floor next to the bedroom door. Mitchell shouted they would stop at the liquor store on the way home.

"Should we start on the shelf?" I asked, feeling awkward, left alone with Chase. Maybe better for Melissa to see something tangible we did while they were gone. I wanted her to come back and see we'd been working on the shelving unit the whole time.

"It's from Ikea. Just warning you." Chase grabbed an Allen key from a cluster of things on the floor and tossed it to me.

As we arranged all the pieces by size, Chase asked, "You doing okay?"

"Yeah, I'm good."

"I meant about Will."

As Chase held two pieces of the black shelf together, I pushed in the screw and twisted it tight with the Allen key. I grabbed another screw while Chase fit another board.

"Yeah, I meant about Will," I said with a laugh. "Just feeling kind of embarrassed about the whole thing."

Chase stopped. "What do you have to be embarrassed about?"

I sat back onto my heels and twisted my hair into a bun. I shrugged and said, "I thought I was stronger than I was. Kind of feel like a fool, letting it go on for so long."

Chase put the shelf down and lowered himself onto the floor in front of me. He was so close I could smell his fresh-showered smell. I slipped back a little further in case Melissa came in.

"You seem pretty strong to me," Chase said. "You came to this city alone. You started a publication. You're doing well for yourself."

"And yet, I stuck around with Will for all this time."

"That doesn't mean you're not strong."

He pushed his hair back from his face. Worry lines appeared across Chase's forehead. "What surprised me was that you dated him at all."

I fiddled with the Allen key in my hand. I wondered if he would pity me, like Will said. I didn't want Will to be right, but I wanted to know.

"Turns out I'm more like my mom than I wanted to admit." I cleared my throat. "I think I assumed I had two options: be like my mom or be like my dad. That's all I knew, really, until recently. My dad, the angry, mean man; or my mom, the pushover."

Chase nodded.

"I would do anything not to be anything like my dad."

"Was your dad the reason you came to the city?" Chase asked.

I nodded.

Chase's eyes met mine. He pressed his lips together and I wondered if he was about to tell me how sorry he was, how sad my life had been. I braced myself for the sympathy statements that often followed a peek into my old life.

"It's amazing what you've accomplished on your own," Chase said. "I'm aware of what I've been given and how it's made reaching my goals so much easier. It always surprises me when I see what people can do without all the resources. I know I wouldn't be able to."

I laughed. "You'd be surprised."

Chase laughed too. "I don't know. I was going to call my dad to fix a hole in the drywall."

I smiled. "I'll teach you."

"Are you qualified to teach me?" Chase asked, his one eyebrow arching up as he looked at me.

"I'm basically a master at spackling," I told him.

Chase grabbed the shelf he'd set down and said, "Then I'm in good hands."

I grinned as I grabbed another screw from the pile. Chase held the shelf still as I secured it.

"What are you doing next Saturday?" Chase asked.

"I have a couple interviews during the day, but nothing after that," I told him.

"Want to come to Melissa's birthday party? It might not be your scene. It's not really mine, but it could be fun." Chase asked.

I slid my body back a little, giving us some distance as I reached for the next screw. "Not my scene?"

"It's at a club downtown," he explained. "Mitchell and Mo are going to be there. I asked Camila this morning, but she said hell no."

I chuckled. "I'll convince her."

Chase held up one finger and left the room. I finished putting in the screw and waited for Chase to return. He came back with a manila envelope and said, "Use this as a bargaining chip to get Cam to come."

He handed the envelope over and I pulled out what was inside. A stack of postcards. I pulled one out and looked at the front: "Greetings from Iowa City" with images of the Liberal Arts Building, Old Capital, and the stadium. I flipped it over to find messy printing dated from two years earlier.

*I love these boys, but if I have to spend one more day in this van with them this band may never survive. I miss Melissa and my parents. I miss my goddamn bed. The show in Iowa City killed though. I hung out with this guy after who said he lost his brother to drugs too. He said our album got him thru. I think I needed that. It hurts, but it rocks too. – Chase*

"Are you sure you want to give these to me?" I asked him. "Are you sure you want me to publish them?"

"I wasn't ready to share the new ones. But maybe in time." Chase turned back to the shelves and said, "So, you're in for Saturday?"

"I'm in."

16

CAMILA FLOPPED BACK ONTO THE FLOOR OF THE LIVING ROOM and asked Kay, "Can I photograph you in here? This place is so eclectic, so *you*. Like, how do you get eight different mirrors to all look like they belong together?"

Kay pushed her hair behind one ear. "On one condition: you guys sell shirts with your logo on them."

"I told you it would come up," I said to Camila with a laugh.

"Okay," Camila said, sitting up. "We'll sell shirts, if you can convince your boss to do an interview with Peyton. She's been blowing us off."

Kay countered. "Only if you agree to give me a discount on a bunch of shirts to sell at the store."

Camila thought about it for a second. "Deal."

Kay gave me a grin and said, "And I told you I would make it happen."

Camila stretched her arms above her head. "I'm gonna head out. My dad's away for the weekend, so my brothers and I are having some one-on-one time with my mom."

I climbed to my feet as Camila did and asked, "You're still going tomorrow, right?"

"To Melissa's thing?"

"Yeah."

Camila shrugged. "Since Chase will only let us use those postcards if I do, then yeah. I think they're going to bring in a lot of viewers, so how can I say no?" She packed up her things. "I'll see you tomorrow for the interviews."

When the door closed after Camila, Kay shut her sketchbook and asked, "Are you sure it's a good idea for you to be going to Melissa's birthday party?"

"What? Why?" I dropped on the couch next to her.

Kay raised an eyebrow. "Chase, and your obvious feelings for him. How are you feeling seeing him with his girlfriend?"

Heat spread through my face. I groaned at myself, but answered, "It's easier to remember he's not single and it's not an option when Melissa's around, if I'm being honest."

Kay gave me a tight-lipped smile and asked, "You okay with that?"

I nodded. "Maybe having a crush on someone who's taken is what I need right now, so I don't jump into something bad for me. Give me time to evaluate what I want out of a relationship."

"I think that's a really good idea. Focusing inward." She held up her pointer finger and flipped back a page in her sketchbook. She turned it to show me. "I did this while you two were working."

It was me. From the mirror I knew my face had filled out after coming to the city, but seeing it in Kay's drawing made me hyper-aware. She'd focused on my large eyes and puffy lips. I let out a long exhale.

"I look like her, like my mother," I told her.

Kay turned to look at the sketch. "Sorry. Uncomfortable?"

I shook my head and took the sketchpad back. I wondered what my mother was doing, if she was okay. If she had got away. I wished I could have one-on-one time with my mother, like Camila had with hers.

"You sure you're okay?" Kay asked.

"I think I want to call my mom," I told her. "Just to check in."

Kay bit her bottom lip in thought and stared into space for a moment before saying, "Don't call from your phone. Since your father seems like a real asshole, call from mine, so he doesn't have your number."

"Are you sure?" I asked.

Kay handed her phone to me, looked me in the eye and said, "If they make you uncomfortable, even for a second, just hang up, okay?"

I took the phone and stared at the dark screen. It hadn't been my intention to call right that minute. I had sort of planned to waffle back and forth on the decision for hours until it was too late to call.

"Oh," Kay said. "You didn't mean right now?"

I held onto the phone. Friday nights my father went out to play poker. My mother would be alone.

"It's okay," Kay said. She put her hand out to take the phone back. After several seconds, when I didn't give it back, she pulled her hand away.

"I'm going to my room."

"You sure?"

"I'll bring the phone back in a minute."

"Take your time."

I got up and walked into my room, shut the door behind me, and leaned on it. I glanced around, thinking if I should sit on the bed or at the desk. Instead, I opted for standing right there with my back against the door. I swiped open the phone and tapped in my old house number.

My finger hovered over the call icon. There were two options. My mother would pick up, like I hoped. Or my father. Waiting until Monday while my father was at work made the most sense, but I didn't know if I'd have the nerve to do it then.

Before I could change my mind, I sent the call. I pressed the phone to my ear as it rang once and then again. I knew my mother would never let the phone ring a third time. I knew she wasn't allowed to.

"Hello?" Her voice was just as I remembered. It was quiet and husky.

"Mom, it's me."

I heard her breath in my ear.

"Are you okay?" I asked her.

"Yes, this is the Young residence."

"Can you talk?"

"No, we're not interested, thank you."

My father was there.

I had counted on him still sticking to the same routine. Still going out with his friends. Guilt tightened my chest. I knew I had to end the call. I knew I couldn't risk anything happening because I called.

I swallowed the lump in my throat. "All right. I'll let you go. I just wanted to hear your voice."

"Okay?" she asked.

Was she trying to get me off the phone or subtly asking me if I was doing okay? I hoped she was asking about me.

"I'm good, mom. I'm really good." I couldn't control the sound of tears in my voice.

"Who is it?" The voice of my father came from somewhere on the other end of the phone. Just the sound of him made me shudder. I shut my eyes.

"Thank you for calling. Have a good night." I heard the shaking of my mother's voice. I'd put her at risk for my own gain.

"I'm sorry. Call this number back and ask for me if you need me, okay?"

"Thank you. Have a good night."

The line clicked as the call ended. I let the phone away from my ear and stared at it. The moment was over.

I'd finally heard my mother's voice after almost two years. It made me aware of how far away she was from me. The distance was much further than I remembered. I could drive to her in an hour and a half, but I wondered how long it would take to really reach her.

WHEN WE GOT TO THE CLUB, I APPRECIATED ALL THE TORTURE Kay had put me through, picking clothes for me. I'd sighed at the process, but the fitted black dress blended in better than my jeans and t-shirt would have. Ignoring her protests, I had paired it with a cropped denim jacket and my high-top Chuck Taylors. The bouncer glared at my footwear, but he let us in after Camila said she had paid for bottle service.

Melissa's booth sat at the edge of the dance floor, black curtains separating it from the booths on either side. The crowd of people in the booth made it impossible to say hello to Chase or Mitchell, who were crammed in the far side, on either side of Melissa.

We were only half an hour later than Chase had said he'd be there, but Melissa was already well beyond drunk. Blowing kisses and laughing, she held up a glass and shouted that we were falling behind.

"We're gonna hit up the bar for some shots," Camila shouted back. "We'll catch up. Be right back."

Melissa let out a *woo* of excitement and collapsed against Chase's shoulder.

Chase gave a short wave and mouthed "hey".

All I could do was send a small smile back, not wanting anyone else to read a response from my lips.

Melissa elbowed Mitchell. "You said you wanted to do shots! Why don't you go with them?"

He stood up on the seat and climbed across the table. Their friends laughed and clapped. Someone took a picture of him in the middle, posing over the bottle of whiskey sitting in the centre of the chaos. When Mitchell landed on his feet, Camila swatted him and said, "Don't mess shit up. They have my credit card on file."

Mitchell kissed her on the cheek. "You know I would never let you take the fall for my shenanigans."

"Saying shenanigans doesn't make it cute. I don't want to pay for a broken table," Camila told him as they walked toward the bar.

I glanced back at Chase and Melissa. Chase took the glass from her hand and set it down on the table. A small gesture, but I felt a vibration of envy.

If I wanted to maintain my friendship with Camila, Chase, and the boys from Forever July, I had to put my feelings for Chase aside. They were important to me already—and on top of that, Melissa was nice. Despite our differences, I could see us being friends. I couldn't allow that feeling of deception to pulse through me every time I saw her and Chase together.

"Peyton!" Mitchell stopped so I could catch up. "You going to do shots with us?"

I followed them to the bar. All around us people were chatting, dancing, and laughing. I wanted to focus on having fun and not the fact that I was celebrating the birthday of the woman who dated the guy I liked. Just the thought made me laugh at myself.

"What shots are we doing?" I asked.

"Burt Reynolds." Camila chuckled to herself. "It's the only one I can stand."

A space opened up at the bar and the three of us slipped

in. In her thigh high boots, Camila stood as tall as most of the men and her shiny gold dress caught the attention of the male bartender. She ordered six shots and passed two to each of us.

"To a ridiculous night," Camila said, holding up one of her shot glasses. We clinked our glasses together before tossing back one after the other. After grabbing drinks, we headed to the dance floor.

"I don't dance," I said with a laugh. The warm sensation from the shots made me comfortable enough to admit it.

Camila tossed an arm around my shoulder. "You can dance. You just need to get drunk enough that you don't care how you look."

Mitchell led us to the centre of the dance floor, where we bumped into a group of people that Camila and Mitchell knew. They introduced themselves to me. I watched the way they moved, swaying their hips and wiggling their shoulders. I drained my drink and told myself I could do it. It would be hundred times easier than going back to the table alone.

Being around people that knew Camila and Mitchell, who seemed happy to have me there, I didn't mind being out of my comfort zone. For one night, I could pretend I belonged there, with people who seemed to have their life together, who spent more than forty dollars on an outfit. I didn't even mind when a man tapped me on the shoulder and asked if I wanted to dance. I thanked him for the offer, but turned back to my friends. He didn't leave. Instead, he bumped into me, his body pressing against my back.

"Hey," Chase said, pushing his way through the crowd. "Does it look like she's interested?"

As much as I didn't need the support, I appreciated Chase stepping in. However, it did nothing to help my goal to put my feelings aside. My stomach fluttered with infatuation.

He glanced back at me, only for a few seconds, but heat spread through my body.

For the first time since showing up, I noticed how different

Chase's clothes were from the norm. He wore black jeans, but instead of one of his many worn band t-shirts, he had on a plain white T and a black blazer. His blonde curls were gelled back from his face, making the worry lines on his forehead more prominent.

"Relax, man," the guy said, holding up his hands in defense. "I didn't know she was your girl."

Melissa put herself in front of Chase and said, "She's not, but she doesn't have to have a reason not to be interested in you."

I heard the emphasis on the first two words. I noticed the defensive stance and wondered if it was about Chase's attempt at heroism, more than defending me.

The man kept his hands up and backed away from us into the crowd.

"Thanks," I said to both Chase and Melissa.

"Oh my god, it was nothing," Melissa said, gripping my wrist.

"You okay?" Chase asked.

I grinned at him. "He'd have backed away if I told him off —but now he definitely won't try again."

Melissa squeezed my wrist again. "Mitchell, you need to stick with her!" She moved me backwards into Mitchell, who chuckled as I teetered into him.

"Hey, I didn't even have time to notice before Chase swooped in," Mitchell said with a shrug.

Melissa turned to stare at Chase. He took a mouthful of his drink, like he was unaware of the conversation all together.

"Want me to give that guy hell?" Mitchell whispered into my ear.

Chase's attention turned back to the conversation. I couldn't help but wonder if it bothered him, the way Mitchell's mouth brushed against my cheek as he spoke. But I also wondered if I was reading too far into it. My feelings for

Chase made me see ulterior meaning in his actions. He was a nice guy, a friendly guy. I was thinking too much about it.

I told Mitchell, "No, I think he got the idea."

"Alright, then you stick with me tonight. I'll be your knight in shining armour."

I gestured to the fabric of his black shirt with print and said, "You'll be my knight in floral print?"

"Hey," he said, puffing out his chest, "It's masculine to wear azaleas, alright?"

"Azaleas? Are you into flowers?" I laughed.

"You should see my apartment."

"It's like being in a green house," Camila chimed in.

Mitchell threw his hands up. "I will not apologize for who I am."

Melissa caught my eye and winked. Chase put his hands around Melissa's waist, but his eyes were on Mitchell and me. For a second, I fooled myself into thinking that it might be because Mitchell and I were standing only an inch apart.

Heat crept up my neck as I stared back at Chase, so I directed my attention to Camila. "Want another shot?"

"Like, another three shots."

"You're not leaving without me." Mitchell offered up his elbows for each of us to take.

"You guys coming?" Camila asked Chase and Melissa.

I thought Chase might say yes, but Melissa stumbled. He shrugged and said they'd be there when we got back.

I was both disappointed and relieved.

---

As the night went on, Mitchell stuck by my side while our friends came and went from the dance floor. The drinks kept coming and I let Mitchell take my hand and spin me around. I forced myself not to look at Chase, not to wonder what he was thinking, to focus only on Mitchell while we danced.

Letting go of being awkward on the dancefloor was much easier than I expected, especially with Mitchell taking the lead. When I returned from a trip to the bathroom, he extended his arms for me to step into him and I did.

At some point, we lost track of everyone else. It was just Mitchell and me on the dancefloor. Even Camila had disappeared back to the booth. When Mitchell pulled my body against his, I allowed it. When he put his lips on the skin just beneath my ear, I tightened my grip on the back of his shirt.

"You look so good tonight," he said, moving his mouth to my jaw. He bit my chin and I laughed.

After things happened with Will, I hadn't allowed myself to think too much about it. I didn't allow myself to think about why I'd allowed things to continue for so long, or happen in the first place. I couldn't remember feeling attracted to Will the way I was with Chase. I couldn't remember how he made me feel, even in the beginning. All I knew was that when loneliness made me uncomfortable, Will made that feeling go away for a while.

I realized that's what I was doing with Mitchell. I used Mitchell's attention to distract myself from Chase, from being single. I didn't want another situation like before.

I ducked my head away. "I think I need some water."

His arms dropped from around me and he took a step back. "We're good, right?" Mitchell asked.

I glanced up and saw concern on his face. His dark eyes looked heavy with worry.

I nodded.

He shifted his weight and shoved his hands in his pockets. "I didn't make you uncomfortable, did I?"

"Not at all. I just got out of this breakup and I think I got caught up in..." I shrugged because I didn't know how to explain it. I didn't want to tell him I was lonely. I didn't want to tell him that until recently, I didn't really understand what it was like to have feelings for someone, but that wasn't him. I didn't want to confess to Mitchell that I liked his very taken best friend.

Mitchell nodded, like he understood. He put both his hands on my shoulders and said, "Listen, if you ever need a rebound, no strings, you let me know, alright? I'd be honoured."

I laughed. "So, we're good?"

"Yeah, definitely."

"I think I'm going to get some air," I told him, "but thanks."

"Find me if you wanna keep dancing. I'm still your bodyguard, but I promise I won't let you touch this." He gestured to his body and bobbing his eyebrows up. His clowning around eased whatever tension might have been there.

I rolled my eyes, but smiled and thanked him for being cool. Mitchell headed to the bar, as I slipped through the crowd toward the booth. I'd almost reached the edge of the dancefloor when a hand grabbed me.

Melissa looked up at me, her face flushed and puffy.

Chase stared over her head at me.

"Oh my god," Melissa squealed. "You and Mitchell are so cute. I can't handle it. Did you make out?"

I feared if I admitted my lack of feelings for Mitchell, it might reveal my true feelings. Even without a word spoken, my heart raced when I stood that close to Chase.

"You looked like you were having a good time," Chase said.

I fiddled with Kay's purse that I had strapped across my chest. "Mitchell was just keeping me company."

"He likes to keep girls company a lot," Chase added. His tone came off as disgruntled.

It surprised me, and despite her drunkenness, Melissa caught on to it as well. She froze in place for a second, as if giving her intoxicated mind a few extra seconds to make a decision. "Girl talk. Let's go to the bathroom."

"Maybe she doesn't want to talk about it," Chase said to Melissa, whispering so I barely heard.

Melissa didn't respond to him. She just grabbed my wrist.

Chase caught my eyes, but I didn't know what he was trying to tell me with his furrowed brow and tight lips.

We made our way through the crush of people toward the women's washroom. The line wound its way from the door toward the belly of the club, but Melissa sashayed past everyone in line.

I apologized and claimed we were just going to use the sink as I rushed after her. I didn't know what to do. I tried to think what Kay did for me in the few times I got uncontrollably drunk after I first arrived in the city. I couldn't remember much—I figured Melissa might not either.

In the bathroom, she slipped between some girls at the bank of sinks. She looked at herself in the mirror and declared, "I'm a mess."

From my purse, I pulled out a small packet of make-up wipes and shook them so she could see the packet in the mirror. When she turned to face me, I said, "I can clean up your eyes."

She stood still with her eyes shut. Her shimmering eyeshadow was smudged, and mascara flaked the tops of her cheeks. I used the wipe to clean away the excess.

Melissa held onto my waist to balance herself, but she still swayed. "I hate being this girl," she groaned after I used a clean corner of the wipe to remove her fading lipstick.

"What do you mean?" I asked her, surprised by the comment. I'd never imagined a woman like Melissa to be insecure in herself in any way. She exuded confidence.

"I hate being the girl that can't hold her booze, who only feels confident when she's with her boyfriend."

I swallowed.

"You probably don't know what I mean." She laughed as she struggled to take the compact out of her clutch. "I always look at you and wish I could be so confident—to just be who I am. I'm terrified that if I wear too much black or getting a nose piercing people will think I'm trying too hard for Chase."

I couldn't help the laughter that escaped me.

When Melissa glanced up, her massive eyes looked so sad. I'd been that drunk girl before. I knew she took my amusement the wrong way.

I put a hand on her shoulder and said, "It's just funny to me, because I always wanted to be as confident as you are. You seem to have it altogether."

Melissa laughed too and fell against me. It took me a few seconds to realize she was hugging me. I embraced her back, trying to ignore the guilt, focusing on the fact that she and I were so different, but we also shared the same feelings, the same insecurities.

"I'm glad you came to my birthday. You're really nice."

"Thank you." I smiled back.

A muscle in her cheek twitched as she glanced down at her clutch. She pulled out the compact she'd been searching for and I saw the shift in her body language. The conversation seemed to sober her up. The way she focused on her purse was the same tact I'd have used if I tried to hide something.

I didn't want to ask. I tossed the makeup wipe into the waste basket under the sink and took the phone from my bag to give her time to process her thoughts.

"So, what about you and Mitchell?" She asked me as she dabbed foundation beneath her eyes. She didn't look at me and I appreciated that.

"There isn't a Mitchell and me. We're just friends and, honestly, that's all I want."

"Is there someone else?"

I pretended to be interested in my phone, even though I

hadn't received a single message. "It's complicated."

Melissa closed her compact and leaned against the counter. Women moved around us to wash their hands and fix their make-up. No one seemed bothered or surprised that we stood in the middle of everything. I thought about excusing myself, but Melissa grabbed my elbow.

"I know about things being complicated." She didn't blink. "This one year, Forever July went on tour for the summer. I took this art class to fill my time, because I wasn't used to doing anything without Chase."

I wasn't sure where the story was headed, but already an uncomfortable feeling settled over the situation. I raised a hand, to tell her she didn't have to go on, but she cut me off.

"I met this guy, James. He was artistic and he was loud and he laughed all the time. Have you noticed how Chase never laughs out loud? He just smiles at everything."

She was right. He never laughed out loud.

"Maybe you want to wait until you're sober to tell me this story?" I glanced around, hoping a member of her birthday entourage would appear and save me from the situation. It didn't happen.

Melissa gripped me harder. "I promise you, nothing ever got physical. We just had this chemistry. You know what I mean? You do, you know what I mean."

"I honestly don't know if I'm the right person to hear this story. Chase is my friend and I..."

Melissa ignored me and said, "When Chase got back from tour, I thought to myself, what if James is just one of those summer things? What if it was a fluke and in a couple weeks, I'll regret my decision? So, I stayed with Chase."

I knew that feeling all too well. But I wasn't the one in the situation. As much as I had feelings for Chase, he and Melissa belonged together. They knew each other so well. They always seemed aware of what the other was thinking. They looked great together.

"You're a great couple though," I reassured her.

"Are we, though? How am I supposed to know if I couldn't be better with someone else?" Melissa let go of my arm. "I love Chase. I always have and I always will, but he and I are the same people. We don't like to step out of our comfort zones. It's a nice thing, but it's also not."

"Melissa, I…"

"Mel!" One of her friends came into the bathroom. "We've been looking for you everywhere. We requested a song for you."

Melissa put on a wide smile and said, "I'll be there in a second. I just need to wash my hands."

They told her to hurry up before heading back out toward their friends and the dancefloor. Melissa turned to look at herself in the mirror. "I don't want Chase to resent me because he was too scared to step out of his comfort zone."

I wondered if she was thinking about what Chase said about Mitchell earlier. I wondered if she read into it the wrong way.

"Chase wouldn't resent you. He loves you."

Melissa smiled and said, "I don't want you to resent me either."

She was drunk, I rationalized. She didn't mean anything she was saying. Just like her story about James, as soon as she saw Chase, as soon as they were back together, she would stop thinking about it.

Melissa took my hand and said, "Come on. Let's go."

It was her birthday. I didn't want to ruin it by asking questions. If she was about to do something irrational, I didn't want to be involved.

I followed her out of the bathroom. When we got back to the booth, Chase asked if everything was alright. Melissa told him she wanted to dance. He looked at me and asked, "You okay?"

"Yeah, I'm good. You okay?"

"Mitchell's at the bar if you're looking for him." Chase ran his hands over his blazer, averting his gaze. I saw the way he fidgeted and wondered if maybe I wasn't overthinking things. The way his eyes connect with mine, it felt like it meant something.

He stood, waiting for me to speak. My mind screamed at me to answer him, but I couldn't tell him that I only danced with Mitchell because I wanted to dance with him. It would be a betrayal to Melissa, Melissa who had been so kind to me, who didn't deserve it.

I glanced away and mumbled a thank you. I was on a mission to keep Chase as my friend and I wouldn't be able to do it if I let myself get too carried away with my thoughts, without any concrete evidence.

"We're going to upload your postcards to the website on Thursday. I'm excited to read them," I said, trying to change the subject. I'd handed them over to Camila without indulging in them, wanting to enjoy it on the day they went live like everyone else.

He cast his eyes down.

"Are you regretting giving them to me?" I asked. "There's still time to take them back down."

"No regrets." He cleared his throat and said, "Could you ask Kay to read them too?"

"Yeah, I can do that."

Chase shoved his hands into his pockets. "Could you give her my number and ask her to text me if she wants to, after reading them?"

I nodded.

Camila squeezed her way between a group of people at the edge of the dancefloor. She pointed at Chase and said, "Dude, we gotta get Melissa out of here. She just puked on the dance floor."

Chase didn't sigh or flinch. He grabbed Melissa's jacket from the seat in the booth and went to find her.

Camila wrapped an arm around my shoulders and asked, "Can I stay at your place tonight? I'm too drunk to deal with the glares of my abuelita when I get home."

I laughed and said, "Of course. But only if we can get food first."

"Pizza or burritos."

"Or shawarma."

"Or just street meat."

I appreciated Camila being there to distract me from all the things that happened that night. It would be easier to stay away from my thoughts while chatting with her.

Camila took my hand and said, "Let's go. I'm starving."

"I like this affectionate version of Camila Gutierrez," I said as we headed toward the exit.

A lot of people stood around the edges, making it hard to move, but being a photographer at shows, she'd mastered the art of slipping through the crowd without getting in anyone's way.

"Don't get used to it. Sober Camila doesn't want to hold anyone's hand," Camila said with a loud laugh.

I gave her fingers a squeeze to revel in the moment.

"Text Chase and tell him we're leaving. I don't know if my message would be coherent." Camila's words came out a little slurred.

I took out my phone and let Chase know Camila was with me and we were heading back to my apartment.

*Can you text me to let me know when you're home safe?*

I smiled at the response. It was nice to know someone worried enough to check in, to make sure I was safe.

"Shawarma," Camila shouted as we stepped out into the fresh night air. "Please tell me we can get shawarma."

I took Camila's hand again. Grateful for her distraction.

18

BANGING ON THE APARTMENT DOOR WOKE ME THE NIGHT AFTER I did inventory at the store. I had no idea who would have gotten into the building without buzzing us first, but I climbed out of bed and stumbled into the hallway. Kay was already at the door in her black robe.

Before she opened it all the way, Camila slipped beneath Kay's arm and said, "I called you three times."

"I was doing inventory," I told her. "I didn't get home until three this morning."

"I posted Chase's postcards early and you need to see our views in the last eight hours." Camila slipped off her shoes while she apologized to Kay. I glanced at the clock to see it was only eight-thirty in the morning. I groaned.

"I'm going back to bed," Kay grumbled.

I put my hand up. "Wait. Chase said you should read the postcards. I've been meaning to tell you all week."

I hadn't heard much from Chase since Melissa's birthday. I wondered if Melissa's bathroom speech had been forgotten. I wondered if she was uncomfortable by Chase's behaviour when it came to Mitchell and me. I didn't know if she would say anything to him, but I sensed something was wrong. Despite that, I still planned to honour what he asked of me.

Kay looked between Camila and me. "He mentioned me by name in these things?"

Camila shook her head. "No, but...I think you'll understand."

Kay stood still for a few seconds too long while Camila shifted uncomfortably.

"Do you wanna read them together?" I asked her.

Camila cleared her throat.

"Yeah. I think so," Kay said. She took her spot in the recliner and wrapped a blanket around herself.

While Camila asked Kay if she could cast her phone onto the TV, I went into the kitchen to make tea. I had a feeling at least one of us might need something warm for comfort.

The first thing Camila did was bring up our website stats. She grinned as she located our unique page views. The graph showed a steady line of views rising across the page from the day we started the project—until the night before, when the blue line careened upwards.

Camila beamed and said, "Do you see that? Isn't that wild? All I had to do was tag the post and every single image with Forever July. The clicks started coming in before I even refreshed the page."

"And that means more money for you guys, right?" Kay asked. "Like, you'll start getting paid more than just a hundred bucks a week or whatever you're up to."

"Yes, if we can keep up this momentum. And I have some ideas to keep it going." Camila clicked onto our website and said, "Peyton, I need you to reach out to bands and see if we can get any of them on board with this kinda thing. Like playlists to go along with their stories, or some grainy Polaroids, multimedia, something. I'm sure there's someone out there with their own unique take that will be willing to share."

I nodded and made a mental note to start sending out emails that afternoon. I already had a vague list of who I wanted to ask and what they might be able to offer. With stats to show them, I could see more and more getting onboard.

"If we can keep this up, maybe I can do less pregnancy photoshoots for income." Camila chuckled to herself. "Honestly, if we are lucky, we will be able to start hiring an intern for a couple shifts a week."

The idea of not only making money, but actually employing someone, made me excited. If we kept up this momentum, we could support ourselves, plus help someone else out too. Of all the things I'd managed to do, the goal of paying someone else, being able to give someone an opportunity, was the best feeling.

"And now, onto the postcards." Camila brought up the first one. She'd posted an image of the front and the back, side by side.

I turned to Kay. "Chase mails himself postcards from where ever they have a gig. Like a journal."

Kay nodded. Her lips were pressed together tightly.

"Chase's printing was pretty legible, but last minute I typed out what they said for people who might not be able to see the images," Camila explained. "I didn't run that by you, but I hope it's cool."

I sat forward to read the first postcard.

*Our first tour as Forever July is off to an awesome beginning. Almost a hundred people showed up in time to see us play. I mean, it was nothing compared to the full house for the Early November, but it was fucking huge for us. It's weird to be playing songs about Danny to strangers, but they seem to like it. He should have been here.*

I glanced at Kay, but there was no change to her expression.

*New York Fucking City.*

*Who knew this was going to happen to us. We had people pumped to see us. Dylan went back to some guy's house. We are gonna razz him so much tomorrow. I asked Melissa to join us in Chicago, but she said she has to work. I don't like sleeping alone.*

I realized it could have been the time Melissa met James. The details she'd given were vague, but it made me sad to think he might have been missing her while she was thinking about someone else. I wondered if she would even remember telling me the story.

*I love these boys, but I'm sick of smelling their sweat for hours in the van. I love these boys, but Mo's sleep farts aren't funny anymore. I love these boys, but if Dylan plays that Taking Back Sunday track one more time, I'm going to drive the van off the road. I love these boys though. I wouldn't want to do this with anyone else. I miss home today.*

*Los Angeles. The city of angels. Mitchell made a mix just for this city. It's amazing. I dreamt about my brother last night, about listening to X with him, and talking about all the places we would see together. I'm so angry with him right now. He was supposed to be doing all this with us.*

*We didn't play a show in Kentucky, but we're sitting at this truck stop on our way home. I feel like an asshole for being mad at Danny all this time. But I feel worse for blaming her, for assuming it was her fault. I tried to call, but she changed her number. It's no one's fault he got hurt. It's no one's fault his body betrayed him. If you ever read this, I'm sorry.*

A sniffle from Kay was enough to make me stop reading. I turned to look at her.

She gave me a sad smile. "I changed my number the first

time his mom called crying to ask why I would leave him with that man the night Danny died."

I hated that she had to relive it over and over again. But I could see a difference in the way she held herself. It didn't seem as defensive or defeated. She sat back against the couch and said, "It's hard, because I thought of Chase and his family like my own family. They loved me for me, or so I thought."

I held up a finger and headed into my room. While searching for the paper with the phone number on it, I heard Camila saying she knows Chase regrets his actions and words even to this day.

When I stepped back into the living room, I handed Kay the paper with Chase's number on it and said, "He asked me to give you this."

Kay stared at it.

"Whenever you're ready," I told her.

I hoped Chase remembered the conversation we'd had and his request to talk to Kay. He hadn't brought it up through text, but our conversations since the weekend had been minimal.

"I might do that now," Kay said, getting up from the couch. She gave my shoulder a squeeze and said, "Thanks for doing this."

"It had nothing to do with me," I told her.

When Kay left the room, I grabbed my phone and texted Chase, letting him know that I'd given Kay his number.

"So, these personal stories, they really resonate with people," Camila said, setting down her phone. The last postcard we read remained on the television screen.

"Yeah, I have a few ideas of bands we might be able to reach out to. I started a Canadian pop-punk playlist for the site, so I thought we could start there."

"I was thinking that you should post that story you shared with me," Camila said. "The one about listening to music from your neighbour's house and... you know, the broken fingers and window situation."

"What?" A jolt of panic shot through me.

"That story about finding punk music from the neighbours," Camila said. "The one you sent a couple weeks ago."

"I...I didn't mean to send that to you. I didn't know I did." My body burned up from the inside out. I tried to stop the bouncing of my knee, but I couldn't. I wanted to ask her to delete it. I wanted to tell her to forget everything she read. But I also wanted to know her thoughts on it, if she had understood what I was trying to write.

Camila studied my face for a second before offering, "I'll remove it from my shared documents."

I'd never shared that moment with anyone. I'd never expected to. But the way Camila remained calm gave me the confidence to ask her a question. "Does it make you feel pity for me?"

Camila didn't respond right away. Her mouth twisted in thought. The longer it took her to answer the more I worried she was trying to find a nice way of saying that she pitied me.

"Pity, no. I have empathy for you, living with shitty parents, and I would say I have a better understanding of who you are. But I definitely don't pity you. You're here, doing your own thing, working hard, and thriving. I don't know what I would pity you for." Camila shrugged. "We all have our struggles. We get so involved in our own stuff that we forget about what other people go through. I think you'd find more connection with people than pity, to be honest."

The way she explained it made so much sense. My past didn't have to evoke pity. I'd become so much more than that life.

"Can I just re-read it before we post it?" I asked.

Camila beamed. "Definitely. I was thinking about putting out a call for submissions, stories about how people got into music, what genres, and how it changed their life. I think a lot of people have stories to share."

I didn't know if I would be able to make the step with people knowing it was me. I didn't want random people to make their first assumption of who I was based on a little look into my life.

I shoved my hands under my legs and said, "Okay, let's do it."

Camila clapped. "This is good. Honestly, this could be our full-time job in no time."

"Do you really think that's possible?" I asked her.

Camila let out a long laugh and said, "One hundred percent. It's already happening way faster than I ever imagined. Like, every day I'm wondering how far we can take this."

Hearing that made me confident in what we'd created, but in myself too. I picked up my phone to make a list of things we needed to do to keep the page views on the up and up. I found Chase had responded with a simple 'thank you,'

*It's the least I could do,* I texted back. *Especially since your postcards are the reason that we've had a record day on the site and it's only nine in the morning.*

I tried not to be disheartened by the thumbs up emoji in response.

19

CAMILA AND I SPENT TWO HOURS AFTER MY SHIFT WORKING ON edits for our personal stories for Eternal Spin. When I suggested cutting the part about my fingers being broken by the window or at least the trip to the hospital, Camila told me to leave all that, it made the finished piece more authentic. As we left the cafe, our hair smelling like coffee, she asked if I'd ever thought about writing a memoir or maybe a work of fiction. I told her no, but once I was alone, walking the two blocks home, that idea was all I could think about.

I opened the door to the apartment to find Kay fixing her lipstick in the mirror. I almost asked if she was going to the DeKay House, but I noticed a few things that told me otherwise. Instead of her sharp, winged liner, she had a soft, smoky eye look going on. Instead of her Doc Martens, she'd set out a pair of black flats.

"I didn't know you owned jeans without holes in the knee," I joked as I slipped off my shoes and walked into the living room.

Kay put the tube of lipstick on her tiny purse. "I texted you a couple times."

"Phone died." I flopped onto the couch and set my laptop bag on the floor.

"I need to tell you something." Kay sat down on the couch next to me and said, "So, as you know, Chase and I have been texting."

I didn't know. It had been two weeks since Melissa's birthday and two weeks since we'd had an actual conversation by text. One night he asked if I was going to a show, which I couldn't go to. Then I asked if he was going to Mitchell's for beers, but he said he couldn't make it. I didn't know if I was subconsciously avoiding him because of Melissa's birthday, or because he was avoiding me.

"And you're going to meet up?" I asked her. Little pangs of jealousy poked at the inside of my chest.

"Yeah. Right now." Kay gestured to her clothes and said, "He's with his mom."

After everything she'd told me about Chase's family, I worried. Despite what Camila, Mo, and Dylan said about Chase's parents, and as much as Chase had turned out well, I didn't want anyone to hurt Kay.

Kay grinned at me. "I'll be fine."

"What?"

"You look distressed, but I promise you, I'll be good."

I let out a breathy laugh. "I'm just worried. I don't want you to feel like you have to do this."

"I want to." Kay pressed her lips together and slipped a strand of hair behind one of her ears. "Chase says his mom wants to apologize to me. And, honestly, I really need an apology from them."

"I'm glad you're getting that chance." I reached out and patted her knee. "I hope it's what you need."

Kay nodded. She glanced up at the painting on our mantel and smiled. I wondered if she thought of Danny every time she walked through the room and saw it. When her eyes moved back to me, she said, "When you first told me you were hanging out with Chase, I wanted to scream."

"You should have told me."

"I was trying not to act irrationally and the more I thought about it, the more I realized it was a sign."

"A sign?" I arched an eyebrow. "I didn't know I believed in signs."

Kay smirked. "No, not like a *sign* sign. More like, I recognized my reaction to you meeting Chase wasn't a healthy response. It made me realize that I was more unhappy than I assumed I was."

The statement resonated with me. I'd been dealing with the same range of emotions, so her situation wasn't a stretch to imagine. We had demons we needed to confront, even if they came in different forms.

"I realized that wallowing in this self-pity wasn't helping me. I'd become comfortable being angry and sad. I want to move forward." Kay shrugged.

"I totally understand that."

"You calling your mom is what made me realize I needed this," Kay told me. "Chase asking me to read his journal entries really drove it home. So, thank you."

I arched an eyebrow.

"You've come so far and made so many big changes in your life in such a short time. It's impressive." Kay leaned in toward me, making sure to look me in the eye. "You've really grown and I admire that. It showed me I was stuck. I owe you."

I pushed my hair behind my ears. "I didn't do anything. I'm not doing anything. Like, I don't think I'll ever be able to confront my dad for the things he's done."

"Do you need to?" Kay asked.

I shook my head. "I don't think so. Especially not now."

"You don't have to, you know. We each need something different to bring us peace. And you know what? That might change over time, but we're moving forward and while we might never stop that journey, I think it's an important one."

I closed the gap between us and wrapped my arms around her. Kay always knew the right things to say, always knew how to make me feel like a better person. I didn't know if I really did anything to help her, but if I did, I was grateful to make even the slightest positive change in her life, after everything she'd given me.

"I do have to go," Kay said, not breaking from the hug. She leaned her head against mine. "I'm glad you got home in time for this chat."

When we fell out of the embrace, she grabbed her phone from the table. "I gotta go, but if you're up, we can talk when I get back, alright?"

I waited until Kay left before stretching out on the couch and retrieved my laptop from my bag on the floor. Kay's words stuck with me. She told me I'd changed, that I'd grown, and that helped her.

As much as I wanted to write off her comments, she made a good point. I'd come further than I'd ever expected. I left Will. I was single and I was happy about it. I'd mustered up the courage to call my mom, to let her know I was there if she needed me. I had a job, a publication, and an apartment I paid rent for.

I might not have a plan for the future or the courage to face my father, but I'd come further than I ever expected and that was something to appreciate. I grinned to myself as I pulled up the document on my laptop. I scanned over the words I'd written before.

*She sat by the bedroom window with all the lights turned off. The music coming from the neighbour's house made her smile to herself. Every time they had a party, she strained her ears to hear the words of who she would learn where punk rock legends. The Ramones. The Misfits. Black Flag.*

While I might have become someone different than that

girl, I was still tethered to her. It reminded me where it all started, where the push came to really make the change.

*If she had been asleep, she wouldn't have woken her father who worked so hard to keep a roof over their heads. If she had been asleep her father never would have slammed the window shut on her fingers.*

I stared at the words. They no longer made me hurt. They no longer embarrassed me. Despite everything, I'd moved forward and I wondered if Camila was right about sharing the details of my life, if they might connect with someone who went through the same thing or still was.

I opened a new document and began typing.

"HAVE YOU TALKED TO CHASE LATELY?" I ASKED CAMILA AS WE stretched out on a blanket in Trinity Bellwoods Park. After several days of rain, the park was filled with people hoping to soak up as much of the sun as possible. People biked around. Kids played. A group of teenagers passed a bottle of pop back and forth so suspiciously, Camila and I knew it was alcohol.

Camila pushed herself up on her elbows to look at me. "I have. You haven't?"

"Not really. Like, he told me he couldn't make it to the Dirty Nil show and when he asked if I was going to Sneaky Dee's with Dylan, I told him we were doing an interview. That's it." I took a sip of my iced coffee. "I think it might have something to do with Melissa."

"What about her?" Camila asked.

I stared at kids chasing each other between all the people in the grass. The little girl screamed and laughed as she went. The boy just beamed in his own quiet way.

"She was really drunk at her birthday thing and she said some things. And I think she thought... I think she got this idea in her head. Honestly, it was all very awkward." I kept my eyes on anything other than Camila in an attempt to control the colour of my cheeks.

Camila sighed. "Well, that explains this." She took her phone from her pocket, scrolled up in her messages, then turned the screen toward me.

*Not feeling up to coming tonight. Melissa ended things.*

I didn't read any further. I couldn't focus on the words of the next text message.

A kernel of excitement expanded in my chest. Chase was single. Melissa ended things. But insecurity pushed in to remind me that just because Chase was single, it didn't mean he was interested in me.

"Thoughts?" Camila asked.

"That sucks. Is he okay?"

Camila flopped back onto the blanket, one arm beneath her head. "Are you really going to pretend like this is bad news?"

I tried to read her tone. I couldn't tell if her response came from being amused or because she knew what happened at Melissa's birthday. They were friends. If she thought I interfered in anyway, she could be upset. Instead of giving a response, I paused, letting her go on.

"We see it, you know. Not just me, either. Dylan, Mo, and I, we all see the way you and Chase look at each other." Camila raised an eyebrow at me. "No doubt, Melissa noticed too."

"I don't think Chase is looking at me in any way."

Camila looked me in the eyes. "And Chase seeing you with Mitchell at Melissa's thing really took those looks to a new level."

I swallowed and tried to ignore the increasing of my pulse.

"Don't look so panicked," Camila said with a loud chuckle. "You like him, don't you?"

Instead of answering, I lay back on the blanket next to her and stared up between branches of the maple. There were small yellowish-green buds, but no leaves had popped out yet. I stared at them, wondering when they were going to be making their appearance. I glanced around, noticing leaves on most of the other trees already.

"You do have feelings, right?" Camila asked.

"Yeah, I have feelings. But, like, what am I supposed to do about it? Even if he's interested… This isn't my forte," I admitted.

It was Camila's turn to be silent for a beat. She inhaled and exhaled deeply and after a while I thought she'd fallen asleep. I didn't want the conversation to end like that. I wanted to know more about the way Chase looked at me. The thought of it alone made me jittery with excitement. I poked her in the side with one finger.

"I was just thinking about ways you could express it." Camila rolled on to her side so she was facing me. "You're both into words. Why don't you tell him it in writing?"

"I guess I could."

"But?"

I didn't know if I had the words to explain how I felt about him. I knew seeing him made me happy. I thought about him when he wasn't around. I wanted to see him happy. Those things felt too private to say out loud.

"Were your parents affectionate with you? Did they say they cared about you out loud?" I asked.

"To the point it's exhausting." Camila groaned. "If I leave the house without saying, 'I love you,' my mom will call me and yell at me."

"I can't remember if mine ever said it," I told her. "I'm sure my mom did—like, even though I can't remember, I have this feeling about it."

"Not your dad?"

"Especially not my dad."

Camila let out a sound of disgust. "Just so you know, they're missing out."

Because I wasn't sure how to express my appreciation for her kindness, I reached over and gave her hand a squeeze.

She squeezed back and said, "See, that's your love language."

"What do you mean?"

"Everyone shows their affection in different ways. I like to show people I care about them by doing things for them or with them. Cleaning their room when they're having a hard time or picking up groceries. And I need that in order to feel love and respected. You know?" Camila tossed an arm over her eyes and said, "Like, you brought sunscreen—and while that might not mean anything to you, you offering it to me, it meant something to me."

"So, if I do things for you, that makes you feel appreciated?"

"Yup. Like, you express a lot by touch. When people return that, does that feel special for you?"

"Yeah. It does."

I watched the clouds drift across the sky. Every day I learned something about myself. Moving forward might been scary, but it was worth it. After everything that happened with Will, I thought I would never get up the courage to get past it, but there I was in the park, thinking about my family, my love language, and how I would take more steps forward.

"You know Chase leaves on tour in two months, right?" Camila asked, keeping her voice low. "Then he's gone all summer."

"I'm aware."

"So, what's your plan?" Camila asked.

I covered my eyes with one arm and said, "I don't know."

I stared up at the sky, between the budding branches of

the tree and processed everything Camila said to me. I wondered if Chase actually had feelings for me and if he did, what I'd done to deserve it. I grinned to myself as I searched for faces in the puffy, white clouds.

WHILE I NEVER REGRETTED GOING TO SEE BANDS, OPENING THE store at eight the morning after a late night took its toll. I yawned as I stepped out into the daylight, almost forgetting how bright it could be after being in the store all day. I'd been too tired to get lunch and ended up closing my eyes for half an hour in the back room. I took my headphones out of my bag and pulled them over my ears. I had albums to listen to, to review for our website, and I had promised myself to never review until I knew most of the words to their tracks. On the walk home, I took in the lyrics, the strong bass, and the hyper-speed drumming—already seeing the track-by-track review falling into place.

The music paused and the ringing of my phone took its place. Kay was calling, so I swiped to answer it.

"Hey. I'm—"

"Where are you?" Kay asked. The concern was heavy in her voice.

"I just left work. I'm still on Queen Street," I told her between yawns. "What's wrong?"

The long pause made the whole start to the conversation

more tense. I couldn't think of anything Kay might call about in a panic.

"Whatever it is, can you just tell me now instead of waiting for me to get home?" I tried to laugh, to make it seem like a joke, but I knew I wasn't fooling either of us.

"Your mom called. She asked me to pass a message along to you. She wants to see you on Friday at noon."

My pace slowed until I was stopped on the sidewalk. Someone bumped into my bag as they passed. I stepped to the side, pressing my back against a store window.

"I offered to buy her a bus ticket, to bring her here, but she said she can't just leave. It sounds suspicious, Pey."

"Did she say when I could call her?" I asked.

"Before four-thirty tonight."

"Okay, I'll grab a ride back to the house."

Instead of waiting for an Uber, I flagged down the first taxi and climbed in.

I wondered if she would do something risky, if she would intentionally put me in harm's way. I couldn't think of specific details, but she never took me away from that place, even when I asked her to.

As the taxi merged into the traffic, I opened the doc I'd been working on. One memory had come, but I couldn't remember when it took place—I wasn't yet a teenager, anyway. I'd come home from a friend's house with blush and lipstick on. My friend's mother had been amused by our attempt to look adult with her make-up. She'd taken pictures of us and told me to run home to show my mom. I wanted to wash my face, but she told me my mom would think it was cute. With her watching, I took short, hesitant steps toward my house. My father's car was in the driveway. Before I even made it up the driveway, my mother came out of the house with a washcloth. How hard she scrubbed my face, how she muttered that I knew better. Tears stung on my raw cheeks.

But looking at the situation now, I understood she was saving me from worse.

"Is this you?" The taxi driver asked.

I glanced out the window—we'd already made it back to the apartment. Handing him a twenty I climbed out, pulled open the door and rushed up the stairs to the apartment.

Kay was on the couch with her phone to her ear. "Well, can I borrow dad's truck then?" she asked. She held up a finger, letting me know she'd only be a minute.

I sat on the edge of a chair and watched as she sighed and told her mother fine, hung up and said, "I couldn't get a car."

"That's okay."

"Are you not going?"

"I don't know. I'm not sure." I set my bag and headphones onto the floor and sat back in the chair.

"Why not?" Kay asked. "It might be a chance to get her out."

"I didn't say I wasn't. I just need a second to process this."

"Okay."

"I didn't think we'd get to this point. I never really expected her to call." Never once did I assume I would hear her voice again. In my mind, she never would have had the courage to call.

"She gave me the name of some park. I wrote down all the details." Then Kay asked, "What's holding you back?"

I picked at the skin around my nails. "My mom kept a bunch of money in a tampon box. It was her escape money."

Kay stayed quiet. I wished she understood what I was implying so I wouldn't have to say the words out loud. After the silence stretched on too long, I explained, "That's the money I took to leave. I don't know where she got it or how she'd kept it from my dad all those years. But she had no one else to rely on—and I just took that money from her."

"How much was it?" Kay asked.

"Almost twelve hundred dollars."

"So why don't you pay her back?" Kay asked. "Do you need some money?"

"No. I've been putting all my Eternal Spin money into savings."

While it wouldn't quench my guilt, it would ease it. If I could pay my mom back, with interest, at least I'd know she had a way out. I glanced up at the clock. There was still time to call, to tell her I could be there.

"I have to figure out the bus schedule. I don't want to tell her I can go if I can't."

Kay cleared her throat and said, "I might have figured out a ride for you already."

My phone vibrated. I took it from my bag and looked at the screen. Chase had texted me.

*I heard you need a ride?*

I glanced up at Kay.

She shrugged. "You can say no if you don't want to."

My fingers hovered over the screen for a few seconds.

*I do, but do you have time?*

I didn't know how I wanted him to respond, but the long wait before he did, made my heart slam against my chest cavity. I watched the three dots as he typed something, then stopped. I wondered if he'd deleted his response—after a few seconds he typed again.

*Just tell me when.*

22

I PACED ON THE SIDEWALK IN FRONT OF THE APARTMENT DOOR. I couldn't tell if I was more nervous about being alone with Chase after what Camila told me, or about seeing my mother for the first time in years. I shoved my hands into the back pockets of my jeans and then took them out again. I tried to work on an article or my personal project on my phone; I gave up and just stood waiting.

When Chase's car pulled up to the curb, half my concerns disappeared. Seeing him took away the anxiety of being alone with him.

He grinned at me as I pulled open the door and he held up a plastic cup from the centre console. "Iced coffee?" He asked.

Before even shutting the door behind me, I reached for the cup and took a sip. I sat back in the seat and said, "You're my hero. I've barely slept."

"I figured, so I went for a double shot of espresso."

With the cup still in my hand, I twisted in my seat to look at him. The three and a half weeks since Melissa's birthday felt longer than when he was on tour. I thought about keeping it to myself, but the words came out before I could solidify the decision. "I haven't talked to you in what feels like forever."

Chase cast his eyes toward the radio, but he didn't move the rest of his body. He was still turned toward me. His hand still rested on the console between us. When he made eye contact, I was glad I'd said something.

"I don't know if you heard, but Melissa and I broke up."

"I'm sorry to hear that," I said. As much as the idea of Single Chase excited me, knowing he was hurting made me uncomfortable. "You okay?"

One side of his mouth tugged up, reassuring me before he sat back in his seat. "I should have reached out to you, but I didn't want to put my relationship troubles on you."

"You could have."

Chase let out a quiet "hmm" to himself.

"I would have listened," I reassured him.

"Oh, I know that. I just... needed to work through some things myself." He drummed his fingers on the steering wheel. "And I just saw the story you posted on Eternal Spin. I read about you finding music, about how your dad…"

I swallowed and nodded.

"I thought, maybe you had your own things going on and didn't really want to deal with my shit too, you know?"

"It was a long time ago," I told him.

"It's still a lot. And I wanted to bring it up, because I wanted to let you know that if you wanted to talk about it, then I want to be there for you."

I found a long thread on the torn knee of my jeans. I picked at it while I tried to think of something to say. Instead, I reached out to Chase's hand on the gear shift and gave it a squeeze.

"Should we…Should we get going?"

"Sure," I said, before taking another sip of the iced coffee.

Heading north toward the highway, we filled each other in on what had happened since Melissa's birthday. Chase had finished putting his apartment together and had been helping his dad with accounting for his business. I told him about all the interviews I'd been doing and the amount of work that Camila and I were putting in.

"I'm glad that you and Kay were able to connect," I told him as we merged onto the highway. The music was playing low in the background.

"And I'm glad that you're getting to connect with your mom," Chase said. "It's been a while, right?"

"I haven't seen or really talked to her since I moved to the city."

The only sound in the car for almost a full minute was the music playing on low. Chase didn't push, giving me a chance to find the right words. I wondered how much was too much to confess. I felt as if I could spill the complete history to him, even if he ended up pitying me. I'd never been so compelled to share.

"I held a lot of anger for her. But I'm starting to wonder if I should have a little more empathy. My memories aren't as clear as everyone else's seems to be. There are also a lot of holes in it. And lately, I've remembered things I thought I forgot. Things with my mom."

Chase shifted in his seat. "It must be painful to remember things like that."

"Yes and no. Without facing those things, would I be able to work through them?" I shrugged, realizing I'd been talking way more about my mom and my family than I'd been expecting to say to anyone. "I don't know."

Will's words repeated in my head. Chase would pity me. He'd realize I'm broken. He would realize I was too damaged. Chase would dip out of my life to avoid dealing with the drama that came along with knowing me.

"I'm not broken though," I reassured him.

Chase took his eyes from the road for only a second, stealing a glance at me. "I don't think you're broken,

Peyton. Just thinking about what you might have gone through..."

"I'm sorry if I made you uncomfortable."

His shoulders tightened. "You didn't."

I chuckled. "Your posture says otherwise."

"Hey," he laughed, "I'm sensitive, alright?"

I smiled to myself. He had no idea how much I appreciated that part of him.

"I'm sorry you had to go through all of that. I wish I'd known young Peyton, wish I could have been there for her." Chase reached over and gave my knee a squeeze, not taking his eyes off the road. For a few seconds after his hand was back on the steering wheel, I could still feel it.

"Oh," I said, reaching over to turn up the volume. "I love this song."

---

BEING BACK IN THE TOWN I GREW UP IN DIDN'T GIVE ME A SENSE of comfort or nostalgia. Chase dropped me at the edge of the park and said he'd be back after grabbing something to eat. While I needed the time alone to calm myself down, I didn't like that he was out of my line of sight. I knew my father would be at work, he'd never run into me there, but glancing around at the apartment buildings I still felt eyes watching me.

I'd become so accustomed to living freely, I'd forgotten what it was like to be in that town. The fear instilled in me had a long reach, but I'd been out of its grip for some time. I'd never expected to find myself back there again.

I took the phone from my pocket and glanced at the clock. Four minutes past our agreed upon time. The minutes changed. Five. I moved from the park bench and to a large, flat top rock. My leg bounced as I glanced in all directions.

When I looked up to check the street signs for the third

time, I saw her standing there. Her hips were rounder. Her hair was greyer, but only around her face. Same pair of faded jeans and soft blue sweater she often wore to leave the house. Purse clutched in front of her like someone might steal it. I noticed the way her grip tightened and released as she stared back at me. I waited for her to speak, but she didn't. I almost feared to say anything out loud, in case she ran away.

"Hi," I said, raising a hand in a stiff wave.

She released her grasp on her purse to wave back.

I stood, because sitting made me feel like a child. I wasn't a child anymore. "There's a picnic table," I told her, pointing behind me. "Should we sit?"

She nodded. We walked, keeping an awkward distance between us. I didn't know if we should hug or if that would be too strange as it wasn't something we'd ever done much of. I opted to keep my hands to myself.

There were so many questions I needed to ask her, but when we sat on opposite sides of the picnic table, I just watched her, taking her all in, while she watched me.

"You look different," she told me.

"I am different." I didn't know how to explain it. I couldn't imagine the old version of me doing this, facing her. I glanced around to see if anyone was watching us, to make sure my father was nowhere nearby.

Her eyes widened as she noticed my actions. "I wouldn't put you in harm's way, if that's what you're thinking."

I wanted to tell her it was hard to believe. My father knew how to manipulate us. He knew the buttons to push to make us do whatever he wanted. I had no idea how things might have changed after I left.

"How...how have you been?" I asked, changing the subject.

She sat with the purse in her lap, both hands still clutching it. Despite everything, I couldn't remember ever seeing her as nervous as she was just to be sitting in front of me.

"Are things better?" I asked.

"In a way, yes."

While I didn't want to hear my mother was still going through the same things she had before I left, knowing that things were better because I was gone, made my stomach clench. I wondered if I had been the cause of most of the trouble. I wondered if one less mouth to feed made my father less angry.

The corners of her mouth twitched, but the smile never came to fruition. "I no longer have to worry about you. That's a huge weight off my shoulders."

I hadn't expected that response. I let out a long exhale.

"Where are you living?" she asked.

"In an apartment, with my best friend. In Toronto." I didn't want to give her specifics. I still didn't want to risk it.

"I never pictured you in a big city."

"Me neither, but I had to get out."

My mother glanced down at her hands.

I said, "It was a good move for me. I have two jobs. I have good friends."

"Do you have a boyfriend?"

I shook my head. "Nope. I've been spending a little time working on what I want from my own life."

Because I couldn't bring myself to ask about my father, I spoke about going to see bands, about getting to meet artists I admired, about the perks like getting free music and merchandise. I spoke about how Kay and I had a cute apartment that I loved being in, how Kay had helped me a lot. I talked about the people I'd met, how they were all different from each other and so accepting.

"You could come stay with me," I told her.

"I couldn't impose," her mother said. "Plus, I don't think your father would like that very much."

I inhaled deeply before answering her. "I mean, for good. You can stay with us until you can find a place of your own or until we could move into somewhere for all three of us."

She looked down at her hands again.

"Mom, you don't have to stay here."

"It's not that simple."

"I never said it was simple. I've been through it. It's really fucking hard. But what's the alternative?"

"Don't use that language."

I let out a long sigh and composed myself.

A car honked and we both looked toward the street. Chase waved from the front seat and held up his phone. I retrieved my own from my bag and tapped on his message.

*Take your time. Checking if you're okay.*

I turned back to him, giving a thumbs up. Before I looked away, he lowered his seat back and closed his eyes. I chuckled to myself, at the ease in which he made himself comfortable in the car.

"Who is that?" My mom asked.

"Chase."

"Is he good to you?"

"He's just a friend."

She raised a single eyebrow.

"But yes. He's one of the nicest people I've met, second only to Kay."

She turned to look at Chase.

"I have something for you," I said, reaching into my bag. I brought out the envelope and handed it to her.

For the first time, she took her hands from her purse. She thumbed through the bills and sighed. Her forehead creased as she looked up at me. "I can't take this."

"I took your money. I just took it and I shouldn't have. It's only right that you get your money back. Use it for whatever you were keeping it for."

She sighed, shaking her head. "Peyton..."

"Mom, please take it. I left you with nothing."

My mother put the money on the table between us and pushed it toward me. "That money was never for me. It was always for you. I knew you were strong enough to get out and do something great for yourself."

To my surprise, she stood. She stepped away from the table and said, "I need to go before your father calls to check in."

I got to my feet as quick as I could. It wasn't enough time. I didn't know what was going on with her. I need more time to convince her that coming with me would be the right thing. I didn't want to leave without her. I didn't want to leave her with my father. I wasn't sure if I could live with myself if I did.

"Come with us. We can go by the house. We can get some things."

"Peyton, no." She stepped away from me when I approached. "What if he comes looking for me? It was already a risk asking you to come here."

"You always told me you stayed because you had nowhere else to go, but now you do. I worked really hard. I have the resources. We can make this work!" My voice pitched upward in desperation.

Her eyes were glassy with tears. "I don't know what I was thinking."

"You missed me. I missed you. Come with us. It'll be hard, but it's nothing we can't handle. You need to get away from that man."

"Don't talk about your father like that. He's not a monster," she scolded me. "He put a roof over our heads and food in our stomachs."

"He also sent us both to the hospital. A lot," I shouted at her. "You know that's not normal? You know that what he's doing is wrong, right? He abused us, time and time again, and you let him."

My mother's eyes darted around to see who'd overheard.

People were staring, but I couldn't take that in. I watched her, hoping she would realize I was right, hoping she would come to her senses. I thought the shock of my outburst might bring her into reality.

"This was a mistake," she said backing away from me. "Goodbye, Peyton."

Her words locked me into stillness. I couldn't bring myself to follow as she pivoted on her heel and dashed out of the park. I collapsed onto the bench of the picnic table.

"Peyton," Chase said, lowering himself onto the seat next to me.

The breeze caught on the tears rolling down my cheeks. I wiped them away with the sleeve of my shirt. "Sorry. Sorry. I never do this."

People were staring. Chase was probably humiliated to be part of a scene.

He put an arm around my shoulder. "You don't usually do what?"

"Cry," I said, forcing a laugh through the tears. I hoped it would force me to relax, making it easier to stop the sobs that rattled through my chest.

Chase pulled me into a hug, wrapping both arms around me. I turned into him, pressing my face into his shoulder. I tried to focus on the smell of soap, of his soft cologne, his warmth that surrounded me, but all I could think about was my mom. My whole body shook with sobs as I realized it might have been the last time I would ever see her.

"I'm sorry," I said into his sweater.

"Don't be sorry," he said, rubbing slow circles on my back. "There's no shame in crying."

The way he said it was so honest, it made it easier to steady myself. After a few more minutes, I pulled back and dried my cheeks with my palms. Chase offered me the sleeve of his sweater to wipe my eyes, which made me laugh.

"Thanks for this. For today," I said. My voice still shook.

Chase pulled a strand of hair from my damp cheek. His fingers brushing against my skin made me shiver. I was glad he was there with me. His level energy calmed me, even if his touch made me flustered. I needed his soothing demeanour.

"Do you want to sit here for a bit?" Chase asked.

I glanced around the park. I used to walk through here after school. Sometimes I'd sit here to do my homework, knowing that when I got back to my house, I wouldn't be able to focus on school. There was nothing about this park or town I wanted to remember.

"I really don't want to be in this town for another second." I grabbed the envelope of money from the picnic table and shoved it into my bag. When I turned back to head to the car, Chase put his hands on my shoulders.

"Are you okay?" he asked. "I don't know what happened or if you want to talk, but can you let me know if you're okay?"

I couldn't resist returning his touch. I put my free hand over one of his and tucked my cool fingers beneath his warm ones. Our eyes met and I smiled, because I didn't know how to tell him the mix of emotions coursing through me in that moment.

"Let's head back then," he said.

His hands fell from my shoulders, but he didn't let go of my fingers. We walked back to his car, hand in hand.

23

CAMILA TOSSED A BALLED-UP PIECE OF PAPER AT ME. I GLANCED up and realized she was waiting for something, whether a response or just a reaction, I didn't know.

I blinked at her. "Sorry. I was elsewhere."

"I was saying your story about listening to your neighbour's music has even more views than Chase's journals," Camila said. She moved from the floor on the other side of the coffee table to the couch next to me.

Camila had spent the last two days at our place, just going home long enough to sleep, eat, shower, and change before showing back up with more plans for the website. She'd come up with an idea for a limited run of a printed publication with the year's great hits in terms of articles, photography, and music. She wanted to make compilations of music from top Canadian artists in the scene as well. It would help bring in the funds we needed to keep the website going and to get the help we needed so that neither of us had to be exhausted.

"Have you seen these numbers?" Camila asked.

"Yeah, I saw them this morning."

Camila closed her laptop and asked, "Should I be worried?"

"What?"

She gestured to me, sweeping her hands from my head to my toes. "Have you showered today?"

I had to think about it. "Nope."

"Chase sent me to keep an eye on you," Camila confessed.

I shot her a questioning look.

She shrugged and said, "I think he's worried—he didn't want to go to Buffalo, because you were going through something."

Hearing that Chase was worried didn't surprise me. In the two days since I'd seen my mother, he had texted me every morning and every night before he went to bed. Both his morning text messages started with, 'how are you doing?' despite me promising him I was fine before I got out of the car that day.

"What happened? You hung out. It didn't go well?" Camila raised an eyebrow and stared at me.

"He didn't tell you where we went?"

"He didn't say. I was hoping you'd give me the details," Camila said with a chuckle. She pulled both legs up on the couch and asked, "Did he kiss you?"

"He didn't kiss me."

"Did you want him to?" Camila asked. She pressed her lips together to keep from laughing.

"What's with the interrogation?"

Camila clapped. "So, yeah, you wanted him to kiss you."

I pulled the blanket off the back of the couch and wrapped it around myself, even though I wasn't cold. "As much as you'd like to hear it was a date, he drove me to see my mom."

Camila stopped grinning. "Oh damn. I'm so sorry. I feel like an ass."

"Seriously, don't. I should have told you." I picked at a loose thread in the blanket and said, "I asked my mom to come here, to leave my dad. She said it was a mistake meeting up with me."

"Shit." Camila exhaled. "I don't know your mom, but I've seen my fair share of rocky families. Maybe she thinks she's protecting you or just thinks it's better if she doesn't influence you or something."

"Maybe, but I'm still angry with her. Like, so angry." I stopped what I was saying and laughed. "I've never talked about my family to so many people before."

"How does it feel?" Camila asked.

It was a complicated thing to answer. I sat with her question for a few seconds, trying to figure out the best way to explain it. "I don't know if this will make sense, but for the past couple months, all the stuff with my family felt worse than it had in a long time. Talking about it didn't seem to help."

Camila gave a heavy nod.

"But," I followed up, "It's become easier to move forward. I don't feel stuck in it in the same way I used to. Like, I don't see this feeling lasting forever anymore."

"It's still brutal that you have to go through all that," Camila said, "But I'm always here to listen, if you need anything."

I smiled to myself as I let the blanket fall off my shoulders. I couldn't have asked for better friends than I'd found. Handling everything from Will to my mom, posting the piece about my past—none of that would have been possible without those people.

My phone chimed and I picked it up to see a message from Chase.

*You and Cam wanna grab dinner with Mo and me?*

"You in the mood to eat?" I asked, turning the phone to show her the message from Chase.

She smirked. "I'm always in the mood for pub food and romance."

I rolled my eyes, which made her laugh out loud. I smiled

as I responded to say we were interested. I got up from the couch and said, "I'm going to shower."

"Thank god," Camila said as she opened her laptop, getting back to work.

---

THE EVENING WAS SO HOT THAT CAMILA AND I WERE DESPERATE for a cold drink by the time we arrived. Chase, Mo, and Kay were sitting at a corner booth. As we squeezed through the packed patio toward them, I wondered how long they'd been there to get a seat. When Chase stood up, face pink, wide grin, I knew it must have been a while.

Wrapping me into a hug, he said, "You're finally here!"

I chuckled. "It's only been an hour."

"I know, but we've been waiting for you guys to come. I invited Kay too." Chase put an arm around my waist and turned me so I could wave at Kay.

She laughed and shook her head. "They've been here for a while." She pulled out a chair for me to collapse into.

"And yet, I'm only two beers in," Mo declared, pointing to the two glasses in front of him. "Unlike this guy."

"I'm just celebrating!" Chase waved at the server nearby.

"What are we celebrating?" I asked.

A set of hands landed on my shoulder. I turned around to see Mitchell and Dylan joining us. With a round of high-fives, hugs and fist bumps, everyone shifted to make space. The server came over and took everyone's order.

"So, what are we celebrating?" I asked again.

"Chase finally finished writing lyrics to all the tracks we've had ready over a month," Dylan said as he reached for the basket of fries in front of Mo. Mo slapped his hand away and explained, "We've been waiting on him so we can get back into the studio. Now we've finally nailed down the final pieces."

"What?" Camila turned to Mo. "You didn't tell me."

"We didn't want to put any more unnecessary stress on our man," Mitchell said, clapping Chase on the back. Chase ran a hand through his hair and drank his beer, still grinning.

The group kept talking amongst themselves, Kay reminiscing about how she and Danny watched them play one of their first shows, when their band was called The J-Walkers.

"That's really awesome you've been writing," I told Chase, bumping his leg with mine beneath the table.

"Thanks. I'm feeling nervous about this one."

"Why? What's making you nervous?"

"When I wrote the last two albums, they were sad songs or songs about my friends. They're easily relatable," Chase said. "This album is going to be more…"

"Introspective?" Mitchell put in.

The server put drinks on the table and said she'd be back with the food.

I picked up my drink. "We'll have to do a piece for Eternal Spin."

"But not you," Dylan said, between mouthfuls of Mo's fries.

"What? Why?" I asked. I looked between Dylan and Chase.

Chase shrugged and said, "Kids in the local scene know you hang out with us. They'll assume your review is influenced by your relationship with the band."

Mitchell laughed. "*Relationship.*"

Dylan smirked and grabbed another fry. Mo moved the basket in front of Camila, who took a few for herself. Camila had been right. I told myself not to read into their laughs, the way Mitchell said *relationship.*

Camila said, "You should do an interview with us anyway. Get some hype going around the new album. Let people know you're back in the studio."

I tried to think about what I could come up with for an interview about the new album, but the way Mitchell had said *relationship* was distracting. If there weren't so many ears and eyes, I might have asked him what he meant by it.

"What if Peyton and Camila document your time in the studio? Forever July gets the promo video and images and Eternal Spin gets the story," Kay offered.

We all sat with the idea for a moment.

Camila was the first to agree. "I'm in if everyone else is."

"We need studio pictures done anyway," Mo said. "And I wouldn't want anyone but you doing them, Cam."

Chase bumped my knee with his. "It would be cool to have you in the studio with us."

If time in the studio was anything like this time together, I wanted to be there. I needed more times like that. Just sitting there with those people gave me a sense of comfort I couldn't remember ever having.

"I'll be there," I told him. It was impossible not to mirror his warm smile. He'd be leaving for a summer on tour and I wanted as much time with him as possible.

The night went on, more drinks and too much food. The dinner crowd left and the rowdier nighttime crowd took their place. The air got cool, but I didn't want to leave. I couldn't remember a time I laughed so much or been comfortable enough to be loud and silly.

"You got a little too much sun," Chase said. His index finger booped my nose.

"Really?" I touched my face. I couldn't tell if it was warm because of the beer or being outside all day. Or from sitting so close to Chase.

He grinned. "You're probably gonna feel it tomorrow."

"Worth it." I grinned back.

Chase turned in his seat so our bodies faced each other. Our friends were talking loudly around us, but their words went inaudible when Chase put a hand on the arm of my chair, barely an inch from my wrist.

"I just wanted to check in and make sure that you're doing okay."

I nodded. "I am. I needed a night like this."

"We should have more nights like this," Chase said.

I don't know if I moved or if he did, but the tips of his fingers touched my arm, causing goosebumps to erupt.

"We should. We should start with going to the Danforth tomorrow."

"Is it the PUP show?" he asked.

I nodded.

"It's a date." His voice was low, just between us. I waited for him to smile or to laugh, but he didn't.

Kay called out to me, reminding me I had to work in the morning. A round of boos sounded from all sides of the table and it felt great. Chase's arm pressed against mine on the arm of my chair and I smiled at how my life finally seemed to be falling into place.

24

IN THE TINY BATHROOM AT THE BACK OF THE STORE, I APPLIED A tinted moisturizer in an attempt to tone down my sunburn before Chase picked me up. The dim light made it impossible to tell if everything was even, but I risked it. I was in the middle of pulling the mascara out of my bag when my phone let me know Camila wanted to video chat. I accepted the call.

"Where are you?" Camila asked as I set the phone on the shelf in front of me. "What bar are you in? Is that a retro Care Bears sticker?"

"I'm in my work bathroom," I told her standing to the side so she could take in the bathroom's extensive sticker collection. Stickers covered every single one of the walls, even under the sink, and they bled onto the ceiling. I'd contributed more than a handful of band stickers to the ever-developing work of art.

"I must photograph you in there one day."

I glanced down at the screen for the first time to see Kay was also on the call.

"What's going on? Is something wrong?" I asked. My eyebrows pinched in the centre of my forehead.

"We're just checking in," Kay said. "You seemed nervous this morning."

"I was hungover this morning," I said, deflecting from Kay's statement. I was anxious that morning as I got ready for work. I tried to pick out clothes to come off, both casual, but also nice. With a throbbing head from the previous night of drinking, it was hard to decide. Chase's words, 'it's a date,' didn't help either.

"You're allowed to be nervous about your date," Camila said.

"I don't think it's a date."

"We heard him. The whole table heard him. He literally said the words 'it's a date.'" Camila smirked at me while fixing one of the curls framing her face.

Kay shrugged. "It's true."

I opened the mascara and leaned in toward the mirror. "It doesn't mean it's a date-date, you know?"

"It is. He asked me what kind of food is your favourite," Kay said into the phone.

Camila let out a loud laugh. "See? Just accept it."

I stood back, forgetting about the mascara for a second. Kay and Camila were amused by the whole situation, but I couldn't be. I stared at the phone and said, "So, I've never been on a date before."

"What?" Camila asked.

"Not even before Will?" Kay seemed surprised.

"Wait, Will didn't take you on dates?" Camila's face moved in toward the camera until I could only see her eyes.

I shrugged. "We hung out. There was nothing formal."

"Well, this is exciting," Camila said in a chipper voice. "You're going on your first date."

I appreciated that they stuck around while I got ready. They helped distract me from the uneasy excitement in my stomach. Their laughter and jokes about their own bad dates kept my hand steady as I applied the mascara and then a deep red lipstick. I looked at the time at the top of my phone screen. It was six o'clock.

"He's probably here," I told them.

"Well, then get out there," Camila said.

"Have fun, okay?" Kay told me. I told them I would see them at the PUP show later and would give updates.

Camila said, "You better," before leaving the call.

Kay stuck around for a minute. She looked at me through the camera and said, "You look cute. Effortlessly. You got this, alright?"

Her encouragement was appreciated. I was excited to spend time with Chase, to hang out one on one. I grabbed my things from the bathroom and break room before heading out onto the floor to say goodbye to everyone working until close.

My heart was pounding harder than normal as I made my way to the street.

Chase stood on the sidewalk outside of the store. When he saw me, a smile stretched across his face. I didn't know if he'd ever smiled wide enough to show off his teeth before. I couldn't help grinning back at him.

"For you." Chase handed me a large ice coffee. "I was thinking we could grab some ramen before the show, so we can actually have some time to talk."

"I'd like that," I told him. "I was too hung over to eat at lunch."

As soon as the words were out of my mouth, I regretted them. Girls in movies didn't talk about how their stomach hurt from drinking beer and eating too much fried food.

"I can't believe you had to work," he chuckled as we walked toward the subway station. "I slept until noon and then I ate toast with a side of antacids and then went back to sleep."

"I'm surprised you remembered we were going to hang out today," I said. I didn't text him that day, curious to see if he remembered, not wanting to make a fool of myself if he didn't. I was glad I'd been alone in the break room when he texted to say he was looking forward to getting together that night. I grinned every time I thought about it.

"I wouldn't forget our date," Chase said, pulling the door to the subway station open for me. I grinned at the word, 'date'. There was no denying it now.

———

THE RESTAURANT CHASE PICKED WASN'T FAR FROM THE Danforth, where we would be meeting up with our friends that night. We slipped into a booth at the back near the kitchen. The smells were rich and they made me hungry despite my nervous, fluttering stomach.

When we were settled in, browsing the menu, Chase cleared his throat. I glanced up to see his serious face.

"What's wrong?" I asked, setting my menu down.

"I just want to clarify something." Chase fiddled with the paper sleeve his chopsticks came in.

His green eyes met mine and I braced myself for whatever might come. I panicked, thinking Will had been right. Chase asked me on a date and now he was regretting it. I sucked in a deep breath and waited.

"I don't know if I was clear when I asked you to hang out last night."

I exhaled.

"With us meeting up with our friends later, I worried this gives off the impression that we're not on a date."

"What?" I wasn't sure I heard him right.

"If you're okay with it, I want this to be a date. A real one." Chase's jiggling leg bumped mine under the table.

I glanced down at the table before looking up at him. "I was hoping it was."

"Thank god." Chase chuckled. "I was hoping it didn't come off too friend-zone-ish."

"Honestly, I wasn't sure," I admitted. "But part of that's on me. I told myself not to read into things."

Chase was about to speak, but the waitress came. We placed our orders. Chase watched me as I spoke, causing me to stumble over my words and laugh.

When the waitress left, Chase asked, "What were you trying not to read into?"

I pressed my lips together to avoid a nervous giggle. After composing myself, I said, "I thought maybe you were interested, but only because maybe I was interested."

"You're interested?" He asked. His eyes widened as he stared at me, waiting for a response.

I covered my mouth with my hand and stared back at him. I didn't know if I had the courage to admit I had a crush on Chase. He had only been kind to me, but saying the words out loud could be embarrassing.

Chase took a sip of his water and leaned forward in his seat. "I just want to make it clear that I like you. Is that a wild thing to say on a first date?"

Seeing the red rising in his cheeks caused a sense of calm in me.

"Maybe a little." I met his gaze and said, "I like you, too."

Chase reached out and covered my hand with his own. His fingers wrapped around mine and gave them a squeeze.

"So, now that we have established that this is a date, I want to say that when we do this again, sober me won't plan a date that ends with us going to a concert with our friends." Chase shrugged.

"It's okay," I assured him. "It's kinda nice."

"I just didn't want to wait with the studio stuff coming up and then the tour." He smiled at me and I smiled back. Despite my crush on him, it never occurred to me that things between us could even get to this point. There had been so many obstacles already.

"Are you excited about playing your new songs on tour?" I

asked him as the waitress set vegetable tempura on the table between us.

Chase waved his hand from side to side. "Yes and no. Some of these songs I've been sitting on for a couple months, but I didn't have plans to release them."

"What changed your mind?" I asked him.

Chase's bottle green eyes met mine. The corners of his mouth tugged upward as he shrugged a little. "It's just good timing, that's all."

I grinned. I couldn't wait to hear the new songs.

Our conversations found an easy rhythm. We discussed books, music, and our friends. We talked about his family and I answered a few basic questions about growing up. Slurping noodles from our bowls made us laugh. Even though we were meeting up with our friends, I was disappointed when our time alone came to an end.

As we left the restaurant, full and content, Chase took my hand. The venue was only a couple blocks away and the show already started, but I made no effort to rush. We had time before the headliner took the stage and I wanted to make the official part of our date last as long as possible.

Neither of us spoke as we strolled along the sidewalk until we stopped across the street from the venue. There was a line out front even though the doors had been open for a while and the music was already blaring from inside.

"So," Chase said, turning so we were facing each other.

"So," I repeated back to him, looking up at the smile tugging at the corners of his lips.

I watched his mouth, the way his lips pressed together and then parted, the way his tongue rolled across them briefly. I reminded myself to steady my breathing.

"I guess this is the end of the date portion of the evening." Chase spoke so quietly that no one passing by would hear.

I took a step closer. "Almost."

"Did you have a good time?" Chase asked.

I wondered if I could say, "hell yes," without coming off silly. I didn't want to do anything to ruin the end of date mood.

"I definitely did," I said. "I enjoy spending time with you."

Chase took a step closer. My heartbeat sped up. His hands moved from mine to my waist. I gave up on trying to steady my breathing. I blinked at him, hoping he would know I wanted whatever came next.

With him standing so close, his hands on me, reality set in. Even several days go, I wouldn't have believed it possible to be on a date with Chase, about to kiss Chase. Our lives were so different I couldn't believe they had merged to this point. So many little details needed to fall into place to make it work.

Chase's whole body moved toward me. I stared at his lips as they inched their way in my direction. Not wanting to wait, I pushed myself up on my toes to meet him.

I closed my eyes as his hand cupped my face.

"Hey, you're Chase from Forever July, right?"

The moment was broken by two teenage boys with wide grins on their faces. They stared at Chase in awe, unaware I stood there, my hands still holding him. Chase slid an arm around my waist as he turned to face them.

"That's me."

"We love your band," the taller one said.

"We've been to like every show you guys played in town. Even one in Detroit."

"When are you putting out a new album?"

Chase's grip tightened on my waist. He looked at me before turning back to the boys. "Thanks for being fans. Honestly. Are you guys going to the show?" He nodded across the street to the venue.

The boys heads bobbed up and down.

"That's awesome. Then I guess I'll see you guys inside. Find me and we'll hang out, alright?"

I smiled at how diplomatic Chase could be despite our moment being ruined. He confronted the situation with grace. I admired him for that. I melted into his side, allowing him to wrap his strong arm even further around me.

"Peyton! Chase!" Mitchell shouted from across the street. He waved his arms in huge sweeping motions as if we wouldn't see him. Camila tugged at him. Even from that distance I could hear her telling him to leave us alone.

"I guess we should join them," Chase said with a sigh.

"I guess so." I smiled.

"I'll make it up to you. Next time." Chase said. He took my hand as we headed toward the venue. Mitchell and Mo were beaming at us, while Camila looked exhausted by the boys' antics.

"I'm looking forward to it," I said. Chase glanced down at me and grinned. It might not have ended how I wanted, but I was happy to be there with Chase and I was happy to be joining our friends.

25

THREE NIGHTS AFTER OUR FIRST DATE AND I WAS STILL THINKING about the near-kiss. With all our friends around, the night ended with a soft peck on my cheek before I climbed out of the taxi with Kay. Despite my determination to not let it get in the way, it occupied my mind at all times, especially when Camila and I sat down to work on Eternal Spin together.

"Hey, did you tell Chase about the studio situation?" Camila asked as she packed up her things for the night. "We're going to have to come up with a backup plan."

Even before Camila showed up that night, I knew I'd have to admit Chase still didn't know about the job offer I'd been given. As much as being in the studio with Forever July was more exciting, it was impossible to pass up the work, the money, and the exposure.

"I'm going to tell him tonight. He's calling me when he gets off work." I glanced down at my hands hoping she wouldn't realize it never crossed my mind to tell him until that moment.

Camila stood up and stretched, a few of her bones making small popping sounds from sitting so long. She bent over to touch her toes. "I hope you tell him tonight, because I need to look for someone for you to collab with, who will do the first four days and you can do the last ones."

"Do you have someone in mind?" I asked, hoping to take her mind off things.

Camila nodded toward my laptop. "In the new folder called Possible Interns. All the submissions we get, I've put them in there. The good ones anyways." She chuckled and started putting everything into her backpack. "I picked the ones I liked, but you're the writer. Decide your top five and if we have overlap, we'll take them out on Saturday and see what they can do."

"I'll do that tonight," I said as I opened our joint cloud storage and found the folder she mentioned. There were already twenty possible interns in the document. It never occurred to me that anyone would want to work for so little per article, but there were the PDF portfolios.

"Since I know you're going to be buried in work this next week and a half, I'm not going to bug you on every little decision. Is that chill?" Camila asked. She slipped her arms into her backpack and stared at me.

I had to admit, the idea of just focusing on writing for two weeks was relieving. As much as I loved working on Eternal Spin, being involved in everything, just writing would be like a mini vacation. I nodded and said, "You got this. This whole thing was your brain child anyway."

Camila stopped fussing and looked at me. Her eyebrows pinched above the bridge of her nose. "What are you talking about?"

"Eternal Spin. This is your idea."

"My idea?" Camila put her hands on her hips. "It's your domain, your blog, your name. Everything that changed you were at least fifty percent responsible for."

"But..."

Camila put up both her hands and said, "No. None of that. This is our project."

I chuckled. "Okay."

Camila's annoyed face didn't ease. "I'm dead serious, Peyton. We have different talents, different priorities, different views, but this is ours, together, equally."

If anyone else said those things to me, I might not have believed them. I might have assumed they said it to save my feelings. Those weren't things I could think when the words came from Camila's mouth. If she thought I wasn't pulling my weight, she would have told me.

I got to my feet and said, "Okay, Camila. We are equal and I'm okay with you taking on more work for the next two weeks."

Camila chuckled and said, "Perfect. Now, I'm leaving, so you can call Chase and get some sleep."

I walked with Camila to the apartment door and pulled it open. She stepped out onto the landing and said, "I'll come by your work with coffee and lunch, alright? I'm forcing Kay to let me do a small shoot at her shop with our shirts in the background."

"We can discuss the intern then."

Camila rolled her eyes. "It's your lunch break. We're gonna talk about boys, bands, and drink coffee."

"No work talk?" I asked, arching my brows at her. I couldn't picture Camila and I going a full hour without talking about Eternal Spin. It consumed so much of our lives, together and separately.

Camila smirked. "For as long as we can hold off."

I waited at the top of the landing as she walked down the stairs and pushed the door to the street open. She turned around and we waved before the door slammed shut behind her. I stood there in the hallway for a few seconds longer than I needed to. Going inside meant calling Chase. Going inside meant telling him my plans had changed, that I needed to put work before going into the studio with the band.

As I forced myself to walk into the apartment, I tried to

think of the best way to tell him. I didn't want him to get upset. Since being offered the job, I wondered how I could change the time frame, to push it until after Chase went on tour. But if I wanted the job, it would be next week.

From the table, I grabbed my phone and tapped on Chase's name in my contact list. Instead of sitting, I paced through the living room.

"Peyton." Every time he answered the phone, he said my name in a way that made goosebumps pop up all over my skin. "You're early."

"Cam left because she wants to go to bed early," I said with a laugh.

"What's wrong?" Chase could sense it.

I stopped in front of the shelf that Kay and I had been filling with random knick knacks, like a black, glitter covered skull-shaped candle and stack of coasters in the shape of records with some of Kay's favourite bands on them. In the middle of them was a picture of Kay standing next to the lead singer of The Distillers, Brodie Dalle. I touched the picture hoping to get some of Brodie Dalle's confidence.

"I'm going to miss the first couple of days in the studio," I said in almost a whisper.

"Everything okay?" Chase asked.

I allowed myself to inhale and exhale before I began explaining. "I know we had plans, but I was contacted by this woman who wants me to write a series of blogs for her company. Each night when I'm done working at the store, I'm going to her office to work on them. And I promise I can still write the article about time in the studio and Camila said she's going to take lots of notes for me. I'm sorry this is so last minute."

"That sounds like a great opportunity," Chase said. "Why did you sound so nervous?"

"I didn't want you to feel let down." By let down I meant

mad, but I'd learned over the years to avoid that word. No one liked to be called out for being angry.

"Let down?" Chase's voice pitched upward in surprise. "Peyton, this is a cool opportunity for you. Wouldn't it be awesome to be writing full-time instead of working retail?"

I didn't know what to tell him. I expected he would be disappointed and upset with me for bailing on our plans. As much as I knew Chase wasn't like Will or my father, I was taken aback by how unaffected he seemed to be.

"Peyton?"

"Yeah?"

"So, you are still there." He chuckled.

"You're not upset with me?"

"Upset? Did you want me to be upset?"

I shook my head even though Chase couldn't see me. I swallowed hard before I explained, "No. I was just worried you might be."

"As much as I want you to be there, it's more important that you're doing what you want and need to do."

"You're gonna be on tour soon, so..." I didn't know what else to say. Making plans for myself would have caused a negative response in my past.

"I might focus better if you're not there." Chase laughed. "I want you there, I really do, but I'm gonna be nervous to hear what you think of these songs."

"I make you nervous?"

I expected Chase to laugh at the statement, but he was quiet for a few seconds, long enough to make me worry.

"I care what you think, Peyton. I value your opinion."

"Oh."

"I really do," he told me. "You may doubt it, but even before I met you, I looked up to you."

I could feel the blush creeping up my neck and spreading across my cheeks. "Why?"

"Peyton, you're smart. You're honest. You're thoughtful."

"Those are big praises."

Will would have laughed if he heard those words coming from anyone in reference to me. Part of me also thought he was lying. But it was Chase and I couldn't figure out why he would say those things to me if he didn't mean them. He'd given me no reason to assume he would lie.

"They're understatements. When I saw you at The DeKay House, I realized two things. One, the picture on your blog didn't do you justice. And two, wow, this person is the whole package. Smart. Thoughtful. Honest. Beautiful."

I laughed in spite of myself. I'd never heard someone speak about me in such a way. If the word beautiful had been said by anyone else, I might have assumed it was a ruse.

"I'm not joking."

I cleared my throat. "It's just that no one has said anything like that to me before. I laughed because I really don't know how else to respond."

My insides tightened at my honesty. The comment came off self-deprecating, but I wanted to be honest with him.

"Maybe I'll have to say it again and again, until you're used to hearing it," Chase told me.

I couldn't believe I was spending time with someone that thought so highly of me. He liked me. He wants to be around me. I made him nervous. He wanted to impress me. I couldn't believe how lucky I was. I didn't understand why it was so terrifying.

"Can I confess something?" I asked.

"Of course," he said. His voice was so deep, so welcoming.

"You make me nervous too."

26

My stomach fluttered at the sight of Chase standing outside of the studio when my Uber pulled up to the curb. The entire drive, I wondered how it would be seeing him for the first time since our date. I wondered if we could finally make up for the near-kiss. I wondered if he would be standoffish and later tell me that we should just be friends. My mind was drowning in all the possibilities, but seeing him made me excited.

When I pushed the car door open, Chase reached out to take my laptop bag before taking my hand to help me out. I grinned at him and said hello. Chase took a step closer to me and said, "I'm glad you're here." I wondered if I would ever get used to the feeling that came over me when our skin touched.

I hoped I wouldn't.

"It feels like weeks since I've seen you. So much has happened since we were last together." He took a step closer. My laptop bag bumped into my thigh, but it barely registered. My focus was on Chase's eyes, staring at my lips. After a week of waiting, I was desperate to feel his lips on mine.

The drop of rain on my forehead caused a sigh to escape my lungs. Chase glanced up and groaned. Within seconds, fat drops collided with our faces and shoulders. Under any other circumstances, kissing in the rain might have been a movie moment to remember, but I thought about my laptop getting damaged and Chase having to perform in the studio with soaking clothes. I grabbed his hand and pulled him in through the front doors. His arms wrapped fully around my body as we stepped into the lobby.

"Is Chase still outside?" Mo's voice carried down the hallway. Chase sighed, resting his forehead against mine. We broke away from each other as Camila and the rest of the band came around the corner. I let go of Chase's hand long enough to hug everyone.

"We're going to grab pizza down the street and stretch our legs. We'll be back in ten to fifteen minutes," Dylan said. His eyebrows bobbed up and down as he walked backwards out the door. Chase shook his head, but I laughed.

"Let's head into the studio," Chase said, tugging on my arm gently.

We headed into a large lounge with black couches, a massive television, and a kitchenette. Everything was wood and black and moody. From the lounge, I could see into the isolation booth where Mo's bass guitar sat. We walked past the isolation booth and into the control room. I inspected the mixing console. Afraid I might touch something and mess it up, I kept my hands behind my back, trying to take it in.

"It's more intense than I thought," I said. I turned to look at a grand room behind the glass. A drum kit was set up at the far end of the space, but there was a grand piano closer to where we stood. Chase threaded his fingers between mine and led me around. I glanced up and noticed the skylight. Even though we could see the rain on the glass, I couldn't hear a sound.

"It's amazing," I said. When Chase let go of my hand to

walk over to the piano, I took the phone from my pocket and snapped a picture of him sitting with his fingers on the keys.

Chase played piano on two of the tracks from Forever July's self-titled album, but witnessing him do so in person surprised me. He played a few notes. They were beautiful. He stopped and tilted his head toward me. With his fingers already in first position, he asked, "Any requests?"

"Anything but Piano Man, right?"

Chase chuckled.

"If you're not sick of your new stuff yet, maybe let me hear one of the tracks?"

"This is the last one I have to record vocals for," he told me. "The rest, I want you to wait until it's done, mastered."

He pressed a few keys as if warming up. After a false start, he started to play. The piano's sound filled the space with deep, rich tones. I stared up at the rain running down the glass of the skylight.

Even before he began to sing, there was a heaviness to the song. The notes were weighted with contemplation. I could already put together the review of the song.

> *Don't know where we're headed*
> *But I know where we've been*
> *From stage to stage, bar to bar*
> *Beneath the lights we spin*
>
> *We pushed ourselves forward*
> *But for what was never clear*
> *When I crashed into her*
> *The future felt so near*

Somehow my legs carried me to the piano bench. I lowered myself next to Chase. His fingers moved across the keys with such a delicate, yet confident touch. I couldn't take my eyes off of them.

*Beneath the red and green lights*
*I found my clarity*
*It was there right in front of me*
*She was there right in front of me*

I swallowed as Chase stopped singing. I knew there were more lyrics. Maybe he sensed it was already too much for me to take in. I thought about what Melissa would think when she heard the song. Would she know it was about her and about me? Would she be mad at me?

The song had distinct highs and lows. I could sense the sadness coupled with the hopeful notes. The whole song was pulling my emotions from left to right.

Chase took his hands from the keys and set them on his lap. I turned my knees toward him, to get a better look at his face and expression. I could see the question on his creased forehead.

"It's an apology song?" I asked.

"Among other things," he said with a nervous laugh. His body shifted until he was looking at me. "Do you like it?"

"I do."

"It will be full band, but I thought you should hear it this way, the way I wrote it." His eyes moved to my mouth again. My body tingled with anticipation.

"Thanks for letting me hear it this way." I pushed my hair behind one ear while I kept my eyes on him. I didn't want to blink. I didn't want to miss a single movement in case he kissed me, like I so desperately needed him to.

Chase put his hand on my knee. Goosebumps erupted over my skin and I braced myself by wrapping my fingers around his wrist. I pushed myself up from the bench toward him, to let him know I was waiting.

"Hey love birds," Dylan called into the room. "We're going to start with drums for the next track, so you'll need to move your love fest elsewhere."

It was another moment of interruptions. I wondered if we would have a single time alone before he left, to take another step forward. The idea of Chase leaving on tour before I even kissed him made me want to drag him, into a broom closet somewhere for a second of privacy.

Chase exhaled. The sound of his frustration spurred me on. I could sense his intent to stand, so I held him still by gripping his hand still on my knee.

Chase took his eyes from mine just long enough to look at the door before bringing them right back to me.

"We're never going to get a moment to ourselves," Chase said.

"I know."

"I don't want to wait to kiss you," he breathed.

My heart raced. I pushed myself up from the bench and clutched his face with my free hand. I pressed my lips against his. They were as soft as I imagined. I took in the way he kissed my top lip and then my bottom. The day's stubble across his chin pressed into my palm, grounding me, reminding me where I was, with who I was. I smiled against his mouth.

A piece of me eased as if I'd satisfied a craving. I realized I'd been waiting for his lips against mine since the day we met. I wanted it to continue forever, even though we only had seconds.

When we pulled back from each other, Chase let out a long breath and grinned. I didn't have to ask if he enjoyed the moment. The flush of his pale face and his wide eyes told me everything. We stood and he took my hand.

We headed back into the control room to find everyone staring at us. Chase whispered that he needed to speak with the sound tech and would be right back. I turned toward Camila who held up the camera display so I could see the picture she'd taken.

A wave of dizziness crashed over me as I stared at Chase

and me in the image. My whole body arched toward Chase, my hand on his face, the piano in front of the shot. If I hadn't lived the moment only a minute before, I wouldn't have believed I was the girl in the picture. The girl – the woman – was confident, happy, totally in her element. My body felt jittery with nervous energy.

Camila whispered, "I can delete it, if it's too personal of a moment."

I shook my head while holding my hands around hers on the camera. "Don't you dare."

"I'm going in," Dylan said, pulling the drum sticks from his back pocket. "I want this done so I don't have to start again tomorrow."

He left the control room to take his seat behind the drum kit. Everyone was starting to take seats on the couches, but I was unsure if I was supposed to sit next to Chase or play it cool and sit next to Camila. Because of my delay, my friends made the choice for me, leaving only one empty seat. I slipped into the spot next to Chase. My body sunk into the couch and into his side.

I was supposed to be there to document their time in the studio, but I couldn't pay attention to anything other than Chase's arm around my shoulders and the tingle of memory on my lips.

---

IN THE STUDIO, WE WERE IN A COCOON OF MUSIC AND ANTICS with people I cared about. I didn't want it to end. I found myself productive in the studio's lounge. In two days, I'd also become comfortable cuddling with Chase in the control room. I didn't get embarrassed when he placed a kiss on my cheek while I worked on their story or pulled me into a cuddle during our breaks on the couch.

After an engaging conversation with their producer and their sound engineer, I decided to put together a series called *Jobs in Music*. After seeing what Camila and I put together in a matter of hours, everyone I asked for interviews agreed. I made appointments with everyone, from Forever July's manager, to the sound tech, a Foley artist, and an instrument tech.

Before I knew it, the album had been recorded and I hadn't spent nearly as much time listening to Chase sing as I'd been hoping too. And now, it was time to break out of the cocoon we'd been wrapped in.

We stumbled into the parking lot at ten-thirty on the last night, disoriented from too long inside.

Camila and Dylan were planning on going to a lounge in the Village. Mo agreed to go with them, if his girlfriend wanted to go as well. Mitchell had plans to go bowling with a girl he'd been talking to on a dating app. I didn't want to go to the bar or bowl.

Chase put a hand on my back and asked, "Are you tired?"

"No."

"Do you want to watch a movie at my place?" He asked.

I inhaled. "Yes."

"We're heading out," Chase called to our friends. "Anyone want a ride west?"

Camila gave me a wide, toothy smile as she linked her arm through Mo and Dylan's. "We're going to take a ride share. You two go celebrate in your own way."

Mitchell spun around and said, "Have fun you two. Do all the things I would do."

I rolled my eyes, but gave him an amused grin anyway. Dylan shot finger guns at us before saying, "I got a good feeling about this album, guys."

Chase gave a low, unenthusiastic chuckle.

"You always say that," Mo said, putting his friend into a headlock. We said our goodbyes before we turned back to the parking lot.

I asked in a low voice, "Are you not happy about the album?"

"I think it's our best yet," Chase said as he walked around the passenger side of the car. He pulled the door open and let me climb in. I expected him to say more when he took his seat, but he got in and the music started when the engine did. He didn't turn the volume down as we drove.

I rubbed my hands on my thighs as we headed toward our neighbourhood. The longer we drove in silence, the more I wondered if I should be worried, if I should be asking for him to drop me off at home. I hoped his mood was only because he was tired.

As we pulled into the city, I watched the shop fronts pass, most of which were closed for the night and the people on the sidewalks heading towards restaurants and bars. I wondered if I should have suggested a night out with his bandmates or called Kay to ask if she wanted to go out somewhere. I didn't want Chase to feel obligated to hang out with me if he wanted to be with his friends or even alone. Neither of us said anything for the entire ride back to his apartment.

Despite my hesitation, I followed him inside when we arrived, but couldn't move from the foot of the stairs. When I didn't take off my shoes, he turned to me and asked. "Is there something wrong? Should I..."

"Are you sure you want me here?" I spoke over him.

Chase's eyebrows pulled together. He seemed confused. "Of course, I want you here. Do you want to be here?"

I didn't want him to think I was needy or fishing for a compliment, but I didn't want to ignore it in case he actually wanted to be alone. I didn't want to be the girl who ignored the signs for a second time.

"I do." I wrapped my arms around myself. "But you're kinda distant. If you don't want to do this, I don't want..."

Chase put his hands on my elbows. His face softened, but I still wasn't sure what he was about to say. "Peyton, I've been waiting to get you back to my apartment for a week."

I raised an eyebrow.

"I wanted alone time with you," he chuckled. His eyes moved to my face and his grin widened. The smile was comforting.

"Is something bothering you?" I asked.

Chase squeezed my elbows. "Sorry. If I gave you the wrong impression and for being quiet. It's work stuff and I don't like bringing negative work stuff into personal stuff."

"You can tell me anything. If you want to, I mean."

He nodded and tugged on my arm. "Come on. Do you want a beer?"

I shook my head. "Just water."

While Chase went into the kitchen to get us something to drink, I slipped off my shoes and made myself comfortable on his couch.

Since my last visit, Chase added guitars and art, making the place look more lived in. There was a black and white picture of Chase, Camila, Mo, and I on the wall. It had been taken in the middle of a mosh pit. Our faces were glowing with perspiration and my hair was a mess. Chase's cheek was pressed against mine.

"That's one of my favourite pictures," Chase said as he handed me a glass of water. He sat next to me and turned so his knee was pointing in my direction.

"It's a good one." I adjusted myself so I could look him in the eye. "So, did you want to talk about...whatever was on your mind?"

Chase leaned against the back of the couch and said, "Nah, it's cool. I'm over it."

Instead of pushing him, I took a long sip of water.

"So, don't get me wrong," he started, just like I thought he might. "The band is my life. I wouldn't give it up."

"But?"

"But I'm worried about what happens if it flops." Chase ran a finger around the rim of his water glass before setting it down on the coffee table.

"It's not going to flop."

"I've built Forever July up as my entire life. People have expectations of my success. It's been going up for a while now, but it's gonna come down. Eventually it'll end and then what?"

The confession took me by surprise. I'd assumed his confidence was default. I assumed he knew his worth. I set my cup of water onto the table.

"I don't think you have anything to worry about. Your family will support you, no matter what," I told him.

The mention of his family caused a physical reaction I didn't expect. Chase sat back and put his hands on his thighs as if to brace himself, but then his shoulders slumped. He seemed to curl into himself. "I'm the only son, now. An only child. There are expectations."

"Are these expectations something they've put on you or you've put on yourself?" I asked him. I didn't know Chase's family. From the things I heard from Kay, Camila, and the boys in Forever July, the Reid's wouldn't hold their son to such a standard. They would support him no matter where he went in life.

"We don't have to talk about this," Chase chuckled. "It's the first time we've been alone together and I would rather just focus on us."

As much as I wanted to agree with him, I knew I couldn't ignore his statements. Dealing with other people's family dynamics made me uncomfortable, but I wanted Chase to feel safe and reassured even if I didn't know what I was doing. I wanted him to share with me like I'd shared details about my mother, even brought him into the mess by having him drive me to see her.

Instead of asking if he was sure, giving him a chance to back out of the conversation, I asked, "Did your parents ever give you a reason to think you had to be a successful musician over something else?"

"No, but..." He paused. His chest rose and fell several times before he explained, "I don't know what else I'd be good at. Music has been my whole life and I'm pretty sure it has an expiration date. What do I do when this is all over? When they stop buying our albums, when we don't get booked for shows, when we don't get invited to the parties. And it's my career. For now."

I couldn't argue with that point. The chances of still being successful as a band for the rest of his life were slim. We both knew it. Eventually the sound would change and they wouldn't keep up or they wouldn't be able to maintain the lifestyle when they started having families, when other things became priorities.

I cleared my throat. "Do you remember the first text I sent you?"

Chase smiled. "How could I forget? You just dove right in there and asked what my life goals were."

"You said you wanted to open your own recording studio. Have you changed your mind?" I asked.

He rubbed the back of his neck. "No. If I couldn't keep playing, I want to stay in the industry."

The facade that Chase Reid had it altogether started to crumble. I thought I'd missed out on planning my life and figuring it all out. I knew I'd missed out on a lot, but it was still a relief to know not everyone knew exactly what they wanted or needed. I exhaled as I watched him pick his words.

"My brother got me into music. I looked up to him, wanted to be like him. After his accident, he couldn't play guitar again, but he always encouraged me to be better at it." Chase swallowed. "I think being in music, especially a band I named to honour him, brought my family closer to him, kept his memory fresh. I mean, it did for me. When I told my mom I was naming the band Forever July, because it was the last good month we had with my brother, she cried, but she was happy. I don't want to let her down."

"I don't think she'll be let down by anything you do. I get the feeling your parents will be happy with however you turn out." I didn't know how to tell him I was sorry for what happened to him and his family, but I hoped he understood.

Chase nodded. "You're probably right. What does your mom think about your work with Eternal Spin?"

I tried my best not to look shocked by the question. I appreciated that he asked me about my family, trying to give me a chance to talk about it, but to avoid discussing it, I inched closer and said, "Talking about her is not exactly what I wanted to do tonight."

One corner of Chase's mouth tugged upward. He slipped his knee under my thighs so that he could get as close as possible. "I didn't plan on this much talking."

Trying to keep a straight face, I asked, "Did you want to keep talking?"

"Nope." He leaned forward and his lips brushed against mine. He breathed against my face, "For now, this?"

He started by kissing my forehead and then my nose. I held still as he took hold of my waist. He pressed his lips against my top lip then the bottom. When he put his mouth on mine, my entire body erupted in tingles. None of the kisses we shared in the studio compared to the elation he expressed in that moment. His hands slid around my back, bringing me against him. It was impossible not to laugh as we fumbled to pull his shirt off. I took a second to look at his bare chest, the faint outline of his stomach muscles, the tattoos I'd never seen before.

He wrapped his hands beneath my thighs and lifted me until I straddled his lap. I grabbed his face and bit his bottom lip with very little force.

Chase tilted his head away from me and said, "Actually, I think I want to talk."

I sat back against his knees and stared at his face. He looked serious for a second. I almost climbed off of his lap, but the corners of his mouth twitched.

"Okay," I said, pulling down the hem of my shirt which slipped up during our moment. "Do you want to talk about your parents?"

Chase cringed. "No, not my parents."

"Are you sure? Do you want to tell me about your mom and dad's first date? Maybe their wedding night?"

I was cut off by his mouth against mine, his tongue sliding across my lips. Chase laid back, bringing me with him. I couldn't remember ever feeling so happy, so secure. After everything that happened, I wondered if I deserved that tenderness all along.

28

I INHALED THE EVENING AIR AS WE STEPPED OUTSIDE OF THE
venue. Camila stood out front already, taking pictures as the
crowd exited. I stepped out of view of her lens and put my
hair into a messy bun on top of my head. I leaned against the
wall of the building behind me and waited for everyone to
meet me there like we agreed upon before the night started.
Camila was the first to join.

"Chase and Mo not out yet?" Camila asked, leaning next
to me.

I fanned myself, trying to cool down from the jumping,
dancing, and closeness of the bodies that had crowded us.
Chase spent half of the night backstage with guys he toured
with before. Camila and I joined him for one of the opening
bands, but since we weren't working, we ended the night
dancing around in the mosh pit.

"Not yet. I'm sure they're talking about the new album and
tour," I said with a light chuckle. Most of what Chase talked
about was the album, the friends he would see on the road,
and places he was going to eat in each city.

As someone who had never left the province, I envied his
ability to see so much of North America with the band. He

joked about bringing me along and while I knew he wasn't serious, I thought about it often. The people I could meet and the places I could see were endless. I hoped that one day I would be able to see those places he went, but also so much more than that.

"I thought you would be with him," Camila said as she tucked her camera back into its bag. When she finished, she turned and asked, "Is everything good between you two?"

"Yeah, why wouldn't it be?"

"I just thought you two would be glued to each other like Dylan currently is with his new boyfriend." Camila laughed, but I sensed she was a little hurt by Dylan's new relationship.

"Are you ladies talking about boys?" Mitchell asked as he came around the corner of the building. Camila and I nodded at him.

"I didn't know you were here," I told him. From the corner of my eye, I noticed a pair of girls inching closer to our group. They talked to each other but their eyes were on Mitchell the entire time.

"That's because you weren't backstage with us. What's up with that?" Mitchell arched an eyebrow at me. Camila pointed at Mitchell and said, "See? I'm not the only one."

I rolled my eyes. "I'm not one of those girls that has to be with the person they're seeing at all times. I'm sure that Chase--"

Camila put up a hand to cut me off. "Don't say, 'one of those girls,' like it's derogatory. There's nothing wrong with being one of those girls. Or any type of girl or woman."

I stared down at my feet.

"Secondly, if that really wasn't your thing, then fine, but you kept glancing up at him at the side of the stage and checked your phone twice."

I knew she was right. I thought about rejoining him twice, but he was with his friends and he was having a good time.

"Don't feel bad," Mitchell said. "Camila loves to point out all my flaws too."

Camila rolled her eyes and Mitchell moved forward and wrapped her in a hug. They stayed like that, tight in their embrace. The pair of girls who lingered finally dispersed.

"Don't be afraid to ask for affection." Mitchell winked. "Chase has made it clear to me that he will take all he can get from you."

"Why do you have to say it like that?" Camila asked. Mitchell, with his arms still around her, rocked her side to side and told her not to worry about it. Camila rolled her eyes.

I wanted to ask what the boundaries were when it came to relationships. Unlike things with Will, there were no guidelines, no rules. I didn't know if I was supposed to ask permission to spend time with Chase, if I needed to draw the line for public displays of affection. I didn't know what was too much and what wasn't enough.

Most of the crowd had disbursed when Chase and Mo came around the side of the building to find us. Neither of them looked disheveled like Camila and I did.

Chase approached and gave me a quick kiss on the lips. He touched my bun and grinned. "You enjoy yourself down there? You guys looked to be having a good time."

"You should have joined us," I told him. As if to remind me why he didn't, a group of people approached. They offered to take us all for beers at a bar down the street.

Mitchell jumped on the chance, saying we'd go, that we'd all have a good night. Chase and I followed our friends to the bar only a few blocks north. The music was loud and fun and for a while, I was able to forget what our boundaries were, what I wanted to expect. The moment was enough. When we stumbled out onto the sidewalk, intoxicated and happy, I kissed Chase on the mouth without a concern over who was watching.

Chase grinned. "Should we walk back to our neighbourhood instead of taking a taxi?"

"Yes," I said leaning into his side. We said goodbye to everyone and began walking west, away from downtown.

We passed bookshops and record stores closed for the night. People mingled all over the sidewalks as the bars closed for the night. We stopped to grab hot dogs at a street vendor before continuing on.

It had been three weeks since our first date and every time I thought about the fact that I was dating Chase, my stomach fluttered. My teenage self would never believe such things were possible. Chase was sweet, polite, ambitious. I'd become so used to all our time spent together, I didn't know what life would be like when Chase went on tour.

"What are you thinking about?" Chase asked. He put his hands out and nodded to the napkin from my hot dog.

I handed it to him. "You're leaving in eight days."

"Hmm." He shoved the napkins into his pocket and took my hand again. We moved off to the right of the sidewalk to let people pass. Their laughter and voices remained audible as we continued down the block.

"I'm going to miss you," Chase said when we stopped at a light. Despite the busy streets and the cars rushing by us, he dipped his head and gave me a kiss. I held onto the hand he used to cup my face.

"I'm going to miss you," I said as we turned back to watch the street for signs we could cross. Without having to look him in the eye, made it easier to admit, "I'm not very good at always saying the things I'm thinking or expressing it."

We began walking when the traffic gave us room to do so. Chase didn't let go of my hand.

"I like spending all this time with you," I explained. "I just don't know all the rules, the boundaries."

"What boundaries?"

"Like, I don't want to miss the sign that you want time for

just you and your friends. Or if you don't like public displays of affection or..." I shrugged.

Chase stopped us in the middle of the sidewalk and ushered me into the dark doorway of a closed dress shop. He put his hands on my elbows to keep me close. My body tensed, prepared for what he might tell me.

"Peyton, honestly, all I've wanted to do for this past month is spend time with you. Hell, even longer than that."

I sucked in a deep breath, trying to keep my heartbeat steady. I feared he could hear how loud it was.

"Me too." My voice shook and I hoped he knew I was being sincere.

"I like you a lot. I wasn't sure if telling you this would scare you off, but I feel like you deserve to know. More than that, I just felt like I couldn't keep it to myself any longer."

I couldn't look away from those green eyes. Green like new summer leaves, bright and welcoming. I reached up and put my hands on either side of his face. I couldn't believe I could stand there and tell Chase Reid exactly how I felt.

"I like you too."

"Yeah?" The corners of his mouth pulled upward.

"I thought it was obvious. I like you a lot."

"A lot, huh?" He winked.

I let out a quiet giggle.

"Like a *lot* a lot?" He waggled his eyebrows at me while grinning.

I too, feared I might scare him away with the truth, but I didn't want to deny it. Putting up a facade was exhausting and I was afraid it would hinder my relationship with Chase. "Like *a lot* a lot."

Because I wanted him to know how I felt, even if I was terrible at expressing it, I pushed myself up on my tiptoes to kiss him.

After a lifetime of hiding my feelings, the moment made me shaky, but proud. I didn't know if I would ever have the courage to tell someone right out how I cared for them. The words were an understatement, I realized, but it took a lot to admit as much.

Chase wrapped his arms around me, pulling me flush with his body. I slipped my arms beneath his and rested my cheek against his shoulder and my head against his neck. I couldn't imagine ever getting sick of him against me.

"Should we get a cab?" Chase whispered into my hair. I squeezed my eyes shut and leaned against him.

"Yes, let's go home."

29

CAMILA AND I SAT IN THE PUB WITH A GROUP OF WOMEN WE GOT together for an interview. We rented a private room, because Camila knew the owner's daughter. Camila didn't say they dated, but something about the awkwardness between her and the owner's daughter told me something happened at some point.

The room started off quiet with Camila and I asking questions, but not pushing anyone to answer. We decided right from the beginning we wanted it to be more of a social gathering and not a straight up interview. The women knew our plans. Everything was on the table and everyone was more than willing to share.

"My suggestion, turn off the recording device and let's do shots," one of the women called from across the table. Everyone cheered. With that, I knew the night was successful. Not only did I get more than enough to write several articles, but our *women entrepreneurs night* brought people together. Those who didn't already know each other, exchanged cards and added each other on social media with plans to collaborate in the future.

"I have to head out. My babysitter can only stay until

midnight," Thelma, the owner of Rebel Hearts boutique, told Camila and me as she approached our seats. We both got to our feet and embraced her.

"Thank you for being a part of this," I told her.

"We really appreciate that you're willing to let us interview you. I know it's not easy to have to put in the labour when you've already done with your workday." Camila smiled.

Thelma looked between us and said, "Honestly, this is what I needed. Running a business can be really exhausting and also super lonely. Sometimes it feels like no one else understands what you're going through, but meeting women who are going through the same thing, it helps."

It never occurred to me that one day I would be thanked for bringing people together, for helping them feel less lonely. I knew I didn't do it on my own. Camila stood by me every step of the way, but it had been my idea and I'd put all the pieces in motion. After relying on people so much, it impressed me to realize I'd developed the ability to help others.

"I'm glad you were able to find connections here," I said, putting a hand on her shoulder and giving her a reassuring smile. "Do you want me to walk you out?"

"That would be nice." Thelma started her rounds, saying goodbye and grabbing her things. While she did, I took the downtime to check my phone. Chase texted me once to wish me good luck and another to let me know he made brownies for a treat when I got back to his place.

With only three days left before Forever July left on tour, Chase and I made plans for each of them. Having someone expecting time of me was both exciting and nerve-racking.

When Thelma approached me, bag and sweater in hand, I excused myself from the table to walk her out. Thelma and I strolled from the private room into the busy pub. The music was louder out there and voices rose to compensate. We dodged tables and wait-staff as we made our way to the exit.

"I'd like to hire you and Camila," Thelma said. We stopped just outside of the building. "My website needs an overhaul, and I was thinking about hiring someone to do blog posts twice a month and some social media work. Camila told me about the work you've done with a few other business owners and I'd like to offer you the job."

"I would be very interested in helping with that," I told her. The offer stirred ideas in me. I'd only been to her store a handful of times, but I already had thoughts of where we could go with the blogs. Showcasing designers, the history of the different subcultures her store catered to, how to put together outfits.

"I'll email you with details?" Thelma offered. I didn't want to pass it up. The more work I could get outside of retail, the better it would be. Camila and I were already making enough money from the site to cut back on my hours, but if I wanted to keep adding to the savings account I started, I'd need more work.

We said our goodbyes. I took a second outside to text Chase about the job offer.

I headed back inside to find Will standing in front of the doors. I froze. I'd allowed myself to forget about my time with him, the concern I always had about his moods, and the breakup that had been a long time coming. Will standing there, looking smug, was jarring. I stumbled back, the handle of the door slamming into my spine.

"What are you doing here?" I asked him, glancing around. If he was with his girlfriend, maybe he wouldn't cause a scene, maybe I would get out of the conversation without much effort. No one seemed to be looking for him.

"Where's your boyfriend?" Will asked. His lips were pursed into a devious smirk. He leaned onto the hostess stand, letting me know he had no intention of leaving the conversation.

"What?" I cursed myself for stammering over a single word.

"Let's not pretend that I don't know you and Chase Reid are a thing. I've seen pictures of you two all over Instagram." The muscles in his jaw tensed.

I shrugged and then shook my head. I didn't know what to say to keep from creating a scene.

"You were just biding your time until you could be with him. Or were you cheating on me with him? " Will hissed. "You think you're better than me, don't you? You're not."

I thought about the way he always talked down to me, made me cancel plans for him, but forgot when he made plans with me, and even the way he couldn't remember how I liked my coffee. I could have thrown all his terrible behaviours back in his face, but I couldn't bring myself to say them out loud. I'd assumed I'd grown and changed, but I hadn't.

"I never said I was better than you." I wrapped my arms around myself.

"Did Chase realize it yet? Is that why he's not here?" He made a production of glancing in all directions to look for Chase. He knew Chase didn't come that night. He smirked to himself, like he caught me.

"Realize what?" I asked, despite not wanting to hear the answer.

"That he's better than you." His laughter was so loud several people turned to stare at us. "You're just the rebound girl. You realize that, right? He's going to go on tour and realize after all these years of being in a relationship, he'd rather be single. The whole time you'll be sitting by your phone, waiting for him to call you."

"Stop," I told him, allowing my arms to fall to my sides. "Enough."

"Did I strike a nerve? You got an ego boost from his attention, but it's all going to blow up in your face. Or wait, has it already?" He leaned toward me to keep his voice low, so no one would hear his manipulation.

I straightened my shoulders. "Go to hell, Will."

Instead of sticking around to find out what he said next, I pushed past him toward the back room. The sooner I joined Camila and the other women, the sooner I would be safe from his tantrum.

Before I could put distance between us, he grabbed my wrist, yanking me backward. I lost my footing, stumbling into him.

Just months ago, I might have allowed him to say all those things to me, because I believed they were true. Another time I might have hushed him, pulled him outside, taken the verbal abuse to avoid causing a scene.

"Let go of me, Will," I warned him. I jerked my arm, but he didn't let go. His face was red with anger. When he didn't release me, I braced myself and said loud enough for half the bar to hear, "I said stop. Don't touch me."

Before I finished, his hand fell away from me. I rubbed my wrist and kept walking. People watched us. I could feel their eyes on me and my cheeks burned. Will would never talk to me in that way again. No one would touch me like that again. I was proud of myself. I wanted to celebrate when I joined the women in the backroom. But when I sat down, his words struck me hard.

---

30

THE SMELL OF COFFEE WOKE ME. I GLANCED OVER CHASE'S sleeping body to check the clock on the nightstand. It was only seven-thirty in the morning. I ran a finger over his muscular arm, over a tattoo of a light house on his bicep, before climbing out of bed. I got dressed in an oversized sweater and a pair of shorts I bought for the gym and never ended up using. To make sure he slept on, I closed the door behind me before heading into the living room. I grabbed the blanket from the couch and folded it, tossing it over the back of the chair.

Kay was in the kitchen making herself a waffle.

"Whatcha doing?" I took a seat at the narrow, two-person table. Kay didn't look up from the waffle maker. She grabbed another plate from the cupboard and set it next to hers.

"If you want whipped cream, it's in the fridge."

"You don't have to make anything," I said between yawns. I leaned back in the chair and that's when I noticed Kay's grip on the spatula. Kay didn't respond to me. She opened the iron and pulled out a waffle. She placed it on the plate and turned to me with it. I noticed her eyes were bloodshot and the muscles in her jaw were tight.

"What's wrong?"

"Nothing. Just couldn't sleep last night," she sighed.

"Was it us?" I cringed at the thought of Chase and I keeping Kay up during the night. I didn't want to think we were the reason she seemed ready to cry at a moment's notice.

"God no." She laughed, but it was cut short. "It's not about you. But at the same time..."

I sat up straight, pushing the waffle away from me. Kay grabbed her mug of black coffee from the counter and sat down in front of me. She wrapped her hands around the mug and inhaled deeply.

I was afraid to ask, but I had to say something, to break Kay from her silence. "What's going on?"

"I'm thinking about turning it down."

"Turning down, what?"

Kay leaned forward, resting her elbows on the table as if to brace herself. I held onto the seat of my chair to do the same thing.

"A friend of mine is opening a gallery. It's her second gallery, so she was hoping for someone to come work with her as her assistant, someone she trusts for when she's going between cities."

If ever a job was right for Kay, it was a gallery assistant. It would turn her passion for art into a career. I couldn't understand why Kay would be upset about the prospect of taking the offer. It was the perfect opportunity.

"In Montreal."

And there it was, the reason for the waffles. I slumped back in the chair. It took me a few seconds to process her words before I was able to push my own concern away and tell her how exciting it would be. Kay deserved a career she loved. She deserved to move forward with her life. After putting other people first time, and time again, Kay needed to put herself first.

"Honestly, that's so amazing."

Kay arched a single eyebrow as she stared at me. As much as I didn't want to say it, didn't want to ruin her news, all I could think about was Kay moving to another province, leaving me in Toronto, alone. I forced a smile in an attempt to hide what I was thinking. She knew, which she made obvious by the long sigh that slipped from her lips.

"When are you supposed to start?" I asked her.

"September third," she told me. First, Chase would be on tour all summer. When he returned, when things would start to look up, Kay would leave me. Leaving the apartment. I realized I wouldn't be able to live in the apartment alone. Sure, I could focus on the fact that the rent would double and I'd have to clean the place all by myself, but none of those things compared to realizing I was most upset about not having Kay around all the time.

"You can say what you're really thinking, Pey," Kay told me. Her voice quivered ever so slightly, but she kept her face even. I admired her for that.

"This is going to be a great opportunity for you. You deserve to do something you really love. And Montreal will be good for you. Do you speak French?"

Kay didn't answer me. She kept her eyes on mine, waiting.

"I'm so happy for you. It's just you're the first family I ever had," I blurted out before I could stop myself. "I honestly didn't know what it felt like to have somewhere I could actually call mine, that felt safe, where I felt loved. You gave me that."

Kay's chin trembled, but she nodded, telling me to go on.

"And I want this for you and I really am happy. I'm just being selfish, because I depend on you for basically everything." I wiped the tears from my cheeks. "I wouldn't have survived without you."

Kay shook her head. "That's not true. Not true. You would

have been able to do so much on your own. I just thought I'd give you a leg up. And look at you. You've grown so much over this past year. You've become so confident, so self-assured." Her own tears dripped off her chin. She didn't wipe them away. She allowed them to dampen the black fabric of the place mat. "You've grown so much and I think you've helped me do that too. Maybe it doesn't seem like it, but you were the first person I could actually tell the story of Danny to. So many people knew him, so many people had their judgements. It might have taken me a while, but I knew I could trust you when I was ready."

I reached out and offered Kay my hands. She took them both, holding them tight.

"I wasn't joking I said you're like my first family. You are Kay. I honestly didn't know I could care about someone like I can now, until I met you."

Kay squeezed her eyes shut as a little sob escaped her.

"I know we never say it, but I love you," I told her. I didn't care that the words tumbled awkwardly from my mouth. I needed her to know, even if saying it out loud was a foreign concept to me.

"I love you too, Peyton. With all my heart."

"I am so happy for you. This is going to be amazing. You're going to get to hang with artists and meet new people. You can get a fresh start," I told her.

Without breaking my hold on her hands, I got up from the table and moved toward her. She stood in time for me to wrap her in a hug. I pulled her as close to me as possible, trying to take in the moment and not think about the distance to come.

"You'll have to come to Montreal," Kay said.

"All the time."

"I'll get a two bedroom, so you know you always have a place if you want it or need it."

I nodded against her cheek. I knew I couldn't leave

Toronto, not after everything Camila and I were building, not with things happening with Chase. But I liked knowing that I had a place if I needed it.

The sound of feet on the living room floor pulled Kay and me from our embrace. Chase entered the kitchen in his boxers and one of my t-shirts. It fit snug on his arms and it made me laugh.

"You two okay?" He asked, looking between our puffy, tear-stained faces. Kay and I nodded in unison and then laughed.

"I'll give you two some space. Want coffee? Kay, you still like cream, no sugar?" Chase asked, glancing between us. He didn't seem bothered by our tears. He didn't seem worried we might pull him into the drama. To others, his reaction might have come off as normal, but to me it was a significant gesture. I couldn't imagine anyone being as lucky as I was.

"Breakfast isn't gonna happen," Kay said, wrapping an arm around me. "Why don't I take you two out for something to eat? My treat."

"It's okay, it's on me," Chase said.

"Nah," Kay beamed. "I'm the one with the fancy new job. I got this."

While Kay filled Chase in on the gallery and her move, I slipped into my room to get dressed. I grabbed my phone from the charger and noticed a series of text messages. Six of them all from Will. I checked to make sure my door was closed before I opened them.

All the messages came while Chase and I slept, unaware. Before I even absorbed the words, I noticed the typos and knew he'd been drinking when they were sent. I sat on the edge of my bed and inhaled in preparation.

*Peytn*

*Answer meeee*

*Your nevrhap ily*

*E*

*Whrn he gone u hve nuthing*

*Your a groupie ad hell have groupies on tour*

I deleted his messages and tossed my phone into my bag. I thought about messaging him and telling him he was full of shit. I thought about responding and letting him know that jealousy looked bad on him. But I didn't want to waste my time.

CAMILA AND MO BICKERED ABOUT DYLAN BAILING ON THEM, AS we walked toward the Reid family home. Even from outside, we could tell there were more people than the last time I'd been there. Cars lined the street as overflow from the driveway. I braced myself for entering. Camila and Mo were too involved in their debate about leaving for a bar in the Village later, that they didn't notice how I put my hands into my back pockets and then removed them again.

We walked into the house and straight into a middle-aged couple who were heading out the front door. I recognized the woman's nose, green eyes, soft features. They were the same as Chase's. The man next to her was just as tall as Chase and with the same broad shoulders.

"Hello there," the woman said.

"Debbie, gorgeous as always," Camila said, tossing her arms around who I assumed was Chase's mom. She moved on, to Chase's father. "John, you're looking handsome."

John winked at her and said, "You're always stunning, Cami. And Mohammed, like the beard."

"It makes me look like my dad, but I'm into it," Mo chuckled, scratching his facial hair.

"And who is this?" Debbie asked, her eyes turning to me.

I wished I'd worn less make-up or at least skipped the red lipstick. It never occurred to me that Chase's parents would be hanging around during a party at the house. People were yelling in the living room, but they were unfazed by it. They trusted them, they respected them. I shoved my hands back into my pockets.

"This is Peyton," Camila said, giving my shoulder a squeeze.

Debbie and John were grinning.

"Mom, Dad." Chase came down the hallway toward us. I exhaled and pulled my hands from my pockets. I expected him to wave hello or even introduce me to his parents. I didn't expect him to squeeze between them and wrap his arms around me.

"Mom, dad, this is Peyton. Peyton, these are my parents, Debra and John."

"Debbie, please." His mother reached out and shook my hand with a firm grip. I appreciated her handshake and the way she told me it was great to meet me. "The picture of you in Chase's apartment, it doesn't do you justice. You're a beauty."

"We've heard a lot about you," John said. He took my hand from his wife's and said, "We were starting to think Chase made you up."

Everyone laughed, but I couldn't force myself to. I nodded and smiled even if I was certain it came off as distant.

"I've read your articles, Peyton. You have a way with words," Debbie said.

"Oh, thank you."

Chase slipped his arms around me from both sides, pulling me until my back was against his torso. He kissed the back of my head. "I was drawn to her words before I ever met her."

"This is the girl that convinced Chase to give up lead

guitar to Mitchell," Mo said with a chuckle. "She works miracles."

"I was just being honest," I told them. I stared at my hands, trying hard to not think about what they were thinking about me. If someone told me they'd be there, I could have prepared. Less make up. More coverage in my shirt. Would my clothes make me stand out against the friends Chase grew up with? Did my shoulders slouch too much? I stood up straight.

"Yes, you're special," Debbie responded. Debbie didn't shy away from my eye contact. If anything, it seemed to make her more confident. She reached out and patted my hand. "I don't want to make things awkward for you. Go have fun and we'll make plans for dinner. Kay's been suggesting we all go out for Indian food sometime before she leaves for Montreal."

"That would be nice." I smiled.

"We're at the neighbours' if you need anything. We'll get them drunk enough that they won't call the cops on your party," John chuckled as he slipped around us. Debbie squeezed my shoulder and stopped to get a kiss on the cheek from Chase. I blushed at the thought of being in Chase's arms in front of his parents even if they didn't seem at all bothered by it.

"To the whiskey," Camila shouted, pointing toward the living room. With their arms around each other, Camila and Mo skipped down the hallway and disappeared into the sea of people.

"I'm glad you could meet my parents," Chase whispered into my ear before spinning me around to face him. I caught the scent of his powdery cologne. I noticed that he'd put product in his waves. I touched his hair and grinned.

"You look really nice tonight," I told him.

"So do you. Beautiful as always."

I blushed.

"I wish I skipped the party this time," Chase admitted as

he ran his hands down my arms, finding a new place for them on my hips. "It should just be you and me tonight."

"I think you'd regret it."

He pulled his head back to look at me. "Regret it? I really doubt that."

"Should we get a drink?" I asked.

Chase leaned down and kissed my neck. "We could stay right here for a few more minutes." His breath on my neck made me giggle.

I took his face in my hands. "When everyone's gone, okay?"

He sighed. "Okay."

---

I CAME OUT OF THE BATHROOM AND COULDN'T FIND A FACE I recognized, other than Mitchell, who had a girl in the corner of the room. She batted her eyelashes at him and nodded at everything he said. I could interrupt, but opted to take a second to sober up and text Kay, to find out if she was on her way.

"I can't believe Chase is actually single," a woman said as my foot touched the first step. They had their backs to the stairs, watching the room. Their attempt at whispering came off too loud like it often did when people were far too drunk to be telling secrets.

"It's too soon though," the friend told her, her voice lower. "He just got out of his only serious relationship. You'll just be the rebound. You'd hate that."

The first woman let out a long sigh. After a few seconds, she said, "You're right. Chase is end game."

I collapsed onto the stair, sitting statue-still as the women discussed how Melissa was taking a trip to Europe that summer to "get over Chase". I didn't know her as well as those women did, but I had a feeling that her Europe trip was more about moving forward than getting over him.

Not wanting to hear any more details, I pushed myself from the stairs and headed toward the back door for some fresh air. I made it halfway there when Chase appeared in front of me. For the first time all night, he was alone and the realization made me smile.

"Where have you been?" He asked as he stepped into my personal bubble. I leaned against the wall and he mirrored it.

"Bathroom," I told him. "I think I need some air."

He took my hand. "Let's go outside then."

I let him lead me through the sliding door out onto the back deck. There were a few people standing out there, but Chase took us past them, toward a big tree at the back of the long yard. As we approached, a swing appeared out of the darkness, hanging from the tree. I climbed onto it without hesitation.

"I didn't know you had a swing back here." I pushed myself back and let the squeaking ropes carry me forward. I stretched out my toes so the tips of my shoes bumped Chase's thighs. He chuckled and walked around behind me, giving me a soft push.

"Danny and I demanded a swing when we were kids, but we almost never used it," He explained. "Our friends used it more than us."

"I would have used it, too. I think I've only been on a swing a handful of times," I told him. Each time I swung back, I was met with his fingers on my back. They pushed me forward again.

"Well, you pump those legs like a pro." He chuckled. I wanted to respond, but something made me stop. I didn't know if it was the lack of pressure in Chase's next push or the short intake of breath from him, but I sensed he had more to say and I planned to give him the chance.

"My parents said they think you're, and I quote, *a real sweetheart*."

"They left pretty quick." I wondered if he'd admit they were uncomfortable or weren't ready to meet someone new, so soon after Melissa. I wondered how Chase explained our situation to his parents. Did he say he wanted his parents to meet *his friend, Peyton* or did he explain he was seeing me, but maybe it was nothing serious? Will's mother liked to pretend I didn't exist. I never found out how he explained our relationship to other people. He'd never really explained it to me.

"My mom thought you were nervous, so she wanted to take the pressure off."

"They seem really nice."

Chase stopped pushing me altogether and walked around, so he stood in front of me again. I brought the swinging to a halt, digging my toes into the subtle indent in the earth. When I stopped, Chase took hold of the ropes and said, "It's nice that you got to meet them before I go on tour."

"Before going on tour?" I couldn't understand what meeting me had to do with going on tour. I wasn't sure why it would matter.

"We've only started seeing each other and I think going on tour will put a lot of strain on both of us and our relationship."

I dug the toes of my shoes into the earth to brace myself. I wondered if what Will predicted was right. Did he think he would be tempted to sleep with other women on tour? Wasn't that what he was supposed to the first time he went on tour after a major break up? The women in the house knew he would need space, would need time to recover from his split from Melissa. Was I the only one who didn't realize it?

"I thought it might be good to establish some things, so we're on the same page," Chase told me. He grabbed the ropes of the swing, holding me still.

It was deja vu. The conversation with Will started almost exactly like that. He wanted to make sure we were on the same page, before he told me he didn't want labels, he didn't want anything serious, that he still wanted to see other people. I couldn't go through that conversation again. Not with Chase.

"It's okay," I told him. "I'm well versed in this situation."

"This situation?" Chase asked.

"I know it's your first tour being single. I know you've never really been able to do whatever you wanted without having someone to answer to. I don't blame you." I wanted to grab him, to tell him that I didn't want him to be single, I wanted him to be with me and only me. But the only way I saw that situation ending was with Chase ghosting me. He would leave on tour and I would never hear from him again.

In a panic, I kept talking, "I mean, you need to get wild eventually right. You don't want to have to make calls every night when everyone else is out drinking. You just got out of that. I wouldn't want you to feel pressured to do that again."

"Peyton..." Chase blinked at me. His eyes were wide with confusion, concern, pity. They moved back and forth across my face.

Then it hit me. I'd read the situation all wrong. Maybe he was going to tell me he wanted to be with me and he cared about me. It hadn't occurred to me until that minute. I opened my mouth to apologize, but I heard Kay calling my name from across the backyard.

I tried to ignore her. I wanted Chase to tell me to be quiet, to tell me I was wrong.

"Peyton, it's your mom," Kay shouted. "Your mom. She's in the city."

Chase held my elbow. I wondered if I was going to fall or if he was trying to tell me to stay. I looked between him and where Kay was waving at me to follow her. I felt myself stagger.

What if my mom was hurt? What if she was at the hospital? What if she was stranded?

"My mom?" I asked in a whisper.

"Come on," Chase said. He let go of my elbow and when I reached back to take his hand it wasn't there.

I didn't want to go. I wanted him to say something, to tell me we were okay, that I was mistaken, that he wanted to be with me. He didn't say any of those things. Instead, he sat in the swing while I walked toward Kay.

THE DRIVER PULLED UP TO THE CURB WITH HIS FOUR-WAYS flashing. I thanked him and climbed out of the car with a promise to rate him with five stars. I rushed into the bus station to find her. I scanned all the seats as I darted from seating area to seating area. None of the chairs held my mother. I wondered if she got off at the wrong stop, if she thought she was in Toronto, but actually took the bus somewhere else. I didn't know how much my mother knew about the city.

Then a new panic set in. It occurred to me that my mother might have used the phone call as a ruse. What if she told my father I would be there? I didn't know what I would do if faced with him. I didn't know if I would run away or give in out of fear. My eyes darted to the exits. They were clear. I wouldn't go with him, no matter what happened. I'd gotten away from him and had no intention of going back.

"Peyton." My mother's voice drew my attention back into the station. Despite the summer heat, she was wearing her winter jacket and had two duffel bags in her hands.

I couldn't help the surprised laugh that escaped me. I

never believed she would do it, but she did. There she stood. She'd made her escape.

There was a possibility that she would go back to him, I knew that, but I couldn't believe she'd made it that far on her own.

"Hey, you made it," I said, as if we had plans, as if I'd been expecting her.

My mother nodded. "Your friend said you were at a party."

"I was."

"Have you been drinking?" She asked. Her voice was weak.

"I have been."

She winced.

"Can I take that bag for you?" I asked, putting out a hand. She didn't move. She clutched both of her bags while staring at me. I wished I'd removed my make up in the car. I wish I'd brought a sweater to put over my bare shoulders. I glanced down at the ground.

"Your eye make-up—" My mother took in my face. I held my breath, waiting for her to tell me it was too much, that I shouldn't be out in public with my face done up like that. She cleared her throat and said, "You look so grown up. It looks nice."

I glanced back up. As much as my instinct was to smile, my lips pressed together. I wanted to take the compliment and not question, but I couldn't hold back the question. "Why did you leave?"

My mother adjusted the bags in her hands before setting them down on the ground in front of her. She was stalling. I kept silent, allowing her time to work through whatever she was figuring out.

"There are many reasons. They accumulated over the years." She nodded as if to tell me she was done speaking. I gave her more time, but she said nothing else. I wanted to hear the real reason. I wanted to know what my father could have possibly done to put the final nail in that coffin. My mother wouldn't share. She was always protecting him, even now.

"Kay is preparing my room for you," I told her.

"I can sleep on the couch."

"It's okay. Kay is staying with a friend for the night."

"It's just for the night," my mother said. "I've already made arrangements for a room tomorrow."

I furrowed my brows. "A room? Why?"

"Why don't we talk about it in the morning, Peyton?" She asked. We both pivoted to look at the departure and arrival screens. It was already one in the morning. While early for me, I knew my mother must have been exhausted. Without asking, I reached out and grabbed one of her bags.

"Come on," I said, motioning her to follow. "Let's get a ride."

---

As I dragged myself out of sleep, I remembered I was in Kay's room, my mother was in mine, and Chase was on tour. Chase was on tour and was still, technically, single. I'd misread the situation and after everything, there was no way to tell where things stood between us. I panicked. I grabbed my phone from Kay's nightstand. There was one message from Chase. Both relief and panic tugged at my brain while my finger double tapped to open the text.

*Hope your mom is ok.*

No mention of wanting to talk. Not a question to be answered. No mention of us being okay. The conversation cut off with one simple message.

Two months he would be gone and I would be there the whole time wondering if he was doing exactly what I suggested he should do. Maybe it was meant to be. Maybe

Chase would meet some girl on tour. Maybe he needed to be wild and free. If he still came back to me, then I was lucky. But if he didn't…

I cursed to myself and dropped my phone onto the bed.

After pulling on a sweater, I headed into the living room. All was quiet. The microwave in the kitchen told me it was already ten o'clock. I didn't know my mother would sleep so long. She'd always been up before me.

I put on coffee and found some things in the fridge to make a small fruit salad. Everything was ready to go when my mom walked into the room already dressed. Her hair was pulled back from her face. Her clothes were more rumpled than she'd worn in front of me before, but other than that, she looked the same. It was strange seeing her in the kitchen, in my apartment. I wondered how long that feeling would last, if she would even stick around until I got used to it.

"Good morning," she said. It felt so formal.

I nodded and pointed to the coffee. "Want some?"

"Yes, please."

I poured us each a cup before filling two bowls with the fruit. We both sat at the small table and ate. Neither of us spoke for far too long.

"So, why don't you stay here?" I asked her, desperate for anything to say.

"Hmm." She kept eating. The lack of an answer made me nervous. With everything she's been through, I didn't want to make her any more on edge. I didn't want to give her any reason to go back to my father. But once the question was out there, between us, I needed to know.

Several times after I arrived in the city, I wondered if it were better to go back home. My money was running out and I couldn't find a job since I had no prior experience. I often wondered how long Kay's kindness would last. The unknown scared me much more than the horrible things I already knew. If my mother felt the same way, I didn't want to be one more reason she had to return.

"I think I need time to find myself," she told me when her bowl was empty. "This is the first time I've lived alone and I think I need to do that for a while."

"What will you do for money or a job?"

"I spoke with a woman at the shelter. She says there are resources for me. I would have gone straight there, but they didn't have a bed for me until tonight."

"A shelter? When you can stay with me?" I tried to keep my voice even, but it pitched upward. "Kay is leaving at the end of summer. Sleeping on the couch wouldn't be forever. We can make it work." I didn't even know if I wanted my mother to stay with me, but I couldn't imagine her in a shelter. My knowledge of the shelter system was limited, being lucky enough to avoid it, but I couldn't understand why she would rather be there than here.

My mother didn't make eye contact.

The awkward silence settled back into the apartment. There was nothing to say. I didn't know what to ask of her. I didn't know my mother, not the way other people seemed to know their parents. My whole life we'd both been in survival mode. I didn't know what that meant for us now.

I cleared our bowls and cups away.

I'd expected too much from her too soon. When I first left, no one pressed me for answers. Kay gave me the option to speak about what happened, but never demanded the story. It took me a long time to get comfortable with my truth. My mother needed the same space.

"I have an old cellphone. I can put you on the family plan with Kay and I," I told her. "It'll be cheaper that way."

"I can pay you back when I get a job," she told me. I didn't know what my mother's skills were outside of the house. I didn't know if she'd even worked before. She hadn't held a job since I was born. My father wouldn't have allowed all the outside influences.

"Why did you leave him?" I asked.

My mother sighed.

"After all these years, after everything that happened, why did you decide to do it now?" I asked even though I knew I shouldn't. A small bubble of anger had risen out of the pit of my stomach and I couldn't stop it. "I begged you to go. Do you remember that? That's all I wanted for my sixteenth birthday."

My mother looked at her hands. I gave her time. I waited for an explanation. It took me a couple of long minutes to realize it wouldn't come.

"I'm going to get ready," I said as I put our dishes into the sink. "I guess there's no sense hanging around."

I went into Kay's room where I'd stacked a pile of my things on her desk. After picking out an outfit to wear to drop my mom off at the shelter, I sat down on the edge of the bed. I opened the conversation with Chase and wrote him back.

*My mom will be okay. I'm sorry about the other night though.*

The minutes ticked by as I sat there, holding my phone. When my mom knocked on the door, I finally put it back down.

SINCE INTERVIEWING A PUNK BAND MADE UP OF TWELVE AND thirteen-year-olds, Kay, Camila, and I headed to the DeKay House. The plan for the night was to drink enough to forget about how I sabotaged things when they were getting good. The beer and the music vibrating the floor didn't stop the thoughts of Chase and my mother, but dulled them enough to smile when Camila took pictures of us.

Camila appeared in what was once a dining room with a refill of beer. "How did it go with dropping your mom off?"

"Fine. The women working there were nice. It's still weird that she'd rather stay there." I took another sip from my cup. Kay gave my shoulder a squeeze.

"Have you talked to Chase?" Camila asked.

I froze. Kay winced.

The question stung.

"He sent me a quick message before sound check. He said we need to talk." The abrupt message said he was glad to hear my mom was doing well and that we needed to find some time for a phone call. He did mention it was going to be hard with the boys around all the time. I kept waiting for him to message me back, letting me know when he found the time.

"You should just call him," Camila said. Her eyes were already glassy from too many beers.

"I don't think so."

"Why?" Kay asked.

"Because maybe I was right to let him go off and do his thing without being tied down. He's never been on tour while he's single. He told me that while he was on tour, he would have to call Melissa every night. I don't want him to feel tied down."

"Would you like it if he called you every night?" Kay asked.

I didn't know if I wanted to admit it out loud, but the answer would be yes.

"He didn't have to call Melissa," Camila said. She furrowed her brows. "Did you know that was always his idea?"

I shrugged. Someone called to Kay and she turned to talk to a guy I'd never noticed before.

Camila stepped closer and kept her voice down. "Chase is that kinda guy. He likes the late-night phone calls. He's all about the gestures, like driving people home and buying them drinks or food. That's how he is."

If Chase preferred gestures to show someone he cared, I needed to find a way to make it up to him with a gesture. To show him how much I cared about him, I needed to come up with something big. Him being on the road made that nearly impossible.

When I didn't respond, Camila turned to a pair of girls standing against the wall of graffiti. With their permission, she took their pictures. The girls asked Camila for her social media, so they could see the pictures when they were posted. "I'm obsessed with this place."

"Kay said you'd love it. It's trashy and awesome at the same time," I told her.

Kay turned back to the conversation. "Trashy and awesome. Are you talking about me?"

I rolled my eyes and smiled while checking my phone. I looked at the conversation with Chase. The last message was a response to me saying he could call me any time. He told me as soon as he had a quiet moment, he would.

*I hope the show went well tonight.*

I hit send before I could change my mind.

I was surprised to see the ellipses pop up right away, letting me know he was responding. I held my breath. My heart rate picked up.

*It was ok*

I frantically looked around the space for anywhere quiet to speak. With the weather as warm as it was, the front and back porches would be just as crowded as the house was inside. I couldn't leave the message on read without a response. I sucked in a deep breath and tapped out a message.

*Can you talk now?*

I wanted to play it cool, pretend that I didn't ruin what we were starting to build. I hoped if I pretended long enough, he would believe it and we could go back to normal. My fingers hovered over the screen waiting for the next message, watching the ellipses appearing and disappearing.

"What's he saying?" Camila asked, glancing over at my phone. I glanced up and Kay gave me a tight-lipped smile. I could feel her pity for me. They knew I messed up. I had someone I cared about, who cared about me, who treated me well, and I allowed my fear to get in the way of that.

*I have a day off on Wednesday and some time before we head to Omaha. Can we talk then?*

Wednesday was too far away. I didn't want to wait until Wednesday to tell him how sorry I was. I wasn't willing to wait until Wednesday to admit everything that went through my head.

*Now's not good?*

He didn't hesitate this time. His reply came without delay.

*In the van with everyone.*

A group of people pushed their way through the hallway where we stood. Kay looked between them at me. I kept expecting her to tell me what to do, but she stood back, letting me struggle.

"What are you gonna do?" Camila asked, glancing away from my phone. Her eyebrows pinched in the centre of her forehead.

I could call him, beg him to take me back, to make it official, to ask me again. I could text him and plead for him to forgive me. The alternative was almost too horrible to say out loud. I could accept whatever he told me. It might mean that I lose him, but part of me could accept that I ruined things.

I shook the thought from my head. There was one other option.

"Thoughts?" Kay asked.

"How long do you think it would take to get my passport?" I asked.

"It can be rushed." Camila beamed. "Twenty-four hours."

Kay tilted her head, not totally understanding.

"Road trip?" I asked her.

Kay looked between me and a giggling Camila. "Is this a good idea?"

"I don't know," I said with a shrug. There was potential for it not just ending bad, but epically bad.

"What if it ends badly?" She asked me. "What if it doesn't work out the way you're thinking it will?"

"Well, I could be broken-hearted in Chicago, a city I've never seen before. But if I stay, I would just be broken-hearted here," I told them as a band rumbled to a stop downstairs. My voice sounded loud without the music.

"Or it could be good," Camila said. "I hope it's good."

"Me too," I said as I re-opened the message to Chase.

*Can we talk Tuesday night instead?*

He responded right away.

*Yes. Set's done at six. We'll talk.*

I turned to my friends and said, "Well, I guess we're going on a road trip."

Camila tossed an arm over my shoulders. "This is going to be awesome."

My smile faded when I looked at Kay. She didn't look too sure.

INSTEAD OF SITTING AT A RESTAURANT FOR LUNCH, MY MOM AND I opted to pick up some food and take it to the park down the street. While it was busy, we were able to find a quiet spot in the sunshine. As I left that morning Kay and Camila told me to be patient with my mom, to give her time. They told me that getting to know my mother as her own person would be a process and to allow the awkwardness and trust it wouldn't always be that way. They were both still hung over when I left the apartment. My mother and I snacked on bagels and drank smoothies while I reminded myself of their words.

"I know you're upset that I don't want to live with you." My mother twirled the straw between her fingers. "I didn't expect you to say yes to getting lunch today."

I shrugged. "You're still my mom."

We sat for a while without another word. I thought about what I should ask her, but I didn't know if I was supposed to bring up my father. I didn't know if I should bring up the shelter. I didn't know what topics were off limits.

"This is awkward," I said after the smoothies were empty.

My mother pulled bottles of water from her purse and handed one to me. "You're not the little girl I remember."

"Definitely not."

"You went above and beyond my expectations."

"And what were your expectations? That I would get married right out of high school and stay with the same shitty person for the rest of my life?" Another pocket of anger burst out of me. I didn't regret what I said, but I didn't like the look of defeat on my mother's face. Her mouth always remained downturned, but the way she slumped reminded me of when my father would come home already angry.

I cast my eyes downward. "Sorry. That came out too harsh."

"You have every right to feel those things. I just want to ask, are you mad that I didn't leave or are you mad that I'm not staying with you?" My mother asked.

"Maybe both. I'm not really sure." There was no sense in lying or sugar-coating it. Eventually, we would have to have the conversation. The sooner it was out in the open, the sooner we could put some of the awkwardness aside.

"I don't think you'll fully understand any of the reasons why I stayed with your father. At first, I thought he would change, but after a while, I was just too scared. I was scared if we left, he would come after us and I felt like that would be worse."

"Hm."

"And that brings me to why I'm not staying at your apartment," my mother told me. "I don't think it's safe."

It wasn't the answer I was expecting. I didn't know what to do with that information. I set down the bottle of water I was holding and rubbed my hands on my thighs, thinking about those words.

"Do you think he's going to come get you?" I asked her.

My mother nodded, glancing down.

When I left, I had the comfort of knowing that he wouldn't hunt me down. It never occurred to me the only reason was because my mother was there to deal with his anger and frustration. I swallowed hard.

"I just want to keep you safe." She took a deep breath. "Despite what you might think, I always tried to do that for you. Sometimes, my options were limited."

"I don't..." I shrugged. "I really don't know what to say."

"You don't have to say anything. I thought I would let you know."

The quiet between us didn't feel as uncomfortable that time around. I drank my water and listened to the sound of kids squealing and dogs barking. I wondered what my mother had to deal with when I left. I contemplated what stress she was under at all times, worrying about where my father was and if he was coming for her.

"I'm going on a road trip for a couple days, with my friends," I told her, worried about leaving when my mother had to deal with the fear of my father's wrath. "I mean, I was going to, but I think maybe I should stay."

"No, I would feel a lot better if you would go." My mother put the cap back on her water. "Where are you going?"

"To see Chase. To Chicago. He's on tour" I gave a tight-lipped smile hoping it would be enough to drop the conversation.

"What happened?"

"Nothing. I just said some stupid shit."

My mom winced.

"I mean stuff." I took a deep breath. "I allowed my insecurities and the words of others to influence a situation."

"Have you explained that to him?" She asked.

I let out a chuckle. "No. He lives a very different life from me. I don't know how to explain this to him."

My mother watched me, but said nothing.

"His parents are so supportive. They have money. They support his dreams. He was with high school girlfriend for, like, ever. He's widely known in our music scene and that alone is kind of weird. And I'm—"

My mother's face slumped so I stopped.

"Go on." She nodded at me.

"Nah, that's okay." I finished the bottle of water and tucked it into my bag to recycle later. "Are you getting along with the other women in the shelter?"

"Do you like this boy?"

I winced. With my eyes still closed, I said, "Very much."

"What are you scared of?" She asked me.

"Everything." I shrugged.

My mother shifted until she moved a few inches closer to me. She looked me in the eye. "You need to tell him that."

"That's the plan, even if it blows up in my face."

My mother smiled. "He would be a fool to pass up such an independent, clever, beautiful woman."

I smiled hard until my cheeks hurt and a little longer after that.

*She wondered how long it would take to stop getting this feeling every time she headed to a new city. Looking out the window reminded her of the time she left the house for the last time. She'd been terrified when she left. So many times, she thought about turning around and heading back. The known might have been awful, but she understood it, she knew how to handle it. The unknown was much scarier.*

"What are you doing?" Kay peaked over my shoulder.

I pulled the phone toward my chest. "Just some words. I'm trying not to focus on the fact that we don't have tickets, the border crossing took almost an hour, and I need to convince Chase that he wants to be my boyfriend."

"Oh, so you're going to use the B word?" Kay asked. She whistled. "I'm impressed."

Before I could answer, Camila hollered out to us from the gate. She waved us over. The woman strapped red bracelets on our arms and told us that we may have to prove, at any time, that we were press. Camila said it wouldn't be a problem and dragged us through the gate. When out of earshot, she told Kay she put her on the website as a writer to get her in as media. Kay and Camila bounced with each step as they moved into the crush of people.

Everyone streamed toward the multiple stages spread out around the park. Music came from all directions. Any other day, any other time, the whole thing would have given me a sense of excitement. That afternoon, I couldn't focus on anything other than what I planned to say to Chase.

We'd driven over night to a hotel just outside of Chicago, not far from the park where the show was taking place. While I napped on and off in the back seat, Camila and Kay stayed awake, talking about everything. I couldn't believe, despite their lack of sleep, they were so energetic, so excited for the day to come. They were excited for the music, to see their friends, and they didn't have the weight of confronting Chase hanging over their heads.

"Alright, so, when are you going to talk to Chase?" Camila asked after paying for a map of the park's new layout and schedule for the day. "If it doesn't rain, Forever July will be going on at six, which means we can head back to the hotel by seven or seven-thirty and get some sleep before the party."

"That I may or may not attend, depending on what goes down after I talk to Chase."

Kay and Camila avoided looking me in the eye. I wondered if they knew more than they were letting on. Kay still talked to Chase from time to time since they patched things up. Camila knew all because of her non-stop messaging with Mo and Dylan. I was under no delusion that they had more insight into what Chase thought about me than I did

"So, do you plan on talking to him before their set? If so, we could always head over to—"

I cut Camila off. "I'm going to wait until after."

"Why?" Kay asked.

"I just want to see them play before..."

"Before you guys talk it out and everything is fine?" Kay

arched her perfect eyebrow. Even though Camila was changing the lens on her camera, she had a moment to look up at me and to nod. Their optimism should have cheered me up, but it only made me more worried about the fallout of my decision.

"Peyton." Kay gave my arm a squeeze. "You got this."

"I got this."

Camila took the cap of her camera lens and said, "At least pretend to look like you believe it."

I sucked in a breath and exhaled as Camila raised her camera. Kay and I squished our faces together. The picture was supposed to capture all the fun we were having or were supposed to have. I hoped I'd be able to look back on the picture and smile.

"Do either of you want to come with me to the heavy stage?" Camila asked.

"One hundred percent, I do." Kay linked her arm with Camila's.

As much as I wanted to spend time with my friends, I needed some time to disconnect, to take in music without thinking about what would happen, what the outcome might be.

"I think I'm gonna go to the local stage and see what Chicago has to offer." I pulled a notebook out of my pocket, waving it in the air. "I'll take notes."

Kay nodded and said, "Text us and we'll meet you here when you're ready."

Camila took another picture of me before we split up. I glanced at the map and followed the directions to the local band stage. It only took a minute to settle into the music. The band jumped around on stage to the crowd of four as if they were in front of a thousand or two. I respected that.

By the time Forever July was to take the stage, I was sunburned despite my SPF and dehydrated despite the two bottles of water I finished. I pulled at my windblown hair hoping to calm it, even a little, so not to look like a total disaster when I headed backstage to see Chase.

I held my breath as the boys walked out on stage. After several years of watching them in clubs and bars around Toronto, I couldn't believe they were there in the middle of the amphitheatre stage. Their fanbase was massive and I knew it, but I'd become accustomed to their attempts to keep their shows intimate, to keep their fans happy with reasonable ticket prices. Festivals were different and I knew it, but I never realized what life was like for him when he was out the confines of our city. The way we talked about our favourite bands, the way we gushed over their autographs on albums covers, it was the same way people spoke about Forever July. Fans were connected to them because of their music, their lyrics. People wanted to know them, wanted to be with them. Chase was an idol, a famous crush.

Chase came out onto the stage last, waving at the crowd as he smiled down at everyone. My stomach clenched as he adjusted his guitar with one hand and grabbed the microphone with the other. It hadn't been a week since he'd left, but it could have been an eternity. There were thousands of people standing between him and me. My body moved me forward through the crowd without even thinking about it. I wanted to be close to him.

His voice sounded hoarse as he began singing one of their older songs. The crowd roared around me. Their hands shot up in the air in excitement. I stopped only a few people back from the mosh pit, not wanting him to find me in the crowd, not wanting him to spot me in the middle of his set.

As they played through their set list, Chase's face became redder, his hair became plastered to his face with sweat. I could see the heat taking its toll on him as their set progressed. I wished I could bring him water. I wished I could put a cold cloth on the back of his neck. I wished I could hold him, sweat covered and smelly.

Between songs, as he tuned his guitar, he leaned into the mic and said, "I just want to thank all of you for sticking around. There are so many other amazing bands you could be waiting for or watching right now and it means the world to us that you picked us."

The crowd cheered. A female voice shouted from the crowd that she loved him. He grinned as he continued to tune, looking down at his pedal board. It occurred to me that he was happy, that he was living just the way he wanted, on tour with women shouting to him that they wanted him.

I took a step back.

No matter how much I thought I grew and changed, the same old concerns flooded back to me. I'd overcome my fear of so many other things, of leaving the only home I knew, of opening up about my past, of finding a goal, and pursuing a dream. Despite all of that, I couldn't even bring myself to ask the boy I was falling in love with to forgive me. I couldn't bring myself to ask him to be my boyfriend, to make it official, for him to commit to me.

The mosh pit opened up around me. I backed up again. I needed to find Kay and Camila. I needed them to convince me that travelling to another country wasn't a mistake.

As I turned, a man the size of a brick house pushed a skinny guy toward me. Before I had a chance to move, the skinny guy's head slammed with my face. The collision knocked me off my feet. The crowd swallowed me up, closing in on me as I fell hard. Hands reached for me and yanked me up almost as fast as I fell. Pain shot up my back and down my legs. My whole body screamed at me. I'd made a huge mistake.

None of the faces were clear as hands passed me from one person to the other. When my eyes focused, I was being passed into the arms of a paramedic. She asked me a few questions I couldn't hear and lead me toward a tent close to the merch tents.

"I'm fine," I told them as the paramedic sat me in a plastic chair. She checked my vitals, my vision, asked me a series of questions I had a hard time paying attention to. All I could think about was how I was a coward.

The paramedic handed me a gel pack and said, "Put this against your temple."

"Honestly." I handed the gel pack back. "I'm totally fine. I just need some water."

I winced when she shone a small light into my eyes.

"There's a good chance you have a concussion." She raised a thin eyebrow at me and said, "Do you have anyone here with you?"

"They're somewhere."

"With a concussion—" I put up a hand to stop her. "Don't drive. Avoid screen time. Avoid caffeine. And in this context, no moshing. If I experience continued vomiting, worsening headache, or seizures I should go straight to the ER or call 9-1-1."

The paramedic stood back to look at me.

"Do you feel safe at home?" The paramedic asked.

I'd seen the look before on many occasions at hospitals, in the office of social workers and vice principals. For the first time in my life, I confessed. "Yes. I wasn't before, but I am now."

The paramedic stared at me for a long time.

"Honestly. I'm safe."

The paramedic nodded and said, "Okay, but I don't want to release you without someone to look after you."

I handed back the gel pack and grabbed my phone from my bag. I typed out a message in the group chat with Camila and Kay. My fingers stumbled over the letters and it took me two attempts to compose a coherent message telling them how to find me.

"Yeah, I'm definitely not releasing you until someone gets here," the paramedic said with a sigh. When I put my phone back, the paramedic handed me a bottle of water. "Drink."

I thanked her between sips of water.

"You're going to have a shiner," the paramedic said as she handed the gel pack back. I sat still in the chair listening to the sounds of Chase's voice in the distance. Tears stung my eyes as I listened to him play songs about his brother, about missing him, about failing him.

Two songs passed and neither Kay or Camila showed up at the tent. I checked my phone to find my messages had failed. I tried again and stared at the screen, hoping to see a response right away. Another fail.

I closed my eyes and leaned back into the chair. I tried to keep the tears from rolling down my cheeks, but the attempt was fruitless.

"Are you okay?" The paramedic asked. I opened my eyes to find her washing out a gash on a teen boy's knee next to me.

"No one is coming for me," I told her. "I can't get in touch with my friends."

I would have blamed the dramatics on getting hit, on having a concussion, but my frustration with myself reached an all-time high. I winced as I wiped the tears from my swelling cheek. If I hadn't been such a coward, if I hadn't tried to flee, I wouldn't have been hit in the face. If I had only let Chase talk that night at his house, I would have a boyfriend.

"Ronnie, can you take over?" The paramedic asked her colleague. When Ronnie took over washing the knee, she pulled off her gloves and tossed them into the garbage. "Come on, sweetheart. Let's go outside and see if you can spot someone you know."

She took me by the arm and lead me to the front of the tent. I scanned the people walking by. I tried hard not to look at the stage, not to look at Chase in the distance.

"This is going to be our last song," Chase told the crowd. The crowd hollered, whistled, and clapped. I winced.

"This is a song about knowing you need someone in your life the second you meet them."

I might not have been able to see more than his blurry figure from that distance, but I could sense the break. The Chase I saw on stage was a performance, his Forever July persona. But there was a crack in it and I blamed myself. I wondered how angry and hurt he was because of me.

> *You pulled me to my feet,*
> *I saw your face in the dim light,*
> *I made a New Year's resolution*
> *As the clock collided into midnight.*

> *I know when the song stops playing,*
> *When the party comes to an end,*
> *I want to be right here with you,*
> *If not as your lover, as your friend.*

My breath caught in my chest. I refused to be a coward anymore.

"Do you see your friends, hon?" The paramedic asked me.

"Yeah." I swallowed hard and pointed toward the stage. "Him."

ONE FLASH OF MY RED BRACELET AND SECURITY ALLOWED THE paramedic, whose name was Delilah, to escort me to the stairs leading to the stage. I couldn't tell if my dizziness started because of the concussion or my anxiety. Delilah and I stood with our backs against the rails. I couldn't look at the stage. I didn't want to misinterpret any of Chase's actions. Delilah would release me to Chase's care, that much I knew, but what would come after was the mystery.

The music stopped. Panic rose in my throat. Chase would allow Delilah to release me into his care, that much I knew, but what came after was the mystery.

When the band's thank yous ended, I stood up straight. I needed to face him and say everything. Running away from it wouldn't help. It would haunt me like so many other things in my past did. I was sick of living like that. I didn't want to feel ghosts of regret everywhere I went for the rest of my life. I turned toward the stairs to find the boys coming down. First Dylan and Mo with their eyes wide at the sight of me. They asked me if I was hurt, if I was okay, if I'd found Camila and Kay who were looking for me. Mitchell, barely noticed my presence as he glanced toward the crowd, still waving.

As always, Chase was the last to leave the stage, tossing his guitar picks into the crowd. He froze on the top stair, staring down at me. His expression gave nothing away. He pushed strands of his sweaty hair from his face. He blinked. I didn't know what to do, so I waved.

"You're Chase Reid?" Delilah glanced between him and me.

Noticing the paramedic, Chase snapped out of it. He took the steps two at a time. Mitchell reached out for the guitar and Chase handed it off without even looking away from me.

I reached for him, grabbing his wrists because I couldn't stand the thought of delaying contact even for a few seconds. I wanted to feel his skin against mine.

"I need to talk to you," I told him.

"What happened? Are you okay?"

I tried to pull him aside, to take him away from the cluster of people who had gathered around us, but Delilah wouldn't let me move. She kept a firm grasp on my elbow.

"She has a concussion," Delilah said. "She should go home and rest."

I didn't want to talk about a concussion. It had been days without a real conversation with Chase. I needed to get it all out. I'd crossed the border to be there, to tell him everything. Spilling everything in front of everyone, wasn't part of the plan, but I was going for it. It had already been too long.

"I'll rest, but before that I have to say something." I ignored the dizziness that was setting in and gripped Chase's arm tight to steady myself. "I don't like the way we left things and I know you said we could talk on the phone, but that didn't feel right."

"Sweetheart," Delilah said to me, "I can't leave until I know you got someone looking out for you."

I waited for Chase to say something, but he just stared at me.

"We got her," Mitchell said, giving me a pat on the back.

"Yeah, we're going to look out for her," Mo promised. "And I just texted the other friends we're with. They're on their way."

I turned in time to see Dylan nodding. My plan had never been to say it in front of all of Forever July, but the adrenaline from the hit to the face hadn't yet worn off.

I thanked Delilah for helping me, but kept my hands on Chase, afraid that if I let go, he would drift away. I didn't know the full extent of the damage I'd done with my words. I didn't know if I could come back from them. All I knew was I had to try.

Chase didn't move. By the way his eyes searched my face, I knew he was worried, but I couldn't tell if it was more than that. I didn't know if he wanted me there or if he was annoyed that his plans changed because we showed up. I knew I couldn't let that get in the way.

"My whole life I've been careful not to upset people. I tried to anticipate what they wanted so that it wouldn't lead to a confrontation. I've never been great at dealing with confrontation."

Someone moved next to me, putting a hand on my shoulder and Chase's. I turned to see Mo. He gave us a nod and sympathetic smile before rounding up the boys and heading away from the stage.

When they were several steps away, I went on. "I listened to what other people said and allowed my history to decide for me. I don't want to do that anymore. I want to be able to say what I need. And what I want. I don't want to let fear push away the things I care about."

Chase finally found his voice. "So, what's changed? What's going to stop you from pushing me away again? I don't want to go through all of this again if you're just going to panic and just leave." He looked away. There was no mistaking the sadness in the heaviness of his eyes.

My fears were materializing in front of me. I'd allowed my

past to seep its way into the present, allowed it to haunt me enough that I ran away. I swallowed down the panic, telling myself that no matter what, I needed to get the words out. Chase needed to hear it. I deserved to be honest with him and myself.

"I can't promise I won't panic again." I tried to keep my voice from shaking, but it was impossible. "I have a lot of things to work through and it's going to be hard, but it's easier with you, Chase. Having you, and Kay, and Cam in my life makes everything so much easier. I have feelings for you, big feelings, and it feels healthy. I'm happy and that scares me."

"I got scared too. Scared that I can't be enough for you. Scared I'd let you down." Chase gripped my arms back. "I let my brother down and I didn't want to go through that again."

My chin quivered as I tried to hold back my tears. The thought of hurting Chase, making him feel like he needed to take that on wasn't fair to him.

"But being away from you reminded me that running away doesn't help either. And when we were going to talk tonight, I wanted to tell you that even if you don't want to be with me, I want to be there for you," Chase told me.

"But I do want to be with you. I want you to be my boyfriend. When I think about the future, when I'm old, when the tours are over, after the parties stop, I just think about my friends, Eternal Spin, and you. Those are the things I want in my life moving forward. And I might sound crazy for saying this even though you haven't even said yes to being my boyfriend, but--"

"Yes, I want to be your boyfriend." He pulled me closer. "And I want you to know that you deserve to be happy. You're a good person, Peyton. You're smart, you're brave, and you're beautiful. Please don't let other people's issues make you doubt that."

Tears rolled down my cheeks. There were so many other

things I wanted to say, to explain, but it didn't all have to come out there now. There would be so much more time and the realization made me smile.

"And I think I'm in love with you," he said. His muscles tensed as he watched me, waiting for an answer.

I never thought I'd hear anyone say those words to me, but hearing them from Chase felt right. I didn't doubt him. I didn't doubt myself.

"Me too," I whispered.

Chase grinned as he slipped his arms around me and pulled me close. "You need to rest."

"I'm okay."

"What happened?"

"I was running away, but some guy's big head stopped me." I smiled up at him, pressing myself against his sweat-drenched chest. I missed the way his arms wrapped right around me, the smell of soap that lingered longer on him than anyone else, the way he looked at me like I was really all the things he said. This time, I trusted that look.

"You have a hotel?" Chase asked.

I tried to nod, but a wave of dizziness caused my legs to buckle. "Yeah, I need to go there."

"I'll come with you."

"You have the rest of this..." I waved a hand at the crowd, the faces watching us. I turned back to him and said, "You have obligations."

"I want to be with you and so I'm going to be with you. Priorities."

My instinct was to argue, to put the needs of others before myself. I swallowed those feelings away and said, "Good, because I have a lot more to tell you."

"You said more words in the last five minutes than collectively since I've known you and you have more to say?" Chase chuckled. He kissed the bridge of my nose. "And I can't wait to hear every single syllable."

THE HOTEL PHONE RESTED ON THE BED NEXT TO ME. THE handset was pressed between the pillow and my ear while I typed out the details of the day into the notes on my phone. I couldn't imagine myself forgetting the way Chase smiled at me, but I wanted to remind myself every time I doubted myself.

The bathroom door was opened a crack and the sound of Chase's shower filled the room. He'd stopped singing Jimmy Eat World songs, so I called my mom.

"Hello? Peyton?"

"Hey mom."

"How are things there?" Her voice was high, chipper. It surprised me.

"Good. How are things there?" There was the sound of children laughing in the background. "Where are you?"

"I'm at the park with Sylvie and her children."

"Is this a woman from the shelter?"

"Yes, from across the hall. I'm meeting with a friend of hers at noon today. A job interview."

"Oh." I didn't know what to say next. I thought my mother might struggle meeting people, might struggle with things like looking for jobs or paying her own bills. Pride filled me. "That's really great. So, no word from dad?"

"No. Sylvie is going to help me set up everything without alerting him. She knows the tricks. She's done this before."

I thought about the offer Chase made the night before. We were on the bed while our friends were sleeping on the couch, the floor, even squished onto the mattress right next to us. He whispered that I should go with him, but I couldn't. I had my mom to take care of.

"I'm really glad to hear that," I told her. "I'm glad you have someone looking out for you while I'm here."

"I'm doing well, Peyton. Are you having fun?"

"Yes."

The water shut off in the bathroom.

"And things with the boy went well. Chase, right?"

I grinned. "Yes. And they're better than well."

"Good. Good."

I could hear the smile in her voice.

"What do you think about Camila and I going on the road with Forever July for a bit?" I asked her. "For work, but also..."

"Because you're in love?"

I laughed. "Yeah. And because of that."

There was a long pause, with just the sound of cars and people on the other end of the phone. I wondered if my mom doubted my situation or if she was unsure about me travelling with Chase.

"And he's a good guy?"

"He's a good guy. I promise."

Her deep inhale almost rattled my phone.

"I know what you're thinking." I glanced toward the bathroom door. "It's not like that. I can't be scared anymore and fear didn't help me avoid the bad ones anyway. Just the good."

"Well, then I'm glad that you learned from my mistakes, Peyton." My mother's voice shook.

It took a minute for me to collect my thoughts. "Do you think we will ever get to a point where we don't think about all the things that happened?" I asked her. My own voice was unstable.

"Honestly, I'm not sure."

The thought that we would carry this for our whole lives terrified me, but I also hoped my mother was right, that I'd learned from the mistakes.

When Chase walked out of the bathroom, still damp from his shower, towel around his waist, I was certain I'd picked a different path. He mouthed, "Are you okay?" while adjusting the plush towel around his waist. I beamed at him, taking in his toned arms, his lean stomach, the tattoos on his ribs. I'd missed seeing him like that.

"I should go," I said into the phone. "But, good luck on your interview, mom."

"Have fun on your trip. I'll be here when you get back."

I grinned into the phone.

Everything fell into place. I was talking to my mom. I was travelling with my friends. I had a boyfriend who was patient and kind and handsome.

I wasn't foolish enough to think it would be smooth sailing from there on out, but I was ready to take it on, ready to face the twists and turns as they came.

I hung up the phone and stretched out on the bed. Chase stepped into a pair of black boxer briefs before grabbing a handful of ice from the bucket and putting it into the towel hanging from the desk chair. He sat on the bed next to me, placing the towel of ice on my face.

"I'm fine," I laughed, but didn't move, didn't swat the ice away.

He pushed my hair back from my forehead with his other hand. "Just for my peace of mind then?"

"I thought we were going to get breakfast with everyone else."

Chase removed the ice from my face, leaned down, and kissed me. Breakfast no longer seemed important. I didn't need to eat when I had Chase's lips on mine. They sustained me.

"I guess we should get ready," he said against my mouth.

"Or we could stay."

Chase didn't put up a fight. He crawled over me and slipped beneath the blankets, getting as close as possible, so our bodies fused together. He buried his face in my neck.

"I wish you could come with us."

I grinned and pulled my shoulders to my ears.

"You're coming?" He reached back to put the cloth of ice on the night stand and turning back to stare at me with hope in his eyes.

"Yes."

"For sure?"

"Twelve days and then I'm helping Kay pack for Montreal." I was excited to see Montreal, to see Kay's new apartment, but I was sad to say goodbye to Kay, and sad to leave Chase for a couple of weeks.

"Good. Okay. That's awesome. Are you going to look for another job when you get back?" Chase asked. He ran a thumb over my swollen forehead and cheek. His touch caused goosebumps, and I closed my eyes.

"I was thinking not looking for a job." I tilted my head back to look at him, to gauge his reaction.

"Good."

"Good?" I arched an eyebrow.

Chase chuckled and snuggled back against my cheek. "Yeah, it's good. If that's what you want. You can focus on Eternal Spin."

"I was thinking..." I closed my eyes and sucked in a deep breath. "I've been putting together these little notes."

"What kind of notes?"

"Memoir notes."

"Tell me more."

Moving no other part of my body, I reached out and grabbed my phone from the nightstand. I opened the document full of little bits and pieces compiled over months.

Chase put his hand over the screen. "You're not supposed to be looking at screens."

With a sigh, I passed the phone to him. Chase took it and rolled over until he was on his back.

"Can I read anything?"

"You can read it all."

Listening to Chase speak my words out loud might have been awkward for the first few seconds, but as he continued, something happened. Little memories popped up, memories I'd forgotten.

"Can you add something? Just add to the document." I asked him.

"I'll hit dictation. You ready?"

"Yup."

"Go."

"I'm twelve and my father got stuck in snow on Christmas Eve. My mother and I slow-danced in the living room to some religious songs that we didn't know the words to, but it was nice." The memory had been so buried under all the other memories, the bad ones.

"That's a good memory," Chase said. He set the phone on my belly. I ran my hands through his blonde waves. I wanted my fingers to get caught in them forever.

"It was. I think I was afraid to remember the good times, because they're so tangled with the bad ones. But things are different now. I think I feel safe enough to explore all those memories, good or bad."

"Anything you need, I'll do what I can to help," Chase whispered.

"Do you have those? The good memories mixed with the bad?"

Chase was quiet for a while. His fingers sketched invisible circles on my chest as he thought about my question. It took a few minutes before he cleared his throat. "My brother called me on New Year's Eve one year. He was at the DeKay House and he was really messed up and scared."

I kept one hand in his hair and used the other to grip his hand.

"No cabs would pick us up, because he was so out of it, so we just sat on the curb together, just waiting for the worst of it to pass. When it hit midnight, the house went crazy and we just sat there, the two of us."

"Definitely the bad, tangled with the good."

Chase's chest heaved against me. "He said this thing to me. He told me that whatever you were doing at midnight on New Year's Eve, whoever you were with, was how you would spend the year ahead, so he was happy he was spending it with me." Chase sniffled. I glanced over to see the tears rolling from his cheeks. I slipped my fingers from his only long enough to wipe them away.

"I was thinking about that the night I met you," Chase told me. "I was thinking about how I made the choice not to spend the night with Melissa, how I wanted to see Kay, reconnect with her and then there was you."

"You gave me a black eye." I gave a small laugh.

He winced dramatically. "I did. I haven't even found the courage to tell my parents that's how we met. I just told them I went to see Kay, to reconnect with the memory of my brother and there you were."

"I'm glad you crashed into me. And here I am again, all banged up."

Chase grinned and squeezed my hand tighter. He said nothing for several seconds and his breathing became shallower. I thought he'd fallen asleep. I was about to close my own eyes, when he asked, "What are you doing this New Year's Eve?"

I laughed. "I'm not very good at planning ahead."

"Yeah, that's fair. It's too far ahead."

I squeezed his hand. "But whatever it is, we'll be together at midnight, right?"

Chase sat up on one elbow and grinned down at me. His lopsided smile could make me smile on the worst days. He planted a quick kiss on my lips and said, "You and me at midnight. But no more black eyes."

"No more." I laughed.

The hotel room door opened and Mitchell busted inside carrying two iced coffees. The rest of the crew came in close behind, not even bothered by Chase's half naked body, not at all curious if they interrupted an intimate moment.

"Get up and get dressed," Kay said as she went to the full-length mirror to check her lipstick. "We have all of Chicago to see and only one day to see it."

Mo sat on the foot of the bed, eating a bagel. Between bites, he said, "Cam found some really good places for some promo photographs."

Mitchell handed Chase and me an iced coffee as he shouted toward the bathroom. "Cam, don't forget the tripod. We need some group shots. All of us and that means you."

Chase gave me one last kiss before he pushed himself off the bed to grab clothes from his duffel bag. I knew I should get up, but I took in the cramped room. There were clothes on every surface, bodies filling up almost every space. I enjoyed our little piece of chaos. I had people who looked out for me. I had a boyfriend who was kind, talented, and handsome. I had people who loved me despite everything.

Chase stopped in the bathroom door with the clothes in his hand. He gave me a quick wink and mouthed *I love you* before going inside to get changed. Kay and Camila flopped on the bed on either side me. Kay rolled onto her side and asked, "So, I was thinking us women should get tattoos together tomorrow before we meet up with the guys in Omaha."

"I'm so down with that," Camila said as she stretched her arms above her head and yawned.

I grinned. "Oh, I'm in."

I couldn't wait to spend the next twelve days on the road with Forever July. There was a comfort having everyone crammed into the hotel room, arguing over who used Dylan's toothbrush, laughing at Mo talking in his sleep.

Chase walked out of the bathroom fully dressed and smiled at me. The way he looked at me brought a sense of calm through my entire being. Dylan stuck his head in the door and shouted at us to hurry up. Kay pulled me to my feet and ushered me straight into Chase's arms.

Whatever obstacle appeared, whatever insecurity cropped up, I wouldn't have to go through it alone.

# ACKNOWLEDGMENTS

All my life, I've spoken about being an author. I've shared some of the roughest drafts with friends and family. I've bugged people for random details I needed to make a scene work. That means there are so many people who deserve thanks for putting up with me. There are just too many people to list, but I appreciate all the support and encouragement.

Before anyone else, I need to thank my family. They always inquired about what I was writing and only seemed a little annoyed when I said I didn't know how to explain it.

Except my sister, Amanda, who asked me how I would ever get this book done if I didn't know what it was about. There's a blurb now, so you're welcome.

Shout out to Sarah Mitchell-Bush for being one of the main reasons I'm actually publishing and not writing only for myself.

During this process, I had the pleasure of working with Marina Endicott, who gave me some of the most valuable feedback and pushed this novel in the right direction. I'm extremely grateful for the expertise she shared with me.

I'm grateful for the people who became resources during

this process; Maxie Mettler, for sensitivity reading this project, and Phil Warner, for editing, and to the beta readers for catching so many little details I missed. This book wouldn't be nearly as polished as it is without your feedback.

And if you made it this far in the book, thank you as well. It means so much.

# ABOUT THE AUTHOR

A.K. Ritchie hails from a small city in Southern Ontario. She loves writing contemporary fiction with a focus on Romance and Women's Fiction stories. Most of what she writes is influenced by the music she loves.

When she's not writing in coffee shops, she's often curled up in bed scrolling through social media or listening to something from her record collection. She's always up for road trips, live music, walks in nature.

To find out more about her and her work:

facebook.com/AuthorRitchie
twitter.com/AK_Ritchie
instagram.com/a.k.ritchie

9 781777 906115